RADIX OMNIUM MALUM
&
Other Incursions

MIKE CHINN

PARALLEL UNIVERSE PUBLICATIONS

Parallel Universe Publications
First Published in the UK in 2017
Copyright © 2017 Mike Chinn
Cover design © 2017

"Radix Omnium Malum" originally published in THE GRIMORIUM VERUM ©2015

"Two Weeks Saturday" originally published in DARK HORIZONS 23 ©2004

"Kittens" originally published in READ RAW ©2009

"Blood of Eden" originally published in THE MAMMOTH BOOK OF DRACULA ©1997

"Suffer a Witch" originally published in SALVO 7 ©2003

"Cheechee's Out" originally published in SECOND CITY SCARES ©2013

"The Owl that Calls" originally published on WikiWorm ©2013

"The Pygmalion Conjuration" originally published in THE TENTH BLACK BOOK OF HORROR ©2013

"To Die For" originally published in BFS JOURNAL 10 ©2014

"Sons of the Dragon" originally published in kZINE 1 ©2011

"Only the Lonely" originally published in DARK VALENTINE 4 ©2011

"Rescheduled" originally published in FINAL SHADOWS ©1991

"Considering the Dead" originally published in DARK MUSES, SPOKEN SILENCES ©2013

"Wednesday Morning at Five O'Clock" originally published in PHOBOPHOBIAS ©2014

"The Streets of Crazy Cities" and "The Mercy Seat" are original to this collection. ©2017

ISBN: 978-0-9957173-0-5
Parallel Universe Publications, 130 Union Road,
Oswaldtwistle, Lancashire, BB5 3DR, UK

CONTENTS

VINTAGE BIPLANES AND NINETEENTH CENTURY REVOLVERS THE ASSORTED WORLDS OF MIKE CHINN

By
David A. Sutton

"If it starts to get preachy,
I bring in a character with a gun and shoot someone"

Mike Chinn is a bit of a chameleon. Not a multitudinous shades of green creature, with big rotating eyes, horny crests and one of those ten-foot long tongues that splat locusts and flies and things... Well, not so you'd notice! No, Mike is a writer I sort of envy a little bit because he can change his literary colour seemingly at will. I'm the sort of traditionalist who writers mostly ghost and horror stories. That's it. Whereas, place Mike against a right backdrop, and he writes fantasy. Put him against a screen as black as hell and horror comes out... Well, despite this tortured metaphor you get the gist.

There are some commonalties between us though. We're both Brummies. Well, Mike would say he was a Black Country-man, and as my forebears hailed from that misty, murky, unknown-borders-land, I think Brummie will do. We both dabble in writing, editing and publishing. And we probably have similar tastes in beer and baltis. And, of course, we have been friends for a good many years. Chewing the cud in Birmingham city centre bars (the now non-existent 'Iron Horse' springs to mind) and later at the Midland Arts Centre, along with some other 'old timers'...

including one or two who departed the genre scene altogether in the late seventies. It's also important to say how modest Mike is. He'll take the opportunity from time to time to describe the mound of rotting manuscripts that are in his desk drawer as 'recyclable'; as in suitable for pulping not reprinting! But this apparent diffidence belies what's in his genre curriculum vitae. Let's take a look.

Mike has been publishing genre fiction since the mid-1970s, with early appearances in the British Fantasy Society journal, *Dark Horizons* ('Designs of the Wizard', 'Shadows of the Weaver' and 'The Closing of the Days' his earliest published fiction). During the early 1980s I accepted and published two fantasy yarns in *Fantasy Tales* magazine (edited with Stephen Jones), 'Sic Transit' and 'But the Stones Will Stand'. Other stories followed in that publication. In all he has published over sixty short stories, including horror and science fiction tales in *Final Shadows*, *The Mammoth Book of Dracula*, *The Black Book of Horror*, *Phantoms of Venice* and *Second City Scares* among many others. Psychic sleuth and Sherlock Holmes tales have appeared in *Occult Detective Monster Hunter*, *The Adventures of Moriarty: The Secret Life of Sherlock Holmes's Nemesis* and *The MX Book of New Sherlock Holmes Stories Part V: Christmas Adventures*. And numerous fantasy and sword and sorcery tales in a variety of publications.

Mike's writing philosophy is that a good writer should be able to write anything and it's a position he's tried to emulate in his output. In 2015, The Alchemy Press published his second collection of short stories, *Give Me These Moments Back*. The book demonstrates the virtue ably, with science fiction, ghost stories, sword and sorcery, westerns and crime fiction all jostling for attention among the eighteen stories in the book.

His first collection, also from The Alchemy Press, was *The Paladin Mandates* (1998). Linked by the characters Damian Paladin and his partner, Leigh Oswin, the half dozen adventures have a flavour of Howard Chaykin's comic book characters Dominic Fortune and The Scorpion, the 1930s costumed, fortune-seeking adventurer. Mike's fascination with old biplanes and '30s detective fiction add plot minutiae. Monsters, Lovecraftian and otherwise, Egyptology, Hollywood movies, the golem and Nazis all nail this collection firmly to the author's avowed mast, his intent to write about anything *and* everything!

With his editing hat on, Mike's first foray was for The British Fantasy Society, editing four issues of the group's journal, *Dark Horizons* in 1979 and 1980. Following this was *Mystique: Tales of Wonder* also for the BFS. An hommage to the pulps of the '30s and '40s, Mike collected six varied stories and again demonstrated his love of our pulp heritage. Five more issues of *Mystique* followed, the last published in 1995.

Anyone would think that Mike was getting a bit of an obsession with pulp heroes. Well, they might have been right when *Swords against the Millennium* was published by Alchemy/Saladoth in 2000. In his introduction Mike expresses his love for sword and sorcery fiction and provides a potted history of the sub-genre, citing Edgar Rice Burroughs, R. E. Howard, J. R. R. Tolkien, Fritz Leiber and Michael Moorcock. After he mourns the passing of traditional S&S, he says, "I'm glad to say the rumours of its death have been greatly exaggerated," referencing this collection. And pointing out that, "There are shelves-full of fantasy novels and series out there, many of them excellent. But remember: it's very difficult to write a good, *short* fantasy story." With authors like Ramsey Campbell, Adrian Cole, Simon R. Green, Joel Lane and Stan Nicholls in the line-up of contributors, Mike ably demonstrates his theme with, as the blurb says, 'high magic and low cunning, thievery and valour... tales that firmly declare: the barbarians have returned!'

Mike's view of fantasy fiction was more recently brought to light in an interview with Nancy A. Hansen, on her blog 'Writing From Home': "I became disillusioned by what felt like countless multi-volume sagas, each book the size of a breeze block... I still buy horror, although I've outgrown the more visceral form, zombies bore me rigid and the way vampires and werewolves have been turned into sexual fantasies for adolescent girls annoys me no end."

In his non-fiction piece (Mike's essays are few and far between as far as I can see, sadly), 'Not Another Bloody Trilogy', in *Dark Horizons* 32 (1991), he cogently puts his case: "Look again at those shelves; are you sure what you're seeing isn't an endless line of toothless clones churned off a conveyor-belt to satisfy an uncritical audience?" In just three pages Mike plots the history of sword and sorcery and along the way lets us know what's wrong with it, at least with its modern evocations. I think Mike's keen perception of the S&S, high fantasy genre allows him to step left of field and bring freshness and variety into his own genre work. "I'll say one thing for S&S – it's damned good at dragging itself down with new clichés!" he reminds us, though we have all experienced the endless sagas that writers are willing to churn out and publishers willing to publish as long as the moribund plots and stock characters continue to sell to less demanding tastes.

These days Mike cites his favourite authors as, Raymond Chandler, Dashiell Hammett, Alistair MacLean, along with some of the better fantasy authors, Joe R. Lansdale, Michael Moorcock, Robert E. Howard, Fritz Leiber, H. P. Lovecraft, Clark Ashton Smith, Ramsey Campbell, Graham Joyce and Joel Lane.

Needless to say, The Alchemy Press came a-calling again in 2012 and Mike began his series, *The Alchemy Press Book of Pulp Heroes*. Two further volumes appeared in subsequent years. For this trilogy of titles Mike has assembled many of our newer writing talents in the genre, as well as some of the bigger names in fantasy fiction. And it's pulp adventure all the way, 'Hard-boiled detectives, sinister vigilantes, bizarre villains: the staples of the Pulp tradition', as the blurb to volume one states.

Writing about Mike's fiction, and the editing of horror and fantasy, I've so far omitted another keen interest he has had and in which he has also been involved since the early 1980s. He has written twenty scripts for the *Starblazer* comic, published by D. C. Thomson, specifically writing for both their 'Anglerre' fantasy and 'Robot Kid' science fiction series. Titles between 1982 and 1990 include 'The Exterminator', 'A Plague of Horsemen' and 'The Robot Kid Strikes Back!' In his blog ('Displacement Activity') Mike jokes that, "I've always thought D. C. Thomson's *Starblazer* picture digest was one of the country's best-kept secrets', as he points out its patchy distribution in the UK. But it was certainly an outlet for comic book writers and artists to hone their skills and, as Mike adds, one of the artists who illustrated his scripts, with increasing flamboyancy, was Enrique Alcatena, who went on to greater things. *Starblazer* started under the influence of *Star Wars* and Mike's science fiction contributions reflected that. Later the magazine's editor, Bill McLoughlin asked him for fantasy material as the publication expanded its remit. For issue 200 Mike wrote 'Demon Sword', the first of the 'Anglerre: the d'Annemarc dynasty' stories, and he admits to his Michael Moorcock influences here. "Once again," Mike writes, "I was blessed to have my scripts brought to (increasingly hallucinogenic) life by Alcatena... I typed up insane, impossible scenes. 'Illustrate that!' I'd chuckle to myself. He would, and the results were far better than my descriptions."

Editor McLoughlin asked Mike in 1987 to come up with a robot/western script and 'The Robot Kid' was born. Mike describes it as, "a clapped-out droid who'd spent most of his life serving in a movie theatre, winds up on a very Western-style planet, instead of the [intended] sheriff they'd sent for." Mike scripted four more Robot Kid stories, but the final two never saw print as *Starblazer* folded in 1990 just after the issue with 'The Robot Kid Strikes Back!'

Mike's script for 'Billy the Cat', an eight-week adventure, appeared in the *Beano* in 2005. The year before that, in 2004 A. & C. Black Publishing invited Mike to edit *Writing and Illustrating the Graphic Novel*, a lavishly illustrated guide with tons of advice for the budding comic artists and scripters. And two years later, with co-editor Chris McLoughlin, *Create Your Own Graphic Novel* was published by the Ilex Press.

A Sherlock Holmes Steampunk mash-up novel, *Vallis Timoris* out from Fringeworks, has the Baker Street detective sent to the Moon (this was published in 2015). A second Damian Paladin book, *Walkers in Shadow*, is due from Pro Se Productions, as is a western, *Revenge is a Cold Pistol*. The mention of Damian Paladin also brings to mind his collaboration with Adrian Cole's character Nick Nightmare in 'Fire All of the Guns at One Time' in the British Fantasy Award winning collection *Nick Nightmare Investigates* (edited by Mike and published by The Alchemy Press/Airgedlamh Publications in 2014). Mike has a penchant for 19th century replica revolvers, locomotives and model kits – as well as biplanes. These interests segue into his fiction from time to time. And his fiction is as various as you will have gathered!

For *Radix Omnium Malum & Other Incursions* Mike has assembled a very different collection to his previous two volumes. Sixteen dark and different yarns, showcasing his penchant for horror fiction. The title story, for instance – where a decorator, Chris, uncovers what looks like a fungal growth behind the wallpaper he is stripping off. The story takes an altogether more malignant turn as the tale progresses. 'Blood of Eden' is a fresh look at the Dracula theme, bringing the count's machinations right up to date in our corporate world. And there's a neat little twist at the end. In 'Considering the Dead' we are taken back to a time before The Old Ones in a phantasmagorical sort of Cthulhu Mythos creation-myth story and, in 'The Pygmalian Conjuration' Dennis Crawleigh tries out Aleister Crowley's sex magick ritual; the results, like the story itself, are unexpected. Then there's the urban horror dished out in 'The Streets of Crazy Cities'. Unremittingly dark right from the beginning, as the wife and daughter of Martyn Turner, are killed in a car crash. He is having a lively affair with her sister, Siobhan. What begins as a love triangle followed by remorse and hatred evolves into rapid mental disintegration and ugly violence. Quite a horror show. So have yourself a roller-coaster read with this new collection from the able pen of Mike Chinn. You'll not be disappointed!

David A. Sutton
Birmingham, January 2017

RADIX OMNIUM MALUM

The stench hit him first.

A huge tear of wallpaper came free, releasing the rank, cloying smell. Chris was glad he was wearing a face mask: even if it wasn't being blocked, pongs like that usually meant rot of some kind. And rot meant spores.

He dropped the strip of wallpaper, picking at a second. It came away just as easily, and Chris saw he was right. Spreading across exposed, discoloured plaster was a fine network of black tendrils, some no thicker than a human hair.

Chris grumbled into his mask. Bad sign, likely caused by damp. It was an adjoining wall, too, shared with a house in an old terraced row. He wondered if the neighbours had noticed anything their side.

He finished stripping the wall. The growth spread from behind the skirting, fanning out from several black finger-width trunks into a multitude of ever thinner branches. It reminded Chris of ferns – skeletal ones, anyway – or a type of coral. Attractive, in its own way. Except for that filthy, bad egg smell.

Chris stepped back from the wall, sweeping the wallpaper into a crude pile with his boot. Most likely have to burn it. "Hello!" he called.

The reply came from upstairs: "Yes?"

Chris waited silently for Miss Jones – Jenny, she'd insisted – to join him. "Yes?" she repeated. Chris had placed her in her early twenties; her partner, Fran, the same. Blonde and blue eyed, she was just the sort he would have made a fool of himself over, thirty years earlier. It was her first house, an ageing three up, two down; likely sold as in need of some renovation. It was going to need a bloody sight more than that.

He indicated the growth. "Think you might have a bit of a damp problem."

She stared at the wall, frowning. "How serious?"

"No idea. I'll finish stripping the rest of the walls, see what they're like. Might even have to get the floorboards up."

"Whatever you think." She clearly wasn't happy about the idea.

"Might need to look at the neighbours' wall, too."

Her head twitched in a brief shake. "House is empty. Half the road's empty."

That didn't surprise Chris one bit. Teller Street was in one of the oldest parts of town, with a correspondingly ageing population. On the whole he imagined the buildings would be sound – structurally in better shape than modern housing – but the decades would have left their legacy. "Didn't your surveyor mention it? The damp."

"Not a word…"

No, anything for a quick sale. Chris's years in the decorating business had made him cynical. "Well, it may be nothing. Seen stuff like this before; usually a bit of fungicide does the trick. At worst, you're probably looking at an injected damp course."

She brightened. "That's okay, then. You fancy a cuppa…?"

*

Is that all…?

What were you expecting? Fireworks? Thunder and lightning? The earth to move?

No, but… It just feels … anticlimactic, that's all.

You've been watching too many Hollywood films.

Nothing feels any different…

Of course not. The change is not within you, but without. Just have patience.

*

Chris stopped off at *The Feathers* for a swift pint on his way home. The wind had come up and the air was full of invisible, irritating grit. He never needed much of an excuse to nip into the pub; shitty weather was as good as any.

He was feeling bad for Jenny Jones. It was clear that half of the ground floor had ferny mould growing up the walls. Chris had pulled up a couple of floorboards and found evidence it was actually rooted in the ground.

It wasn't his field of expertise, but he was pretty sure that whatever was wrong with the house couldn't be cured with a chemical damp course and fungicide. A fractured water main, perhaps, or worse, a cracked sewer pipe. It was going to need structural work anyway. He'd made a couple of phone calls:

Fergie, an old mate who knew everything there was to know about damp, would be calling round tomorrow.

He took a sip of bitter and grimaced. He could still smell that sodding mould. It was one of those whiffs he'd be smelling and tasting for hours.

He gulped another mouthful to try and clear his mouth and throat. Didn't help. Even *The Feathers'* ancient bouquets of stale beer and long-banned cigarettes couldn't mask it. Probably meant he was just imagining it.

His fingers felt gritty, too, even though he'd rinsed them before ordering his pint. Bandy Mandy might not care about work clothes, but she was a stickler for clean hands. Chris glanced at his fingertips, rubbing his thumb against them: there was definitely a roughness, though he couldn't see anything. No bits of sand, soil or old plaster. It had to be off the wind. He'd wash them properly when he got home.

He finished his beer and had a second. Anything to drown that smell.

*

"Well I'm buggered if I know." Fergie straightened up and stepped out of the gap in the floorboards. "Far as I can tell the ground's no wetter than it should be, so I think we can rule out leaky pipes..."

"That's something," Jenny murmured softly. Chris couldn't miss how pale and grey her face had become overnight. Fran was standing at Jenny's side, gently squeezing her hand. She was as dark as Jenny was fair.

"You don't think it's damp, then?" said Chris.

"Not any kind I've come across." Fergie brushed at his knees. "If anything, I'd say your wall creeper is some kind of plant. A nasty variety of weed."

"What kind of weed could germinate under a house then grow under a layer of old wallpaper?" Fran demanded.

Fergie shrugged. "Sounds crazy, I know. But look—" He knelt on the bare boards, pointing his torch into the hole. He ran the beam up and down a gnarled shoot twisting out of the earth. "If that's not a plant stem I'll buy Chris's beer for a month. There are two more: here ... and here." He picked them out with the torch beam. "They're woody, with a pretty tough dermal layer. Tried cutting through one with my penknife – not a chance."

"Could it be coming from next door?" asked Chris, remembering it was empty. During the summer of his first marriage one lot of neighbours had done a moonlight flit. Their deserted house was soon overrun by mice and the little bastards had found their way into Chris's place. He glanced at Jenny. She was fidgeting with a length of hair: twisting it endlessly around her forefinger.

Fergie shrugged. He was obviously stumped and didn't want to admit it. "I know some people in the Council. They'll have a better idea of what's needed. Digging the stuff up, probably. Maybe laying down a membrane and solid floor." He slipped the torch into a pocket, wiping his hands on his jeans. "Have you got anywhere you can stay?"

Jenny blinked. "Stay? Why…?"

"The whole floor will have to come up, I'm sure of that. You won't be able to stop here."

Fran took a deep breath. "My mother, I suppose…"

"Good." Fergie sniffed, pulling a sour face. "Get you both away from that smell for a while, anyway."

*

The invocation was successful?

I believe so.

Was he satisfied?

Not entirely. Like so many on the minor levels he has a poor grasp on…the big picture… and he has a novitiate's typical expectations. You know: all shock and awe.

Indeed. What's the projected window?

Anything between two days to a week.

Not very precise.

Nothing like this has been attempted before.

Very wel … report back in three days.

Of course…

*

Two days later, Chris drove past Teller Street on his way to a new job. Jenny and Fran had paid him for what he'd done – Christ knows that was little enough – and that was it. Except Chris couldn't help wondering what the Council had found.

Professional interest. Nothing to do with Jenny Jones' blonde hair and blue eyes.

He parked the van and stepped out into a depressing drizzle. All of the terraces, not just Teller Street, looked forlorn and grim in the rain. There was a reflective plastic barrier across the street's entrance along with a *No Entry* and contractor's warning signs, although there was no evidence of contractors.

The street was deserted; the terraced lines looked tired and sagging, ready to fall any moment like twin rows of dominos. Chris found Jenny's house – there was an additional yellow and white barrier across the door – and pushed his way indoors.

The smell was worse. He gagged, bunching a handkerchief against his mouth and nose. It was dark inside. He flicked at a light switch several times before realising the electricity was off.

All of the ground floor had been torn up, just a few boards propped between door frames as makeshift walkways. The growths were everywhere: poking through the exposed ground, spreading up walls, arching across one door lintel like roses on a trellis.

There were even a couple of flowers dangling from the stems: pale purple, trumpet-shaped blossoms. They nodded in a breeze too faint for Chris to feel. Thickening waves of stench rolled over him.

Throat tightening, he backed out quickly, almost colliding with a figure outside: a contractor in a hard hat. A Hi-Viz jacket stretched around his burly frame.

"What you doin' 'ere?"

It was a good question. "I was— I just wanted to see how things were going. I discovered that stuff..."

"You want a fuckin' medal?" The contractor stared at Chris for several seconds, rain dripping from his hat's dirty white peak. "Well, you shouldn't be here, mate. Didn't ya see the sign? Place is dangerous. We'm probably goin' to have to knock it all down."

Chris wondered who 'we' were: the street was deserted except for the two of them.

"What happened to everybody? The people still living here?"

The contractor shrugged. "Nobody around when we got 'ere, mate. Fucked off, likely. Like you should. Right now."

Chris nodded and returned to his van. In truth, he was glad to be away. The place spooked him; those – flowers, or whatever they were – spooked him. And that stench was unbelievable. It smelled worse than his mouse-infested neighbour's had after an exterminator had killed the lot, but not bothered coming back to clear away the piled up carcases.

*

Jim Casherton, head of Housing & Redevelopment Services, pushed the pile of newsprint aside. He tapped at the newspapers for a moment before sweeping the lot into his waste bin. At least the Press hadn't got hold of it yet. Even the local rags had buried it inside, along with the over-zealous traffic wardens, bakery competitions and letters pages. He should have felt relief, but there'd been a constant knot of anxiety in his gut ever since the affair had broken.

And if it got any bigger…

There was a knock on his office door. Before he could respond, Matt Foynes charged in. The younger man, a senior technician from the Environmental Health section, placed an opaque, shoebox-sized plastic box in front of Casherton. He peeled the lid back; Casherton bent to look at the contents. A gnarled lump of something around the size of a baby's fist, it looked and smelled very dead.

"What's this?" he asked.

"A chunk of what's growing under Teller Street." Foynes grinned back. "Tough little bastard – needed a chainsaw just to hack that off."

Casherton recoiled from the box's contents. He'd once said the younger man should have been a mad scientist in an old black and white horror film. This just proved it. With an effort he managed to sound unconcerned. "Wonderful. So?"

"So?" The younger man deflated a little. "I thought you'd want some. For analysis, like."

Casherton slowly flattened himself against his chair back. "I want it analysed, yes," he said, his voice a little too shaky. He could feel sweat starting to prickle under his greying hairline. "But *I* don't want it!"

"No. Sorry." Foynes clipped the lid shut again. "I just thought you might want to take a look at it…"

"Foynes – I don't give a yard-long crap what it looks like." Casherton felt his body relax, hoping the other man hadn't registered his discomfort. "Any idea what it is yet?"

"Ah, now there's the thing. We don't exactly know."

"Exactly?"

Foynes perked up again, obviously the mystery appealed to him. "From the DNA it seems to be related to the *solanaceae* – you know: the nightshades. Tomatoes, spuds, aubergines, peppers. And belladonna, of course: Deadly Nightshade…"

"But?"

Foynes cleared his throat. "Yes. We have no idea which part of the *solanaceae* family it comes from. It's a unique find, Mr Casherton."

"I'll be sure they include that on our dismissal forms, Foynes. Can you kill it?"

"We've tried a range of herbicides: glyphosates, Imazapyr, paraquat, glufosinate ammonium, TCDD, Tordon … even sodium chlorate. Nothing touches it."

Casherton waved the meaningless terms away. "Okay, it's indestructible. How far has it spread?"

"Teller Street's riddled with it. There's no indication it's appeared anywhere else, though."

"Can you be sure?"

Foynes perky manner evaporated again. "No, sir."

"No, sir." Casherton stared hard at the box and its sealed contents. "Then it sounds as if we have no choice but to demolish Teller Street."

"That's won't be hard. All the foundations are shot; the stuff's growing up the walls like ivy. A good push should bring the whole street down."

"Still leaves us with the roots."

"Excavate the whole area and burn them." A ghost of Foynes' smile reappeared. "Napalm."

Which would *definitely* attract the attention of the nationals, thought Casherton. He picked up the box and tossed it towards Foynes. "Here, take this away."

"And do what with it?"

Casherton shrugged. "Drop it in a furnace. At least that will tell you if it'll burn, won't it?"

*

I think you have good news?

With regards to the working, excellent news. The spread has exceeded

17

all of our projections. Full insertion is expected in less than a fortnight.

I sense a qualification…

Yes. The novitiate for whom we performed the invocation is growing increasingly taciturn and unpredictable.

I suspected as much – the man has little moral fibre. Certainly no backbone. No matter – he can't alter the inevitable, and the more he tries the more certain is his … failure.

I believe he will request an audience again.

Let him. I enjoy our little chats.

*

Fergie strolled into *The Feathers* and dropped onto a ratty chair opposite Chris. "Knew I'd find you in here." He wrinkled his nose. "Christ, it's a fusty old pace. What do you see in it?"

"It's quiet." Chris emptied the last drop from his glass. "Get you one?"

"Brown and mild, please." Fergie was, in Chris's experience, the last man on the planet still drinking brown and mild. "There's quiet and there's quiet, old son."

As Chris approached the bar, he admitted Fergie had a point. *The Feathers* never was a bustling pub – not since the old Queen died, anyway – but tonight it was deathly. He ordered the drinks, commenting to Bandy Mandy: "Quiet tonight."

She pulled a face. "It's getting worse. Place has always been an old man's pub – present company excepted, of course." Her grin was lascivious. "But each night there seems to be less of the regulars. Like they've all decided to fall off the perch together." She placed two pints on the bar. "Soon be just you and me, chuck."

Chris winked. "I look forward to it." He paid up and carried the drinks back to Fergie. "So … to what do I owe the pleasure?"

"Huh?" Fergie licked at a foam moustache. "Oh – yes." He took another deep pull on his pint before continuing. "That weird business on Teller Street."

"Jenny Jones' place? What about it?"

"Ha! As if you haven't been thinking about it all week! And her. Irene'd tear you a new one if she suspected."

"I'm hardly her type, am I?"

"Like that'd stop you."

Chris made an impatient sound. "What about her house?"

"They bulldozed the whole street, did you hear? Although the word's going round that they didn't actually have to demolish the place."

Chris hadn't heard. "Wasn't in the papers."

"Course not. Council's keeping the lid on. Can't last, though. Even the dozy bunch at the local rag can't miss a whole street falling down."

Chris polished off half of his pint, wincing at the flavour. It had tasted manky for a few days now; no wonder the clientele was disappearing. Mandy was losing her touch.

"That's not all." Fergie leaned closer. "I've heard – on the QT – that those weeds are spreading."

Chris frowned. "In the streets next to Teller? Roots must be pretty extensive."

"Aha!" Fergie drained his glass. "That's just it. Clear across town – nowhere near the Teller Street area."

"Gossip, Fergie. I'm surprised at you."

His friend looked hurt. "The Council exists in a permanent state of paranoid secrecy, old son. There's far too much they don't want getting out. Gossip is all that's left. And —" he raised a finger "— you'd be surprised how much turns out to be true."

"Whatever." Chris stood. "Anyway, I need to water the flowers. Back in a bit." He made his way to the gent's. The overwhelming smell of bleach cut through the pub's personal fug, almost like fresh air.

It wasn't until he was drying his hands under the blower that he spotted a familiar fan of dark tendrils nestling against the tiles beneath the washbasin.

Fergie had gone when Chris hurried back to their table. It felt like a fucking good idea; and Chris was pretty certain he wasn't coming back to *The Feathers* again.

*

Is this important? I am extremely busy…

Aren't we all…?

This will be about the invocation, of course?

Damn right! That stuff is cropping up all over the place…

Is it? Then consider it your bonus.

It was supposed to be contained, in one small area – not popping up in desirable residential areas!

Indeed. 'Slum clearance', I think you said.

19

I do not recall using those words! The idea—

I am aware of the idea – while you seem to be forgetting your position.

—I'm sorry. But the whole thing is out of hand. The nationals have got hold of it now, with the tabloids blaming everything from GM crops to freak weather to immigrants...

Does anyone actually care what the tabloids say...?

It doesn't matter. It must be stopped—

I'm afraid it isn't that easy. The genie is out of the bottle, as they say.

You invoked it – you can send it back!

Mandragora potentator *cannot be dismissed so easily. It answers the call freely because of what it finds on this side. It is a collector. It has little interest in returning.*

There must be some way to destroy it? Fire? Everything is susceptible to fire...

Oh, my dear fellow—

*

Matt Foynes hunched in a corner of his small lab. Although the ambient temperature was in the low twenties, he looked cold: his arms crushed hard around his torso, hands buried under his armpits. He was rocking slightly; as time passed his foetal swaying grew more pronounced.

He had no idea how long it had been since anyone had been down to see him. He had a vague memory of trying, unsuccessfully, to phone Casherton. It could have been ten minutes ago, or a week.

Lying open on a Trespa work surface was the empty plastic box, the small knot of stem nowhere to be seen. Even so, Foynes couldn't take his eyes away from it.

"He knew," he was muttering. "That bastard knew. Wouldn't go close. Oh yes, he knew. Never went close—"

He'd been unable to phone Casherton. Where was he?

"'Drop it in a furnace'! Bastard knew!"

He slipped his hands out from under his armpits. A quick glance and he rammed them out of sight again.

"Never went close..."

*

Chris settled back in front of the telly while Irene started the washing up. She called something he didn't hear. He paused the action with the remote, giving the contraption a curious glance. The plastic felt sticky, like something had been spilled over it. "You what, love?"

"I said, have you seen those flowers growing up by the greenhouse? You any idea what they are?"

Chris shook his head. As if he'd have the faintest idea what some particular flower was. If it wasn't a rose, he'd be clueless. "No idea. Sure they aren't weeds?" Not that any sensible weed would try it on in Irene's garden. "What they look like?"

"Sort of lilac coloured. Trumpet-shaped. Quite pretty – though the rest of the plant's not much to look at. Like ratty black ferns."

*

—*I'm sure you are aware it's being described as a crisis.*

Strong words.

Nevertheless, surely it's time to rein it in?

Not possible.

Not—?

When the mandragora *was first invoked, perhaps. Then it was small; weak. Now it has outstripped all of my projections. Its growth is exponential. Quite remarkable. I fear there are simply too few of us. It will resist…*

You must have known…!

I have to confess what I know about the current crisis is that I don't know very much.

You—?

No artist can foresee the outcome of their work. Genius is unpredictable, you see … this so-called crisis, as with all pivotal events, is the moment of truth for real collectors and true artists —

*

Fergie wandered through the deserted corridors. He'd never known the Council House to be so quiet – even at the weekend there was a skeleton staff. There'd been nobody outside, so it couldn't be a fire drill. As far as he knew the building didn't have a bomb shelter – not that the powers that be would admit it, even if there was – so he didn't think they were practising for the four minute warning, either.

So where in hell were they?

He climbed the ornate staircase, feet silent on the thick red carpet. Although he was spooked by the emptiness, he was also relishing it. He'd never had the run of the place before, might as well enjoy the freedom. He checked the offices, conference and reception rooms: nothing. There was a faint smell of coffee coming from somewhere; he never located the source.

Fergie jiggled the mobile weighing down his coat pocket, wondering if he should call someone. But who? *Can I have the police, please? Yes – the entire Council House staff seem to have buggered off somewhere. Just thought you should know…*

His random search brought him to the top of the staircase. Only one door led off, and Fergie had absolutely no idea what was behind it. Inside the dome which crowned the old building? A *camera obscura*, perhaps? That'd be fun.

He tried the handle, expecting the door to be locked. It wasn't. With the faintest of squeals – deafeningly loud against the unnatural silence – it opened onto a black, claustrophobic void.

Fergie stepped inside, shivering for some reason. The place was oppressive: felt more like a dank basement than the top floor. It wasn't entirely black, though: his eyes caught the glimmer of numerous candelabra lining what he assumed were the walls. Dark candles guttered, their tiny flames struggling to provide illumination. Two steps into the room, and Fergie was pretty sure he should be somewhere else. Anywhere else.

Mr Ferguson.

The voice was maddeningly familiar. Fergie knew he should recognise it, but there was something— "Hello?" he called, wondering why.

Please come in – we don't stand on ceremony here. Although I wasn't expecting you.

"Ah – sorry. Yes." Fergie looked around, wondering where the voice had originated. The dark confused his hearing. He took another, involuntary step into the room. "I needed to speak to someone."

You are.

"Someone from the Council."

Go on.

As his eyes adjusted, Fergie thought he saw movement – just off to the left. A flickering, even more insubstantial than the feeble candles. He couldn't tell if they were small portraits hung on the invisible wall, or crude statues propped in niches. Whichever, they were so poorly lit that even the pale, guttering candlelight made them dance, giving them a pallid illusion of life.

Mr Ferguson?

Fergie began to retreat. There was something very wrong here. Masonic rituals, secret kiddie porn rings – nothing like that would have surprised him – but this… This was something else entirely. "It's okay. I'll speak to someone tomorrow—"

His hand fumbled behind him, but couldn't find the door. He'd become totally disorientated.

That won't be necessary, Mr Ferguson. We'll see you now.

He recognised the voice, finally: Ellery, the Council's CEO. The smug arrogance; the little catch that sounded like he was trying hard not to snigger at a world of inferiors. It was unmistakable but … wrong, somehow.

It's about the mandragora, *isn't it? The working…?*

"The what?" Fergie thought he heard a faint rustle above him; the brush of something against his cheek. His eyesight seemed to be getting clearer: he could make out the thick billow of drapes covering the wall.

Don't concern yourself, my dear fellow. It's all in hand, so to speak.

Fergie blinked. It wasn't his eyes. The candelabra flames were increasing in brilliance, the candles themselves seeming to darken. The domed room grew clearer. The portraits or statues against the walls, sprang into focus. It wasn't the candlelight making them writhe.

We have branches everywhere.

Fergie stared up into the thing which radiated above him, choking the curved walls and ceiling; realising they weren't drapes at all.

*

Chris drove aimlessly around town. There'd been no work for a couple of days, but he couldn't bring himself to tell Irene. She'd say he wasn't looking hard enough. He passed Teller Street: it and half the roads were like bomb sites. He was reminded of the film clips from the Blitz that were aired on the box, whenever a shorthand image for the last war was needed.

The Feathers was gone, too. It was reduced to a pile of bricks and jagged pegs of wood. He stepped out of his van, standing for a moment like a mourner at the graveside. He could hear flames snapping somewhere, and smelled blistering paint. Occasionally sparks spiralled upwards, a miniature firework display that crackled for a moment before the breeze snuffed it, floating the ashes away.

Back in his van he came to a decision and drove home. The whole town was going to hell, an irate wife was the least of his, or anyone's, worries. But Irene wasn't there. He couldn't remember if she'd said anything about going out; it wasn't the day she normally went shopping.

He stepped out into the garden. The pale purple flowers nodded alongside the greenhouse as though in greeting. The plant was taller and much denser than it had appeared in the torchlight last night.

He stood and watched, unconsciously keeping at least a yard away. He noted absently that the greenhouse's concrete floor was splitting, and a couple of glass panes had cracked. There was a pair of gardening gloves dropped carelessly on the path, next to secateurs. Irene must have been trying to cut the black growths down, and got called away in a hurry. Maybe her sister was ill.

The trumpet-shaped flowers bobbed in the wind – though to Chris it looked more like they were twitching. Watching him without appearing to watch him.

He wiped his hands nervously down his jacket and made for the garden shed. There was a five litre bottle of white spirit tucked away under the jumble. He carried it back to the purple-flowered plant and emptied the contents over the fucking thing. It recoiled, flicking drops of solvent back at him.

Chris slipped a box of matches out of a pocket, striking one. The white spirit ignited eagerly; the whole plant was engulfed in a roaring sheath of flame. It thrashed; it roared; it screamed like a new-born baby. It crackled and spat bright sparks. One flailing knot of tendrils lashed across Chris's right hand and he leapt back, dropping the empty bottle. Blue flame rolled across his exposed skin: the splashed white spirit flaring to life. He batted the flames out before they could burn him, but his fingers stung.

He stepped further away, nursing his throbbing hand, wondering why the bush wasn't shrivelling in the heat. Why it seemed to be surrendering itself, mote by mote, to a swirling curtain of sparks which rose up endlessly. Cooling to a fine mist that dissipated on the moist breeze.

The pain in Chris's hand soared. He stared at his fingertips: a network of fine black shoots sprouted from each one, spiralling up his hand, growing thicker, denser. He rammed the hand under an arm, hiding it from sight. Denying it. A paralysing numbness flowed up both legs and he stumbled, crashing to his knees. The agony that was his arm spread, washing through his torso, dashing itself against the numbing paralysis. He doubled up in foetal terror. He would have gasped in relief as the paralysis deadened his agony, but his vocal chords were frozen.

Black, dancing motes clotted his eyesight. The stench of rotten eggs filled his head. By the time the burning *mandragora potentator* had been reduced to hot spores, there was another mass of black, twisted roots sprouting by the path.

TWO WEEKS FROM SATURDAY

Cliff has long since passed the point where he wants to disembowel Bryan. Now he would much prefer to poke out both of his eyes with a rusting screwdriver and dribble battery acid into the sockets.

"Pity you can't use that imagination of yours when it counts," he mutters at his blank computer screen. The machine doesn't bother to reply; nor does it magically begin to generate the story he's been trying to write for a fortnight. Damn, damn, damn!

Christmas parties, Cliff decides. They are to blame – not Bryan. Or rather, the alcohol. That's it.

Bryan is standing with the owner's son – Graham Murdoch – slightly out of the press of enthusiastic drinkers. Vista Signs have hired the top room of *The Abbot's Mill* for the company's annual Christmas do. The common room which had been the normal venue in all of Cliff's three years at the place is undergoing drastic refurbishment. The drink is free – or as free as it can be when everyone contributes a quid a week all year – and somebody's wife has organised a buffet that can rupture an elephant. The pity is: no one seems to want to eat, just drink. It is Christmas, after all. What else are you supposed to do for two weeks?

Bryan spots Cliff as he wanders in search of conversation: preferably with one of the young, unattached girls that dot the room in tiny clumps. Bryan waves, beckoning for Cliff to join him and Graham. With a hopeless glance towards the spot where gorgeous Debbie Nash is talking with the equally arousing Julia Ellis, Cliff moves toward Bryan and Graham. He's drunk enough to feel irritable about the summons; not so much to know you don't ignore an office superior.

Besides, Debbie and Julia are nothing more than fantasies. Things to keep him awake at night.

"Cliff!" Bryan calls when he is close enough to hear above the crowded room. "Graham and I were just discussing nutmeg."

"Nutmeg?" Cliff is baffled. What the hell are they talking about that for? Is it some forgotten '70s band?

Graham is already speaking: "I say that it's a mild

hallucinogen; Bryan here says it isn't. What do you reckon?"

"All bollocks!" laughs Bryan. "Else every time you ate rice pudding, you'd get stoned!"

"Quiet, Bryan," Graham shushes him. "Let the scientist speak."

Cliff doesn't bother to remind them that it's *political* science he'd been studying: no one ever listens. Anyway, he'd failed his second year, which was how he ended up an office junior in a minor advertising company.

"I've heard something similar," Cliff admits. "I don't know how true—"

"There you are," Graham says, giving Bryan a smug look, ignoring whatever else Cliff wants to add. "You know I'm always right."

"Except when you aren't," Bryan adds. Cliff wonders how he manages to have the nerve to be so familiar with someone on Graham's position. It's something he admires in Bryan: his ease in all situations. "How many fingers am I holding up?" Bryan continues, waving his left hand in the air, two fingers raised.

"It's when they turn into Atomic Kitten you have to worry," Graham says.

"Or Nuclear Pussy as they were originally called!" Both men burst out laughing; even Cliff feels himself grinning broadly. If only he could think so fast.

"Good, Bryan; very good," Graham says when the laughter dies. "I must remember that." He swings his attention back to Cliff. "What are you drinking?" Perhaps he considers Cliff's part in his minor victory deserves a reward.

Cliff looks at his half-empty glass as though the answer is written on it somewhere. "Er – Stella," he mutters.

"Stella it is. Bryan – you're on Speckled Hen, I think?"

"Right again," Bryan says with a faint smile.

Graham turns away and makes his way towards the bar. The crowd lets him through; for a moment Cliff is convinced it rears up on both sides – like the Red Sea parting for Moses.

"Sucking up to the boss, eh?" Bryan's voice brings him back sharply.

"No – no," he mutters, embarrassed at the thought.

Bryan laughs. "Don't blame you if you do, kid. It's the only way round here, believe me." He drains the last of the bitter from his own glass. "How's the writing coming?"

Cliff takes a drink of his own. "Oh, you know… not too bad…"

"Sold anything?"

"Not for a year or so." What is this sudden interest? Cliff wonders. It's no secret that he likes to write – it's on his CV, after all – but no one asks him about it. There seems to be a general rule at Vista Signs: if it isn't work, or you can't sound like an expert, don't mention it.

"Sold what?" Graham is suddenly at Cliff's side, holding two pint glasses. He hands one to Bryan and the other to Cliff.

"You didn't know our Cliff was a budding Jeffery Archer, did you, Graham?" Bryan puts his empty glass at his feet and starts on the fresh one.

"Really?" Graham sounds as though he's really interested. "Novelist, eh?"

Cliff shakes his head, wondering how in hell he's found himself in this position. "Just a few short stories."

"And Bryan says you've sold them? Well done."

"Not for a while… and then just in amateur magazines. Home-produced things…"

Graham surprises him with a genuine smile. "Know them well, Cliff. Used to edit one myself back in my student days. I published a piece by Clive Barker before he made the big time." He turns to Bryan, whose face is growing the blank expression of someone who has lost the thread of the conversation. "Friend of mine was at university with him."

Bryan nods; but it's clear to Cliff that he's never heard of Barker.

"Do you… er, do you still… Are you still involved in editing?" Cliff thinks it a forlorn hope, but one still worth following. Besides, it seems polite to ask.

"Good god, no!" Graham laughs. "Don't have the time, anymore. Still write a bit though, despite Dad." He lowers his voice, as though Vista's owner is standing within hearing distance – as if Charles Murdoch would ever lower himself to step into a public house. "He seems to think that all writers are a bit… you know—"

"Light in the loafers," Bryan supplies. "Limp-wristed. Shirt-lifters…"

"Thank you," Graham says – a little abruptly, Cliff thinks. "You and I are proof that isn't true. Eh, Cliff?"

"If you say so."

"The boy's learning, Graham."

"Get off his case, Bryan. Listen, Cliff, every few weeks I get together with a few friends – fellow dabblers – and we read out our fiction. Then we take turns in pulling it to pieces."

Cliff nods. He's heard of those workshops, but up until now hasn't known anyone who is involved in one. Besides, the thought of reading out something to complete strangers terrifies him.

"How about if you come to the next one?" Graham forges on, oblivious to the cold sweat he is provoking in the younger man. He digs inside his jacket and pulls out a business card. "Here's my address. The next meeting's – when is it? – oh, yes: two weeks from Saturday. Come along; bring something with you. Your most recent piece, preferably. You can watch us flaying each other's egos, and if you feel up to it, have a go yourself. What do you say?"

As Cliff takes the card, it starts to sag – drooping like a Dali clock – before snapping back into shape.

"Sounds perfect, doesn't it, Cliff?" Bryan leaps in while Cliff is still staring at the card. "You were just telling me how you felt you could do with some help."

Cliff blinks. When did he say that? Perhaps he should eat something after all: the lager was definitely playing silly buggers with his mind. Before he can say anything for himself, Graham moves away and starts to loudly congratulate some other minor boss.

"Got yourself a step on the ladder there, son," Bryan says with a wink. "Go for it." Then he backs into the crowd as competently as Graham, leaving Cliff in a mild panic and a growing sense of paranoia. A paranoia that hasn't lessened over the days as he tries to come up with something he can write; something that he won't feel too embarrassed to present at the workshop. Assuming he ever gets up the nerve to read it.

Because the truth is, he hasn't written anything worth the name in months. It isn't writer's block – at least, he's pretty sure it isn't. He has ideas by the cart-load, but none he can see developing into a decent vignette, never mind a short story.

On top of all that, he isn't sleeping well. He can't believe he is so worried about a stupid story that he can't sleep. After all, he doesn't have to go to the damned workshop! Graham isn't going to sack him for not going, but what else could it be? Cliff never thinks about Vista Signs once he is out of the door; he has no love life to moon over, and he stopped fretting about the lack of it some time ago. There is nothing to keep him awake each night, glaring at the dim ceiling, his mind flickering from thought to thought, never settling long enough to relax. Nothing.

Except the damned story.

Cliff shuts down his computer. As the screen darkens, Dana Scully's voice asks him to promise this isn't leading to anything embarrassing. Once, he'd found that amusing; now it isn't even ironic. He looks at the wall-clock: 11:30. Another night gone, and nothing to show for it. He should go to bed but despite his lack of sleep, he doesn't feel tired. He never does.

He walks across to the small cupboard where he keeps his meagre supply of drink. A half-empty bottle of sherry, an empty tequila bottle which he keeps simply because it's wearing a sombrero, an untouched litre of scotch, and two sets of wine glasses. Also untouched. His parents had bought one set when he left home – for all the parties he was going to be giving – and the second from a girl who never quite made it to girlfriend.

Cliff pulls out the scotch and a glass. What the hell. He can't make it to sleep the usual way; maybe he'll try drugging himself. He almost fills the glass, ignoring the layer of pale dust collected on the sides.

He goes to bed, giving his flat the usual once-over: checking everything that has to be is locked, his computer is switched off, and the few sticks of furniture disguising the naked floor are tidy. It is an empty routine, but he's grown so used to it that he can't feel embarrassed by it any longer.

He takes a stinging gulp of scotch and flicks out the light. He makes it to his bedroom in the dark: it's not far to walk after all. He puts the glass down next to a table-lamp, undresses and crawls into bed, waiting for his eyes to adjust before raising the glass again.

He takes another mouthful; it doesn't burn quite as much as the first. Eventually you can grow used to anything, Cliff thinks bitterly. After a third swallow, he replaces the glass, lies back, and wonders if sleep will come.

All that do return are the endless, prancing thoughts.

Once again Cliff wonders why Graham Murdoch has invited him to the workshop; he wonders why Bryan has been so keen to get him along. Nothing seems to make sense.

"You were just telling me how you feel you can do with some help," Bryan says. "Got yourself a step up the ladder there, son. Go for it."

"Feels more to me like I'm being pushed," Cliff murmurs,

reaching for the glass.

"What are you drinking, Cliff?" Graham's voice comes from nearby.

"Bloody whiskey." Cliff takes another swallow. He feels it burn all the way down; it makes him feel faintly sick. "What's it look like?"

"The boy's learning, Graham."

Graham glances at Cliff and frowns, pursing his lips. "But *what* is he learning, exactly?"

"Don't you know?" Bryan drains his pint and tosses it over his shoulder. It bounces off the bedroom wall and rolls along the carpet.

"That political science and nutmeg don't mix?" Graham suggests.

"He needs a taste of nuclear pussy." Bryan shouts into the darkness: "Debbie! Get over here!"

"Quiet!" Cliff tries to shush him. "The walls aren't made of paper, you know!"

"Even if they were, you couldn't do much with them." Bryan grabs at a girl who appears at his side. "Here, Debbie – don't be embarrassed."

He pushes Debbie towards the bed and she stumbles. She lands almost on top of Cliff, her hands punching the bedclothes either side of his hips. For a moment, Cliff imagines her face is going to fall into his lap. She raises her head, and Cliff finds himself gazing into Dana Scully's eyes.

"Eyes forward... put your hands where I can see them... don't turn around or I'll blow your head off...!" she snaps.

Cliff jerks awake, dropping the glass on the floor. For a moment he is totally disorientated. Where is everyone? Where's Debbie—?

He takes a deep breath, suddenly aware of how ragged his breathing is. The oily sweat coating him. It had been a dream – a bloody bizarre dream. Which means he'd actually fallen asleep and now he's awake again and—

"Shit, shit, shit!" He swings himself out of bed, stepping on a patch of whiskey-soaked carpet. "*Shit!*"

He weaves into the tiny bathroom and tears off a long strip of toilet roll. Wadding it, he returns to the bedroom, flicks on the main light, mops up the stain. The back of his hand touches glass; for a moment he actually believes it will be the pint jug Bryan tossed away. But it is only his wine glass: unbroken and empty.

Cliff replaces the glass on the bedside table. Leaving the wad of tissue on the carpet to draw up whatever spillage it can, he crawls back into bed. Perhaps sleep will return? But he doubts it; he's certain there will be no more dreams tonight.

He's not disappointed.

The morning arrives, grey and unpromising. Cliff drags himself into the flat's kitchenette, but can't face anything other than black coffee for breakfast. Leaving his mug in the sink he grabs a coat and makes for the bus stop. Standing in the cold air, wondering if the bus will ever arrive, he leans against the metal post. It tries to twitch out of contact: wriggling like a fat, rust-coloured, well-fed snake. He hangs on with both hands. Finally the thing gives in, but he's left sweating and breathless. He feels unclean and gritty, and wonders why he didn't have a shower.

The bus appears around a far corner. It shudders to a reluctant halt by the stop, throbbing impatiently as Cliff pulls himself into the thick, sweaty interior, fumbling for his pass. The driver accelerates away from the stop before Cliff makes it to a seat, and he clutches a polished steel upright with complaining fingers. Barely balanced, he swings into a seat, banging against a seated passenger. Cliff mumbles an apology.

"Damn' nutmeg tilers!" grumbles the passenger. "Ivory bargain painted fine!"

Cliff glances around. The passenger nods its huge mushroom head towards him. An instant later it explodes, showering the bus with fine spores.

Cliff screams and lurches to his feet. Everyone is staring at him: the rough-looking passenger on the seat glaring especially hard. "What the hell's the matter with you?" he shouts. His voice is peculiarly high.

Cliff looks about wildly. Debbie is standing next to him, her left hand half-raised in a gesture of stunted concern. "Cliff? Are you all right?"

"Debbie? What are you doing on the bus?"

"Bus? Cliff, are you feeling okay? You look bloody awful!"

He blinks hard, rubbing at his neck: it's starting to ache. He's in the open-plan office at Vista, standing right above his own, kicked over, chair. A whole ream of paper is scattered across the floor; Debbie looks like she's standing in a field of shattered ice.

"I thought I was on the bus…" he mumbles. "Coming in…"

"You were lying across your desk." Julia steps around Debbie.

"Moaning and crying…"

"We thought something was wrong," Debbie finishes.

"I… I've not… er… been sleeping too well," Cliff mutters around a tongue that is far too big. He scrubs at his eyes and looks at the chaos he's caused. Everyone is staring at him.

"No kidding," Julia says. She comes closer, her face two inches from Cliff's own. Her huge, violet eyes seem to be sucking him dry. "Anyone we know?"

"I'm jealous," Debbie's voice comes from somewhere behind Julia's head. "I haven't had a decent shag in weeks."

"Well – we can always do something about *that!*" Bryan slips an arm around Debbie's waist and pulls her away. Just before they are absorbed by the crowd, Cliff sees Bryan squeeze one of her breasts, none too gently. Debbie giggles and flutters her tongue at Cliff. At least, he thinks it's for his benefit.

"Not having one, Cliff? We can't have that: it's Christmas!" Graham pushes a slopping pint glass into Cliff's empty hands. "Here, drink up!"

"Yes, two weeks Saturday…" Cliff murmurs, mostly to himself. He can't shake off the feeling something is very wrong.

Graham is frowning. "No, in two *days*, Cliff. We'll be back at work in three weeks. Hard at it, eh?" He swings his head back and forth like a radar dish, scanning the crowd gathered at the bar. "Any idea where Bryan is?"

"Hard at it," Cliff says, and raises his glass.

The bus jostles to a halt. Cliff lowers his hand – he expects it to contain something – and gets on. He's glad he has a bus pass, realising he has no idea how much it is to Graham Murdoch's house, or even the name of the road on which the nearest bus stop is. The younger Murdoch lives in a somewhat more exclusive area than Cliff, but still nothing like he could probably afford. Perhaps he is making a statement of some kind.

Cliff huddles in his seat, staring out of the dirty window. He has the oddest feeling – like *deja-vu* – that something is about to happen. He can't imagine what. Somewhere, in the core of his being, he doesn't want to.

All that he does know is he's going to Graham's workshop after all, despite having written not a word. He'll just ask to be allowed to watch: get the feel of how things work; maybe come back another time with something worthwhile.

The bus arrives in the tree-filled suburb where Graham lives.

Cliff gets off and heads in the direction of the house. Constantly, he looks over his shoulder, expecting to see something. He forces himself to stop, wondering what he's doing, and why he is both alarmed and relieved that the grey sky stays overhead, the street remains under his feet, and the houses grow ever larger.

The Murdoch home is a small detached building in ample grounds. Despite its modest size, it's obviously an individually-designed, exclusive house. Nothing of the residential development area about it.

Cliff walks up the gravel drive and rings the bell. For some reason he's surprised when Graham himself answers the door.

"Cliff! I was beginning to think you weren't coming! Come in, come in—"

Graham takes his coat and ushers him towards a spacious lounge half-filled with people. Cliff is about to sit in the chair Graham indicates when he recognises the faces. There are many people from the office, some whose names he still doesn't know. Bryan is there, as are Debbie and Julia. No one seems to have anything like pens or notepads, and there are no manuscripts of any kind in sight.

Debbie smiles at him: slow and provocative. She flicks her pink tongue. Suddenly, Cliff remembers.

Graham throws himself into a wide, comfortable-looking armchair and grins up at Cliff who is still standing uncertainly. "So, Cliff. Shall we begin with your piece?"

Cliff tries to swallow: all the saliva has dried in his mouth. "I'm afraid I haven't been able to produce a thing—"

Graham's smile grows larger. Cliff is aware of Debbie – just visible out of the corner of his eyes – wriggling to the edge of her seat in anticipation.

"Now, Cliff – we all know that isn't true." Graham lies back, templing his fingers, looking around at a mosaic of eager faces. "So, who would like to start the discussion…?"

KITTENS

As Chris stepped out of *The Mirrorball* pub, he felt premature slivers of winter cutting into his face. Too cold to rain, the weather had obviously decided to go for ice-showers instead. So much for global warming, Chris thought. Get them grit-bins filled: soon be Christmas.

He glanced up and down Hagley Road, absently noting the traffic into Birmingham was thin for the time of night. After taking a sip from his almost empty can of Diet Pepsi, he shrugged the large, battered Head bag full of his paraphernalia more comfortably across his right shoulder. Turning left, he strolled away from the main road, down the slight hill towards his bus stop.

I've got to get a car, Chris thought. No one's going to take a music promoter who goes everywhere by bus seriously! Chandelier Promotions: Chris Chandler and his own, unique chauffeur-driven vehicle, courtesy of Travel West Midlands. He turned up the collar of his black raincoat and hunched his shoulders against the late-night cold. With his long dark hair flowing to his shoulders, he almost faded into the evening. Only his face was left: an untethered, pale balloon, drifting against the night.

It had been a typical enough Friday night. He'd got Ménage-A-Ray a gig at *The Mirrorball*, turning up to watch them and negotiate a few more deals for the several other bands on his books. And the miserable bastards hadn't even offered him a lift home. Wrong side of town, Ronnie had said. Well, that was true enough: they all lived in Dudley, and Chris wanted the suburbs of Birmingham. But all the same—

He upended the Pepsi, sucking out the last drops. There was an aluminium recycling bin on the way to the bus stop; he'd be a good boy and toss the empty in there. Do his bit for the environment, and all. The only problem was, the bin was just past the bottle-banks.

He took a few steps closer to the three plastic igloos, one for each colour of glass: green, brown, and white for clear bottles. With each foot-fall, his chest grew tighter. It was all Ronnie's fault, telling him that bloody stupid story.

There had been a litter of kittens, Ronnie had insisted, face stiff as a church sermon. Someone had dumped them in a bottle bank, instead of the river or motorway like normal. Must have been around six to start with, it was reckoned; by the time the bin was emptied, only one was left. Along with the cleaned bones of its litter-mates.

Stupid, Chris knew. It probably wasn't true: sounded too much like one of those urban myths that seem to grow out of nowhere. But he'd never felt quite the same about bottle-banks.

He drew abreast of the three domes, his feet tracing a wide orbit quite independent of his self-conscious feelings of ridicule. Just as well there was no one about; what the hell would they make of him?

He was past the bottle-banks. Stepping up to the aluminium bin, he dropped his empty can through one of the holes. As it fell, Chris distinctly heard a sound from one of the bottle-banks. A steady, shifting crunch. As though something inside was changing position. Making itself comfortable.

He backed away; suddenly aware of how quiet and empty the streets were tonight. His shoulder bag threatened to slip off. Unconsciously he shrugged it back into position, rattling the loose contents. Turning his back on all four recycling bins, he made for the empty bus stop.

He tried to wrap his coat tighter around himself. Once it had hung off him like a tent, now he could barely button it. Too many late night chip suppers. *The Mirrorball's* spot-lit car park, right behind the bus stop, was empty. The huge, ancient pub was a lock-up; no one could afford to live over it any more. And even John, the head barman, had buggered off to Pedmore, or wherever it was he lived, without so much as a kiss-my-arse.

"I've got to get a car!" Chris repeated aloud, the words coming out as cloudy whorls. A couple of times, Ronnie had let him have the loan of his twenty-year old Mini van, when the drummer wasn't working with Ménage. Typically, the coldest night of the year so far wasn't one of those times.

It was too bloody cold for September. The few deciduous trees amongst the thick stand of cypresses at the far side of the pub car park were already showing signs of yellowing leaves. They formed points of contrast against the otherwise dull, impenetrable mass of evergreens. *Cypressus-depressus*, he'd heard them called. Seemed appropriate on such a cold, bleak evening. The lone spotlight only helped to make the night beyond darker; it certainly didn't light up much of the deserted car park.

It was then he saw the boy. Chris was surprised, to say the least. Two kids had already gone missing in the past couple of weeks, the second only three days ago. The body of the first boy had been discovered on the same night; police considered that significant. Especially as the body had turned up in a black refuse bag just inside the gates of a council tip, half a mile from the second disappearance. The prevailing view was that the bag had been tossed over the locked gates, late at night.

All the local papers had a field day with a rumour the body had been found with no head. Police had refused either to confirm or deny the rumour, automatically giving it greater credence.

Yet here was a boy, not more than eight years old, walking past a deserted car park at half-past eleven at night. Didn't his parents care? Or were they just stupid? Chris sighed. Some people didn't deserve to be gifted with children. They didn't seem to appreciate just what delicate, fragile things they were.

Chris watched the boy closely. He was heading for the bottle-banks. A bulging carrier-bag clutched in both hands kept banging off his left leg with a harsh rattle, forcing him to hobble. Chris couldn't believe it. They'd sent him out in the middle of the night to throw a bag-full of empties away!

The boy stopped by the first of the truncated cones: the white one, for clear glass. He placed the bag at his feet. There was an upended milk-crate nearby; the boy stepped onto it, raising a hand to check he could reach the circular opening near the top. Satisfied, he bent down to pick up his carrier bag and began to feed in empty bottles, his expression solemn.

Chris noticed more than half of the bottles looked green. Naughty, naughty, he thought. But under the circumstances, he couldn't blame him for wanting to dump them all in one go. Besides, for all Chris knew, the different colours got mixed together anyway, once the glass reached wherever it was recycled.

"That's how he does it!" The words, bellowed into Chris's left ear, were followed a moment later by stale, yeasty breath. "I saw it!"

Chris hadn't thought people could actually jump with fright, but he managed it. He spun around: a drunk was leaning precariously towards him, the harsh planes of his face splintered by cracks.

"What?" Chris gasped, his voice breaking with each panicky rattle of his heart. There was a sour lump rising in his throat.

"Glass!" the drunk answered, beer-soaked breath fouling the air in front of Chris's face. "All over. I saw it!" His unsteady legs caved slightly, sending the drunk a few precarious steps away from Chris.

"What was?" Chris wanted to know, but the drunk had forgotten him. He weaved up the street towards the bottle-banks and the boy – who was eyeing him intently, an empty bottle clutched protectively in two hands.

Chris watched the drunk draw closer to the boy. His right knee seemed to lose its strength and he staggered past in an untidy circuit. The boy didn't take his eyes off the drunk until he'd reached the top of the road and disappeared around the front of *The Mirrorball*. Neither did Chris.

His heart was still beating painfully. What had the stupid twat meant? And what the hell had glass got to do with anything? Get a grip, Chandler! The old fart's pissed as a rat; he's got an excuse. All you've had is two pints of Black Sheep, so don't start getting paranoid!

The boy had finished loading his bottles into the bin and was carefully folding the carrier bag into a small, neat square. He stepped off the milk-crate and began to walk back towards Chris. He had passed the car park safely, when Chris realised he was holding his own breath. He imagined something was about to charge out of the darkness – all sharp edges and prismatic reflections – and snatch the boy.

Fucking idiot! he thought.

The boy passed the bus stop without looking in Chris's direction. His face was set; eyes locked forward. Probably on the houses nearby; one of which was almost certainly his home.

About half an hour later a number 11 finally pulled up, and a shivering Chris leapt gratefully aboard.

*

Late Saturday afternoon, Chris got back to his dingy Hall Green flat from his usual ritual: shopping in the city-centre. Everybody who knew him thought he was crazy: who went into Birmingham on a Saturday afternoon voluntarily? But Chris enjoyed it; the crowds, the overall insanity. Besides, this time he was feeling extra delighted: he had treated himself to his one indulgence.

As he pushed the front door shut, he noticed the *Evening Mail* jammed through his letter box. He yanked it free, walked through into his tiny living room and tossed the paper onto his well-worn sofa. He was more interested in the small parcel cradled in his left hand, wrapped in a plain plastic bag.

Chris sat in an armchair that matched the sofa in general wear, if not design, and pulled a box out of the bag. Letting the plastic carrier float to the dim carpet, Chris opened the box, carefully peeled back the crinkled layers of packing, and took out his prize: a piece of ruby crystal. Resting it on his left palm, he turned the piece slightly, watching the play of refracted light through the globular, faceted body. He had no idea what it was supposed to be: that was half the fun. He'd seen all the twee, pretty shapes in jewellers' windows: mice, dragons, teddy bears— All so predictable; so safe. Chris preferred the unusual, the downright weird. The obscurer, the better. His latest prize could be a piece of bloated fruit; or an organ, ripped from a living body; or an overfed, blood-soaked cat—

He shook his head, trying to dislodge *that* image.

Chris got to his feet and placed his newest acquisition on the mantle-shelf, next to his other two beauties. The first piece he had bought looked vaguely like an owl: facets cut to resemble huge, blank, but somehow threatening, eyes, and crude, sharp feathers. The second piece could have been meant to be a crucifix: its harsh edges and twisted form symbolic of Christ's agonies. Chris just saw a warped human shape: an alien from a superior science fiction movie.

Chandelier Promotions might not be making a fortune yet, but whenever Chris felt he could justify the expense, he bought another crystal shape. Some people collected sculpted cottages or models of classic cars; it was crystal that drew Chris. He loved the sparkle, the cleanness of it. Even naming his own business wasn't just a pun on his surname. He had always promised himself that, come the day he made it – financially speaking – he'd have a huge crystal chandelier: the kind they had in old costume movies. Something huge and gothic, hanging from the ceiling, scattering rainbow light in all directions. He'd even begun saving; although at the present rate it would take him years. Decades. Not that it was the kind of thing he talked about much. First time he'd mentioned his collection to the lads, they'd given him funny looks.

He sat down again, picking up the *Mail* and rested his feet across the sofa.

It was all over the front page: a third boy had disappeared, while a second body had been found earlier that day. This time the police weren't even trying to pretend the victim hadn't been decapitated.

Two blurred faces stared up at Chris. The one on the right – the most recent disappearance – was the boy Chris had seen outside *The Mirrorball* last night.

He had to read it all. The recovered body had been wrapped in a plastic bin-liner, already part-filled with broken glass, and left on top of a bottle-bank outside half-completed, one-person flats in Yardley Wood. It was a mass of cuts. There was no evidence of sexual assault; though the report neglected to say exactly how the body had been identified. Clothing, Chris supposed; and DNA. All that stuff.

Needless to say, the *Mail* was outraged, demanding to know when the police would start to protect Birmingham's children.

Bottle-bank. Chris knew those flats: they were less than five minutes' walk from his own. Too new for his erratic income. The old drunk's words suddenly replayed themselves in Chris's head.

Glass! All over —!

He let the paper drop to the carpet. All he could think of were those deserted kittens.

Chris got to his feet and wandered through into the kitchen. He filled the kettle and plugged it in. Tonight he was going to go into Digbeth; pleasure, for once. Vincent Black was playing one of his semi-regular gigs at *The Kerry Man*, and he wanted to hear him again. Chris had even bought a copy of Vincent's CD, *Poison Road*, the last time he'd caught his act. And that was something he didn't normally do. But he was going back to *The Mirrorball* tomorrow night. Mayan Surprise was playing, and he wanted to check them out.

Had that drunk really seen something? Or someone? And where had he been when he saw it? If Chris saw him tomorrow, he was going to have to ask.

*

Chris left *The Mirrorball* early. Mayan Surprise had been a good band, but the gig was lousy. The pub had only half-filled, leaving the atmosphere flat and uninspiring. Surprise's particular brand of Latin American influenced R&B needed more from its audience than polite applause.

He dodged across a Hagley Road streaming with traffic, heading towards a chip shop he knew well. He bought himself a large bag of chips and a stubby bottle of Pepsi. Shoving the bottle into a raincoat pocket, he strolled leisurely back in the direction of the pub, eating the white hot but somehow undercooked chips. Chris had talked Ronnie into lending him the battered Mini for the night – Ménage-A-Ray weren't doing anything, after all – but the drummer loathed the smell of stale food in his van. Chris couldn't see why Ronnie was so fussy: the thing was a half-rotted rust-bucket already. But it'd be more than his life was worth to sit inside, eating.

Chris stood on the corner for a while, near the pedestrian crossing, watching the twin lines of traffic: one heading into the city, the other out to Quinton and the Clent Hills. As he finished off the chips he wondered if Clent was a decent place to live. Mostly countryside; loads of empty, green space where you could lose yourself. Probably expensive, though. Chandelier Promotions would need to do bloody good business to reach those heights. And that meant dealing with better bands than Ménage-A-Ray and Mayan Surprise. No, not better: more commercial.

Art for art's sake; but money for God's sake. Art was his crystal collection: this was business.

Chris tossed the balled-up chip paper into a waste-bin and pulled out the Pepsi. As the man in the pedestrian lights changed from red to green, Chris twisted off the top and took a deep pull on the bottle. He trotted over the crossing smartly, knowing how little time they gave pedestrians, continuing on past *The Mirrorball* and down the hill towards the car park.

He paused reluctantly at the array of bottle-banks, mouth suddenly dry. Swirling the last mouthful of Pepsi around his arid tongue, he jerked the bottle into a bin, and backed rapidly away. He heard the bottle hit, and a sharp, piercing avalanche of noise. As though something had been jolted awake.

Glass! All over —!

Crap! That was just settlement. His empty bottle had shaken a load of others loose—

A whole litter of kittens —

There was another harsh rattle as more bottles moved, deep

inside the bin.

Bin-liner partially filled with glass…left by a bottle-bank—

More glass shifted. Chris heard the brittle detonation of something being smashed. He backed further off, feet pulling him towards the car park and back of the pub. Never mind what he thought he heard: business first.

He found the ladders exactly where he'd left them. John the barman had asked Chris to stow them away for him one night. It was useful knowledge. Chris grabbed the ladders, careful not to drag any part of them on the brickwork or cratered tarmac. He circled around the far side of the car park, skirting the dense stand of trees. No one could see him – not with his long dark hair and black raincoat – and the ladders were too weathered to catch any of the thin light cast by the single spotlight.

At a precise spot between a laurel bush and stark clump of privet, he pushed into the thick, concealing mass of conifers. He raised the ladders, sliding them with difficulty between the black, dusty fronds of two cypresses. Once they were positioned as safely as they ever would be, he dragged himself up. His shoulder bag caught on a branch, half-slipping. The loose contents seemed to screech shatteringly loud. By the time he had reached the top he was breathless and sweating, despite the cold. The resinous stench of conifers blocked his nostrils.

Chris heaved the obstinate needles aside, and relief flooded him. It was still there: exactly where he'd hung it Friday night. His crystal ornament. The latest instalment on his chandelier.

The boy's body was still attached – pinned up among the branches by a short length of electrical cable – but now he'd got Ronnie's van, he could sort that out. Like he had before.

It was the head he coveted: encased in a mosaic of glass shards, each lovingly inserted and positioned to best catch the light. Clear, green and brown glass; and some freshly-stained ruby glass. A brilliant glass bauble, decorating the tree. His third.

A whole litter—

And best of all: there for Chris alone. After all, he had promised himself. No one could see this chandelier unless they pushed their way into the heart of the conifers. And why would they?

Chris slowly climbed back down the ladder, aware of how quiet it had grown. The city-bound traffic was tailing off at last. He stepped out into the car park, eyes squinting towards the quartet of shapes on the edge of the kerb: the bottle-banks, the aluminium can drop. They were so obvious from here: highlighted by the street's sodium glow. But there was something new: something that split and threw back the light in razor-edged patterns. Its brilliant, serrated T-shape incongruous amongst the ugly plastic bins.

He began to step, cat-silent, across the tarmac.

It was waiting for him. Yellow and white light stabbed off its myriad facets. The slightest movement threw a million tiny spotlights across the pavement, sharp-edged as ceramic wind-chimes. Chris's eyes glinted with tears as he neared the patient cruciform.

"Perfect," he whispered. He reached out to touch it, feel its keen smoothness. Another step, and he was within its embrace.

Glass daggers enfolded him. It swallowed him. He felt each sliver finding its home in his flesh. It was exquisite. He threw back his head to laugh, but foot-long splinters of green bottle-glass slid up through his throat, pinning tongue to palate.

As he grew increasingly rigid – ever more chunks of glass sinking deeper, setting themselves in his bones – he thought he could hear distant purring.

BLOOD OF EDEN

Cydonian left his two backups to wait in the basement parking garage. They weren't happy. Which makes three of us, Cydonian thought. But the short goon in the Armani suit insisted, and there had been enough assurances and pledges from both sides. All he could go on was trust. It didn't feel like so much.

The runt rode the elevator up with Cydonian, standing by the doors, hands clasped lightly in front of him. The car had mirrors on two sides, which surprised Cydonian – though maybe it shouldn't have. This was a public building, after all. He caught sight of his reflection: big, solid, crop-haired, his charcoal suit probably costing a fraction of the Armani – but his face was oddly corpse-like in the car's light. He shook his head; he didn't believe in premonitions.

There weren't many days when he envied his sister's husband, Jon. But at that moment, sitting behind a desk, signing dockets that moved freighter-loads of merchandise in and out of the country – with just a little creamed off now and then – seemed pretty good.

The car jolted to a halt. The doors slid open onto a small room with all the charm of a washroom. But it was bright and warm-looking, and half-filled by a giant.

Tall and wide, a grey vest tight across his massive torso, his bare arms were heavily tattooed. Dragons: three-coloured, one twining up each arm. His shaved head gave no clue to his racial origins; though the broad face and harsh cheek bones suggested Slavic, if not further east. Cydonian felt there was something ritualistic about the way the giant was standing: like a half-baked sumo wrestler thinking about tossing another handful of salt.

The giant waved a ham-sized mitt towards Cydonian, palm up. The gesture was unmistakable. Cydonian reached under his jacket and slid out his automatic: a SIG 9mm, their latest model, nickel-plated and custom-gripped. Jon had gotten it for him – sneaked into the country in his last freighter load from Europe – as a birthday present. It dropped into the giant's hand and lay there like a kid's water pistol.

Moving with a speed and delicacy Cydonian wouldn't have imagined from the man's meat-hook fingers, the giant ejected the magazine, working the breech to check there wasn't already a shell loaded. Cydonian felt vaguely pissed they considered him so unprofessional.

The tattooed giant tossed the automatic to the runt in the suit, and thumbed each slug out of the magazine. Satisfied, he reached over Cydonian – handing the emptied clip and shells to his partner. To Cydonian's surprise, the reloaded gun was offered back to him a few moments later.

Thorough, he thought, and confident. Hence the check for silver bullets. He didn't have any; and they obviously didn't believe ordinary slugs were a threat. Maybe they were right. Cydonian knew all the rumours; the stories taken for gospel. When it came to one who the Director called the Prince of Darkness, even the craziest urban legends started to sound true.

Cydonian reholstered the automatic just as a door facing him – previously unnoticed – swung open. The tattooed giant stepped back and indicated he should go through. Not ready to argue, Cydonian did just that.

The room he entered was dark, almost black after the antiseptic whiteness of the cubicle behind him. Then lights came on: shielded wall lights that grew steadily brighter. They reached the moody level of an expensive cocktail lounge and didn't go any higher. All the room contained was a leather chair, low drinks table and three panelled walls. The fourth wall, facing him, was still black and featureless. It might just have been a perfectly flat sheet of obsidian.

"Sit down, Mister Cydonian," came a voice. It was warm, cultured, accentless. Whatever PA system he was using, it sounded expensive: there was no sense the words were being filtered through speakers. "Have yourself a drink. You'll find a wide selection of spirits and mixers under the table in front of you."

"Thanks." Warily, he walked to the chair and lowered himself into it. He didn't believe there was a disguised trapdoor waiting to drop him into oblivion, but he couldn't shake the habit of a lifetime.

There was an impressive collection of bottles on a shelf under the table; along with tumblers, an ice-bucket, shaker, slices of lemon and olives in glass bowls, and several mixers.

"Bourbon and branch, if I'm not mistaken," came the assured voice. Cydonian smiled to himself. If Dracula was trying to impress him with his wealth, taste and background knowledge,

Cydonian was the wrong guy.

He finished mixing his drink and raised it at the dark.

"I come to you in trust, with my defences down." He took a sip of the bourbon to mask the discomfort the words stirred in him. It was the correct greeting – they'd drummed it into him often enough – but it sounded so trite.

"You are welcome, Mister Cydonian. May a little of the joy you bring remain forever with us."

Cydonian took another drink. This was dumb! Swapping quaint phrases with a dead man. So far nothing had dissuaded him from his original belief: they should have come in force; loaded for bear. He had seen only two goons – though he guessed there would be plenty more stashed away somewhere – but surprise would have been enough. This building was too old and rotten with narrow corridors for anything like a decent defence to be mobilised in time.

Except that wasn't the way you went for someone whose megacorporation, Paradis-LaCroix, contributed nearly seventy percent of Switzerland's gross national product. He near as dammit owned the country; and that meant he owned Zurich. And the banks.

Cydonian took another mouthful of bourbon, and waited. He could afford that. It had taken years of move and counter-move, threat and direct action to get this far: a face-to-face with the Count himself. He could be patient a few more minutes.

Not that Dracula used the title anymore. The world had changed since he'd left his ancestral lands a century ago: titles meant nothing. It was all about money. And the power that went with enough of it. Families weren't things of blood: families were corporations.

Things of blood, Cydonian thought, chuckling to himself. Blood-ties. Yes – he liked that one. He'd tell it to the Director when he got back.

"Something amuses you?" The voice soothed through his thoughts.

"Just thinking." Cydonian placed his almost empty glass on the table. "If the social amenities are over, I'm eager to get down to business."

"Why not."

The black wall in front of him began to lighten. Shapes slowly formed out of a gradually paling background: a desk, functionally stark; two dark walls with more of the subdued lights. The third wall – to Cydonian's left – was a single plasma screen: a mosaic of smaller images. They blinked and flickered, too small and too fast to mean anything to him.

And behind the desk, a silhouette outlined against a high-backed chair by the screen and wall-lights, was Dracula. It was hard to make out details, but Cydonian got the impression of a tall, thin man, much younger than he should be – but that could have been the poor light. Just as the faint luminescence of the vampire's eyes was probably Cydonian's imagination.

For a few seconds, he was fooled; then Cydonian noticed the faintest distortion just where the video wall ended. He checked the other side, and the ceiling. Both had the same unfocused edge – as though the room had been sliced neatly down the centre, then inexpertly patched up.

Holy shit, he thought, trying not to be impressed – a hologram. Good trick. Despite the inexact blending of the rooms, the image was far and above anything Cydonian had seen. And he had seen plenty. Dracula had money, and obviously bought outstanding talent with it.

No wonder he had proposed the New York meeting: he could go anywhere he wanted, without moving from his office in Berne, or Tirana, or Beijing – or Samarkand, for all anyone knew. It would take just a few days' notice – enough time to rent office space and install the appropriate equipment.

But why then, Cydonian wondered, the shuck-and-jive with his weapon? If Dracula was sitting in the Australian Outback, silver bullets wouldn't mean diddly. Cydonian reeled back his memory, trying to find a clear image of the only two he'd met so far: the giant, and the Armani-suited runt. Did either show the signs? If they did, Cydonian hadn't spotted them – and neither had seemed to care squat whether his slugs had been silver. If one had been a vampire, just brushing the precious metal would have melted flesh like shit through a tin horn.

"Were you surprised that I requested this meeting?" Dracula asked. There was a note of amusement in his voice; or was it the kind of barely-hidden contempt some Europeans showed towards Americans?

"To be frank, yes. Especially the mano a mano bit." Cydonian picked up his glass and drained it. He waved it at the holographic screen. "But I see you got around that."

"I believe in taking precautions, Mister Cydonian. And it does no harm to… show off, once in a while."

"We know all about what your various corporations can do," Cydonian said. "And how many thumbs you got stuck up whose asses."

"You're hardly in a position to be superior. What about your own Agency's investments?"

"National security." It was the pat answer. Nobody believed it anymore, but Cydonian had seen it scrawled on the toilet-paper dispensers in enough washrooms back at Langley.

"Fascinating how far around the globe the USA seems to feel its national security is threatened."

"You going to tell me you're no threat?"

"Not when your Director seems to feel otherwise."

"With respect, Count, that's no answer."

"I asked for this meeting because I've grown tired of your constant interference in my affairs." His voice was curt and business-like suddenly. If Dracula was irritated by Cydonian's blunt manner, he wasn't showing it. "Having to constantly keep an eye open for your frequently inept attempts at subversion is proving too large a drain on my resources…"

"Thinking of giving in, Count?" Cydonian allowed himself a chuckle.

Dracula's outlined head tilted fractionally. "Hardly. But I think the time has come to call for a cease-fire. Perhaps just a temporary one. A break in hostilities."

"For what? You to regroup and plan another attack? Your friends in the Balkans have been playing that card for the past ten years."

"I've not been travelling in that part of the world for many decades, Cydonian." He paused and raised a hand to where his lips might be. "Ever since I quit my estates, in fact. How time does fly. They seem to be doing well enough without me, though."

Cydonian resisted the urge to laugh. The constantly changing demands of the factions in that particular shitstorm had the vampire's MO all over them. The latest cease-fire – to mark the birth of a new century – didn't look as though it would be any more permanent than the previous ones. "Maybe the generals are quick studies."

Dracula waved the hand. Cydonian saw long nails, and in the back-lighting they looked odd: more like a rat's claws. "You credit me with too much influence, Cydonian. Humanity has rarely needed prompting to go to war."

"Is that why you involved yourself in World War Two?"

The vampire laughed, this time in simple appreciation; there was no mockery involved. "So you found that out?"

"Didn't look as though you meant to hide it. A volunteer RAF pilot, enlisting in 1942 under false credentials. You got a couple of medals."

"In wartime, Cydonian, medals are handed out like candy. It gives the cannon-fodder something to strive for. I simply survived all the night raids on cities such as Dresden and Berlin. Bomber Command seemed to think that was a feat worth celebrating."

"Why should you care?"

Dracula leaned on his desk. Even though he knew the vampire was probably miles away, Cydonian felt himself draw back in his seat.

"Are we going to play dumb and dumber, Cydonian? Will you pretend that, at the time, the OSS didn't know what Hitler's more … unorthodox scientists were trying to do? *Projekt Nachtzehrer*: the systematic eradication of all vampires throughout German-occupied Europe. While at the same time trying to isolate whatever factor it was that created the Undead."

"Would these be the same scientists working on the flying saucers?" Cydonian began, then his mouth slammed shut at what he was seeing. Mary, Mother of God! he thought, his eyes really do glow!

"Under the circumstances," Dracula said, his voice low and velvety, "knowing what we both do of the Agency's involvement in military Black Projects, I would not consider it wise to mock." He leaned back, some of the light fading from his eyes. "The Führer's astrologers forecast that an army of vampires would sweep out from the heart of Europe and conquer the world. Hitler chose to interpret that as meaning a personally selected regiment from the Waffen-SS: vampire warriors who truly could be called *Tötenkopf*!"

"So you joined up. Didn't think you were the vengeful type."

"Then you've not done your research thoroughly."

Cydonian didn't rise to the bait. He wasn't going to question why the vampire's reprisals waited until all of his Undead cousins had been beheaded with axes. Buried in huge pits filled with poppy seeds, coins placed under each head's tongue – none of them was ever going to rise again. Despite the Count's spoken sentiments, Cydonian couldn't help thinking the vampire had let the Nazis do a little house-cleaning for him.

And maybe Hitler's crazy egg-heads had gotten closer to some kind of vampire factor than Dracula liked.

"Tell me, Cydonian," the soothing voice interrupted his thoughts again. "What do you think is my greatest desire?"

Cydonian thought hard before replying. He had seen a phrase years ago, and it had sounded so right! Ah, yes – that was it...

"Illimitable dominion over all?" He couldn't help being smug.

"Don't try and sound literary, Cydonian. It ill-suits you."

He watched as the rat-claw hand dropped to the desk. Immediately, the light in the holographic room grew. No longer an outline, Dracula's face was gaunt and pale. His lips looked too dark against the pallor, as did his eyes and hair. Cydonian was surprised to see how little he had of it: just a thick fringe, leaving the top of his skull bare and shiny. He was wearing an expensive grey jacket, grey shirt and a chaotically patterned silk tie. Just like any other middle-aged businessman. You could pass him in the street and never know.

"No, Cydonian, just like any other thing on this planet, I want to see myself reflected in my children."

"Vampires don't have kids."

"Not in the ordinary sense, no. But we can reproduce, as you know."

"If you're trying to tell me you want to turn the whole world into blood-suckers, that's old news, Count."

Dracula's dark lips thinned into a warm smile. It got nowhere near his eyes. "I'm the new red menace, am I? And you're wrong, Cydonian – all of you. What use to me is a planet of vampires? Off what would I live? Or any of us? If you'll forgive the analogy, the human race wouldn't survive long if it killed and ate all of its cattle in one go. The predator must allow some of its prey to survive."

"What are you trying to say? That you don't intend to prey on us any longer?"

Dracula leaned back in his chair. He waved an arm at the room. "This is the twenty-first century, Cydonian. The rules have changed; are changing all the time."

"So?"

"A few years ago someone, I forget who, commented that each century has its own sciences; disciplines which define that particular era. In the nineteenth, it was engineering; in the twentieth, chemistry and, naturally, physics; but the twenty-first would have biology. In the new millennium, man will not only conquer all disease, but find new ways to exploit the foundation of life itself."

"Like bio-chips."

Dracula waved an expansive hand. "Already a reality, to all intents and purposes. Several of my subsidiary companies own the patents on thirteen processes which are part of a bio-chip's manufacture."

"Useful combination of interests, right, Count? Paradis-LaCroix gets an arm-lock on wetware manufacture, while all the satellite, communications and electronics businesses you own tie up the hardware."

"Which of us can exert the most influence on the modern world?" Dracula's smile broadened. Cydonian thought he looked like a Great White about to strike. "Me, or the Agency?"

"You might have Wall Street and the London Stock Exchange kissing your ass, but we have all the secrets no one wants told." He turned the facts over in his mind. "I guess it's a stand-off. Between us, we've got the world tied up: finance and intelligence."

"Quite. While a stalemate continues, neither of our great houses can hope to benefit. We are like two giants throwing rocks at each other: neither can hurt the other, but the irritation value is high."

It all seemed so clear, suddenly. The Company had something the vampire wanted, or he thought he could buy himself some kind of angle. "What do you have to trade?"

"I have no need to trade. I give you a present." He steepled his long fingers. "The cure for AIDS."

Cydonian remembered in time, and stopped himself jerking forward in his seat. It wasn't smart to show too much interest. "Just like that?"

"Call it a show of faith. Faith in the future. And a demonstration that whatever bungling strikes your department tries to make at me, I am quite capable of setting it right."

Cydonian settled back in his chair. He wanted another drink, but didn't dare make one. It didn't surprise him the vampire knew of the Company's involvement in the AIDS disaster.

"Of course, I could always send my gift elsewhere – China, for example – while letting it be known exactly who released the HIV variants. Black Projects initial coding *ASV2a, b* and *c.*"

"No one would believe it. That rumour's been doing the goddam rounds since the virus was identified."

"I have proof. Memos from your own department, balance sheets, Presidential authorisations. The idea that the government could release a deadly biological agent before it had been adequately tested – or even an antidote prepared – would sound perfectly reasonable to some paranoid minds. Although, I would draw the line at who the original target was. I doubt even the most rabid conspiracy buff would swallow the idea of an anti-vampire virus."

Cydonian licked his lips. "If you're going to let us have the cure anyway, why the threat?"

"To show you what Paradis-LaCroix can do. As I indicated, I hope the new century will see an end to all disease. I want PLC to be the lead player."

It didn't ring true. No one was that generous. "What do we have to do to get it?"

"Get it? Nothing. Watch." Dracula reached down below the desk surface and looked as though he slid out a drawer. His clawed hand dipped out of sight and touched something. All the images on the plasma wall blinked out, and then came on again. Parts of one image. It looked to Cydonian, more than anything, like a huge computer monitor.

Dracula touched something else, and words scrolled rapidly down the wall. Much too quick for Cydonian to make them out. But some kind of programme was active.

"Twenty years ago, who would have imagined sending massive packets of data along telephone lines, or satellite links?" the vampire was saying. The image changed. Now Cydonian could make out diagrams and formulae, columns of figures and scatter-charts. Dracula tapped out more commands on what Cydonian had belatedly realised was a keyboard, and the lines of text vanished. A confirmation note flagged up.

Dracula returned the keyboard under his desk and leaned back in his chair, steepling his fingers again.

"There. Every item of data on the cure is now awaiting your Director's attention on his private terminal. Formulations, test trials, methodology. Call it a present from the Paradis-LaCroix corporation. And don't worry about eavesdroppers: all of my lines are perfectly secure."

He was baiting Cydonian again; Langley had been trying to bug PLC for years without success. "Call me cynical, Count. But I can't imagine you just throwing something that's potentially worth billions of dollars to us. Does it kill the patients after ten years, turn them into shit-eating zombies or something?"

The vampire laughed softly. "I admire your bluntness, Cydonian. I always have. No, it's a genuine therapy, with few, if any, side-effects. Nothing worse than those associated with, say, chemotherapy."

Cydonian changed track. "If you think this makes up for all the past years—"

"I know: the Agency cannot be bought. Such quaint devotion to a demonstrably untrue concept. I repeat: this is a gift. All I ask is a—" he waved a hand as though it helped him frame an unpleasant request "—small favour."

Here it comes, thought Cydonian. The horse-trading. "How small?"

"Nothing that will cause any drastic alteration to the Agency's foreign policy."

"Which one?"

"Russian."

"I can't make promises."

"You're trying to be clever again, Cydonian. You're fully empowered to deal, or you wouldn't be here."

Cydonian took a deep breath. "What do you propose?"

"Russia is about to suffer the worst civil war since the final days of Rome. It's likely that the recent terrorism will escalate into open rebellion. Every general who can find so much as a working tank will make a bid for the Kremlin."

"That's not exactly insider information, Count. Anyone with two eyes and an IQ bigger than a shithouse rat could figure it out."

"Perhaps. But they wouldn't appreciate how large a part the Agency has in Russian destabilisation. The policy for the past decade has been to keep Russia on the brink of collapse, constantly warring with itself, to prevent the resurgence of its old Imperialist dream. Good as the game was, no one wants to see the Cold War back. Not when the same methods can be used to keep an old enemy on its knees and helpless."

"Excuse me while I stand and applaud your grasp of politics, Count. What's all this got to do with your favour?"

"I want a small nuclear war."

Now Cydonian did lean down and pick up the bourbon bottle. He poured himself a stiff one and took a mouthful.

"You're fucking crazy!" he said, after the bourbon's heat had eased off. "The radiation – fall-out!"

"Do you really think I would jeopardise the hub of my operation in Switzerland? My calculations indicate that the risk to the Northern Hemisphere is minimal. Certainly no worse than the Chernobyl incident. Inconvenient, but not terminal."

"You can't calculate risks like ball-game percentages!"

"For twenty years or so, it has become increasingly difficult for me – and my contemporaries – to step outside," Dracula replied calmly. "Even on the most overcast day. I have every reason to believe this is due to the constant erosion of the ozone layer. You see, Cydonian, vampire and mortal have much in common: the sun is lethal to us both unless it's shielded effectively. Thanks to humanity's usual carelessness, we are all in some danger."

"Then just come out at night, like your legend says you do."

"Difficult, when I am supposed to be the owner of a vast corporation."

"My heart bleeds."

"I know. Even through a hologram, I can see it."

Cydonian gulped at his drink. The fear was back. "But I still don't see the connection."

"Nuclear winter. Even with a strike as small as the one I propose, the amount of ash and dust thrown into the atmosphere will blanket the sun for years."

"Further damaging the ozone layer!"

"I'm impressed, Cydonian. Yes, for a few years the ozone layer will be severely compromised; but it can repair itself. During the decades of nuclear winter, the damage will be fixed."

"By which time you and all the other nightcrawlers will have taken over the fucking planet!"

"Of course, I cannot rescind my gift. Regardless of your decision." Dracula waved a hand at the plasma wall. "It's too late for that."

Cydonian wanted to fidget. He was sure there was a trickle of sweat starting at the base of his neck. The leery old son-of-a-bitch wouldn't give in just like that!

"What's your game, Count?"

"I don't play games, Cydonian. You should know that." His eyes were red now: dark and hot. "If you won't instigate total civil war in Russia, I will be forced to cause the war myself. It will be a little more difficult – I don't have a seasoned network already established – and take a while longer. But the results will be the same. There are, I believe, many in the Ukraine who would dearly love to make their old masters a present of the millions of tonnes of nuclear missiles they inherited. Do you doubt I can arrange it?"

Cydonian thought about Paradis-LaCroix: how much of Switzerland Dracula's corporation owned. And he thought about how many leaders of the old Soviet Union had siphoned off funds into private Swiss bank accounts. Accounts that could be drained, or expanded, by someone with the vampire's influence.

And he thought about the tonnes of communications hardware orbiting the Earth, and about how many were built by the countless businesses hidden behind dummy corporations, themselves a front for PLC. Satellites that could relay plenty of signals, other than multi-channel television systems. Signals such as missile launch codes.

Yes, he believed Dracula could do it.

Cydonian started to rise. "I don't think we have anything more to discuss, Count. If—"

"Sit down."

Cydonian dropped back in the seat as though a weight had been dropped on him. Even though Dracula hadn't even raised his voice, Cydonian responded automatically. He was a kid again, hugging concrete because his drill sergeant had ordered another hundred push-ups.

"I have no interest in an unhealthy world. Once the Russian civil war is under way to my satisfaction, I will pass on to the Agency effective, total cures for all serum-carried disease. Like the hepatitis variants. Not simple vaccines, you understand: methods to eradicate the diseases entirely. Plans to destroy bacterial and viral disease are also well in hand, although here we must go carefully. PLC doesn't want to release another HIV on the world. Not even deliberately.

"In the meantime, one of my subsidiaries – known world-wide for its confectionery – is going into the soft drinks business."

Cydonian shook his head. "Soda?" This was getting beyond him.

"After the war, while the Americans and Soviets were busy stealing rocket scientists from the Nazis, I was much more interested in their biochemists. Many were helped across the border into Switzerland, where their research was allowed to proceed unchecked."

Cydonian made a connection. "The vampire factor!"

"Indeed. Once the war-time bombing raids – those in which I had a hand – removed all records of their work and experiments, there was nothing left for anyone to pick over. I had the scientists; I had their minds. The memory of *Projekt Nachtzehrer* died with the Third Reich."

"You already owned Laboratoire Paradis," commented Cydonian, thinking back to what he'd read.

"And a smaller concern in Spain. Both counties – Spain and Switzerland – escaped the ravages of the war. By 1946 work into the vampire factor was well beyond anything Hitler had managed."

"And you found it." Cydonian tried to move, but found he couldn't twitch much more than a finger.

"Better yet: I discovered the Dracula factor!" The vampire stood, and for the first time Cydonian got a real sense of his height and presence. Even from a hologram.

"You know that before a human can be reborn a vampire, they must first drink a vampire's blood. Only then can they experience the little death: be brought across to the world of the Undead." Dracula walked around to the front of the desk and sat casually on it. "It took years for research and techniques to catch up with the idea, but eventually we found it: the factor in my blood which makes me who I am, and ensures my disciples need never die. Biology, Cydonian. I told you it would define the twenty-first century."

"What you going to do with this … factor? Poison the water?"

"I told you: we're going into the drinks business. Americans so love their soft drinks. The factor can be included perfectly safely in just about any drink you might name. Colas, club soda, root beer." He gestured towards Cydonian's empty glass. "Branch water…"

The only part of Cydonian moving was sweat: trickling down his back. That and his eyes. They flashed back and forth between the glass and the Count's smug face.

"You may already have noticed one effect: even across this satellite link – through a holographic image – you are subject to my will. Intriguing, isn't it. How the most recent advances in technology can still be vessels for the most ancient gifts."

"You're going to make me a motherfucking vampire! You bastard! You gave your word you—!" Dracula paralysed his larynx. Cydonian was left silently flapping his mouth like a beached fish.

"Please, Cydonian. I abhor profanity; no matter the situation. Rest assured you have my word: I have no intention of bringing you across. That would serve no purpose. I told you I have no use for a world filled with vampires; mortal servants are another matter. The blood factor gives me total control over the human mind. A constantly reproducing pool of labour, any part of which can be brought across as the whim takes me.

"Hitler's astrologers were correct, in their way. But it begins in Switzerland, not Germany.

"What I do need is a salesman: someone who will persuade the Agency's Director my civil war is justified; ensure the FDA finds nothing to alarm it. Perhaps buy anyone who becomes too annoying a soda…

"I can provide the advertising: make the market secure in what it's buying. Your brother-in-law is in imports, I believe?"

Cydonian mentally raved and tore at his paralysis. He'd been set up from the start. His position in the Company; Jon…

Light spread across the holograph screen from over Cydonian's shoulder, instantly destroying the 3-D effect. Two shadows briefly fluttered against the ghostly image of Dracula. His two goons. Cydonian felt hands locking under his arms, raising him up.

Something approaching control returned to his legs, and he could just about stand. He found himself looking up into the face of the giant. There was something wrong; something different.

It was the teeth. The fangs. The giant grinned, displaying enlarged, needle-sharp fangs. He looked like some kind of blunt-headed shark.

Cydonian couldn't speak, couldn't express his confusion. But it must have shown on his face.

"Biology, Cydonian," Dracula's assured voice came to him as the giant raised a huge hand, and carefully peeled the skin off like a pale glove. "Grown in PLC laboratories from human stem cells. For a short period, it gives us tolerance to some of the more traditional methods of detection."

The skin dropped to the floor like a snake's discarded scales. The giant took Cydonian's shoulder and gently guided him towards the white cubicle. This time, the light looked much too threatening.

"Adam was rejected from the Garden for disobeying his master," the Count was saying. "I will be taking no chances."

SUFFER A WITCH

He watched her flinch away from the first cords of wood hitting the ground. She tried to draw back as the growing pile of kindling battered her already grossly abused feet. Yet all the while her gaze never left the window through which he observed the preparations. Surely she could not actually see him through the heavily leaded pane? But her eyes seemed to find his, holding him snared and breathless, even now. Those wonderful eyes, still not condemning him; nor confessing. Eyes so full of life and beauty, staring out from a face and body ruined by days of careful questioning.

She never confessed.

Was it that, or the lack of condemnation that made him so uneasy?

The door behind him slammed. He turned – almost jumping around – trying to disguise how startled he was. It was Noordijk's *burgemeester*, Joseph Groen, smacking the dust from his broad hat as he stepped into the tiny room.

"A grand day, *Meneer* van Haardt," Groen said. Despite the friendly words, his hard, flat tone made no effort to disguise his true feelings.

Pieter van Haardt grunted and returned his attentions to the scene through the window. He had no more love for Groen than the *burgemeester* had for him. And no more regard for whether it showed or not.

"You appear vexed, *meneer*," Groen continued, joining him at the window. Was he trying to provoke van Haardt? "I would have thought you looked forward to this day."

"And why would I?" van Haardt favoured the older man with a cold glance.

"Your first witch tried, convicted and about to be destroyed. Your position in Noordijk secure. Is that not cause to celebrate?"

"One less, that is all, *meneer*," van Haardt mumbled. His eyes were drawn back to the spectacle outside: the pile of faggots reached halfway to the girl's waist. It wouldn't be long, now. "What is one less? The Low Countries are plagued by them." *And she never confessed*, a silent voice added. *No confession; no condemnation. No hatred...*

"Surely not plagued?" Groen was saying, his tone baiting. "You exaggerate."

And it may be that van Haardt did, but he would be the last to admit it. "Last year, in Amsterdam alone, there were twenty-three burnings, *meneer*," he commented, as though counting off livestock. "In Utrecht, sixteen."

"Amsterdam is a large city, Pieter; feelings run high—"

"Are you implying the creatures burned were not witches, *meneer*?"

"Not at all!" Groen was eager to deny any such claims. Given how van Haardt had aroused the people of Noordijk, he could easily have the *burgemeester* arrested, tried and be in exactly the same straits as the girl in less than a week. As far as witches were concerned, van Haardt's word was the law. Where he had found one witch, he could easily find another.

The *burgemeester* was still talking. "I was simply observing how a certain... objectivity could disappear in such cases."

"Then I am guilty of a lack of objectivity?"

...She never confessed...

Groen sighed. "Hardly that, Pieter. The opposite, if anything."

Van Haardt grunted. "The Lord's work must be carried out, *meneer*. I can show neither fear nor favour."

...Despite all the beatings, the red-hot irons applied to her soles, the needles eagerly applied to find the Devil's mark... she never confessed...

"Then you are either made of steel, *Meneer* van Haardt, or ice." Groen replaced his hat, tugging the wide brim down across his brow. "I could never do your job." He left, slamming the door again.

...So she had been thrown from the dyke into the nearest canal... and in the deep, clean water, had floated...

...As he had known she would...

Van Haardt smiled for the first time. "That you never could, *Meneer* Groen," he agreed softly.

*

The eager volunteers had finished building the pyre. Now the girl was buried to her waist in bundles of wood. Her broken hands were bound to the stake above her head, at van Haardt's suggestion. He didn't want even the remotest possibility the ropes could burn through before the fire had done its cleansing work.

The people of Noordijk were standing at a respectful distance, all eyes fixed on the victim in the centre of their square: some eager, some sickened – a few afraid. They knew that having found one witch in Noordijk, and tasted the power, van Haardt was unlikely to leave it at that. Any one of them could be next. There was more than one person gathered that morning who knew the true reason for Anna Roosendaal's trial and conviction. It would not be wise for any of them to discuss it aloud.

As van Haardt stepped into the square, he could feel every one of those mixed emotions; smell them. He breathed in deeply, savouring the fear, envy and hatred. It was something new to him, this power; this reaction. He considered he could grow to like it. He could like it very much indeed.

He walked slowly towards the bound figure, Anna watching him calmly. She was the only one who seemed able to meet his gaze. Of all the eyes in the village square, hers were the only ones that held no feelings for her executioner. No love; no hate. It seemed that, even now, he meant nothing to her.

"Come to gloat, Pieter?" she said, her voice meant for him alone.

"It is not too late for your immortal soul, Anna Roosendaal," he spoke loudly. He had no desire to be seen having private words with a convicted witch. Everything had to be proper and legal. "Confess yourself a witch. Tell us where your familiar has fled. Renounce the others of your coven. Renounce your Infernal Master. Throw yourself on the eternal mercies of our Lord Jesus Christ, and you may yet save yourself from the flames of Damnation!"

"What a hypocrite you are." She smiled, a strained and poor imitation of the brilliant one he remembered so well. He could only guess what such a small movement cost her, and for a moment, his heart wavered. Then a blaze of anger burned the indecision away.

"Witch!" He turned to the crowd, arms spread wide. "See how she revels in her unhallowed allegiance! It seems she welcomes her imminent reunion with Satan!"

"Tell me," her heard her soft voice from behind him. "What would have happened if I had submitted to you, Pieter? What would happen once you tired of me, or begun to think me below you? Not only are you cold and cruel, you are too ambitious. How long could you tolerate a simple Friesian girl for a wife, or even just a lover?"

He spun back to face her. "You could have had it all, Anna!" he hissed. "As my wife you could have seen the world: Den Haag, Paris, New Amsterdam! But you preferred to throw cow's-eyes at that milk-sop van Drunen."

Momentarily, something like emotion coloured her pale, bruised face. "Where is he, Pieter? Did you murder him, too?"

For the second time that day, van Haardt smiled. "Our merchant fleets always need volunteers, Anna. I imagine your boy lover is halfway to the New World by now."

"I pity you, Pieter van Haardt," Anna murmured.

"Pity yourself, witch!" He raised his voice to a self-righteous roar. "You tried to bewitch me, hag; the whole of Noordijk knows it! But I was too strong in the Lord's might. Now you are tried and convicted of the heinous crime of witchcraft. You will neither renounce nor recant your sins, and so we have no choice but to order your death by the prescribed means. You will be burned to death."

He began to walk away, and then stopped and turned to face her again, as though struck by a final thought. "Enjoy the kiss of the flames: they will be as lover's caresses compared to the eternity of torment awaiting you!"

"Goodbye Pieter." Her voice was so soft; he could believe he had imagined the words.

Van Haardt raised a fist, instantly wondering why. He dropped it limply at his side, and stood uncertainly, taking a long, last look at Anna. Then he backed away.

He found himself standing at the edge of the crowd, next to Joseph Groen. The *burgemeester* was holding a burning torch. He held it towards van Haardt.

"Do you not wish to be the first?" Groen was taunting him. His tone and face might be expressionless, but the mockery was there nevertheless. Van Haardt felt it as keenly as he had the crowd's anticipation a few minutes earlier.

"I was the accuser and witness, *meneer*, not judge and executioner!"

"Even at the last, dirtying others' hands with your work." The *burgemeester* stepped out of the crowd, making his way towards the pyre. Several others, similarly armed with brands, appeared out of the press.

Van Haardt's gaze was nailed to the stake, and the torn figure bound to it. He found it impossible to blink as Groen and the others thrust their torches into the kindling. Within seconds, flames were eating their way greedily through the dry wood. There would be no smoke to mask Anna's final agonies.

The blaze grew, but Anna did not move. Even at this distance, van Haardt was sure he could see the serenity in her eyes. He wanted to rage, to curse – but he dare not. This was not right! This was not what he wanted. Anna was supposed to scream: to cry upon heaven, beg him to put the flames out.

…Confess, vilify him, blame him… Anything…

She said nothing; failed to acknowledge the flames even existed. She simply gazed calmly at him from the square's heart, and refused him the pleasure of her accusation.

Then the blaze erupted like a volcano. Anna and stake were swallowed in a white-hot glare that drove the citizens of Noordijk shrieking from the square, hands and arms shielding their eyes. Only van Haardt stayed, his gaze fixed and rigid.

The sky grew black. A vast shadow enveloped Noordijk; and a cold no less intense fell on van Haardt.

As though doused by the terrible cold, the huge blaze guttered and died. Stake and pyre were gone, but Anna stood there: her naked body no longer scarred by the brand and lash. The flames had cleansed her after all, but not in the way van Haardt had expected.

She stepped forward, seeming to glow in the intensifying darkness.

"Poor Pieter," she said. Her smile was no long pained, distracted. Its brilliance tore at his heart. "In your petty jealousy, you hit back with the surest weapon you knew."

Van Haardt looked up into the sky. It was almost totally black: the morning sun had vanished, and nothing else was visible. But for all that, he had the feeling that the darkness was somehow solid. It was as if something – so huge it was formless to a human eye – had risen from the horizon, blotting out the entire sky.

Anna was no more than an arm's length from him. She followed his gaze into the lightless sky, and cocked her head to one side.

"The irony of it all, Pieter, is that you were right," she said, her tone light. "And to answer your questions – or at least one of them – here is my familiar…"

CHEECHEE'S OUT

Anwar checked the time on the ticket machine: still seven minutes to go before his bus was due out. No one was waiting at the Abbey Street terminus stop. Time for a smoke.

He slid from his seat, stretching cramped limbs. It was a quiet night. The only sounds were from the kids sprawled over the dual carriageway's central reservation: coarse laughter, muted shrieks, and harsh obscenities. Anwar tugged a packet of cigarettes from his tunic pocket, flicked one out and lit it. The lungful of tobacco smoke was like – what was it? – nectar. This ban on smoking was killing him.

He froze with the cigarette halfway to his mouth. Sounded like there was something inside the bus, on the top deck. A muffled giggle, he thought, followed by a rustling, shifting sound. Anwar frowned; there couldn't be anyone upstairs: he'd come straight from the garage. Though he supposed it wasn't impossible for someone to sneak on while no one was looking. A tramp; couple of kids having it off…

He started up the stairs, wondering if he should have called in on the radio first. He poked his head up from the stairwell cautiously: the deck was empty.

Hearing things. Late nights'll do that to you. He realised he was still carrying his cigarette and decided to get off before leaving too strong a tobacco smell. Halfway down the stairs he heard something again. Strange liquid, snuffling sounds. A dog?

Anwar was back up the stairs in a moment. "If some dog's shitting all over my bus…!" He stared hard between every bench as he moved towards the rear.

Then he found it, huddled on the floor, apparently wedged under a seat. It moved restlessly, but with a fluid grace, as if nervous of the driver's gaze.

"What the hell—?" Anwar had no time for another word as it embraced him tenderly.

*

DI James Ibbotson weaved his old Ford through the assembled police cars. Their blue lights stippled the night with random

64

patterns. A small crowd of onlookers gazed morbidly beyond the police cordon. Their eager features pulsed on and off: immobilized dancers in a mute disco.

Ibbotson heaved himself out of the car and nudged its door shut. He walked slowly towards the nearest clump of officers, fastening one of his overcoat buttons as he moved. The coat was tighter than it used to be. And to think he was known as the thinnest streak of piss in the force when he joined. Grey hair and a beer gut: that was all he'd collected after more than twenty years with West Midlands police.

A round-faced CID man with cheeks red as his mop of curly hair glanced up, rugby-player frame made larger still by a bulky ski jacket. Ibbotson groaned silently: that was all he needed. Detective Sergeant Glyn-bloody-Conway. Possibly the most insensitive idiot in the Division.

"Evening, guv." Conway's accent hadn't changed a bit, even after years of living in the Midlands. Ibbotson believed it was sheer bloody-mindedness.

"Sergeant. What have we got? They wouldn't tell me over the phone."

Conway guided the Inspector towards a covered ambulance stretcher. "Nasty one, guv. Paki bus driver, sliced to ribbons. Woman who runs the supermarket there called us when the bus hadn't moved for half an hour."

"Which was when?"

Conway glanced at his notebook. "Call timed at 22.41."

Ibbotson took hold of the stretcher's blue sheet, checked none of the rubberneckers could see anything, and pulled it back. What lay underneath had given up all claim to humanity. Only the few remaining slivers of skin and shirt identified it as ever being anything more than a glistening knot of flayed, crimson rope.

"Christ." He dropped the sheet quickly

"Even his own mother wouldn't recognize him." Conway sounded quite cheerful about it. Two paramedics wheeled the anatomized remains away. A third man in ill-fitting white coveralls that made him look like a deflated Michelin Man stood back to let them pass: Dr Les Taylor, duty forensic pathologist. Ibbotson had always thought Taylor looked the part: tall and cadaverous. Even the crappiest TV police procedural would have avoided such a walking cliché.

"Evening, Jim." Taylor's warm Edinburgh accent clashed with

his gaunt appearance. But then, Ibbotson reflected, hadn't Burke, Hare and Dr Knox all come from the same city? "A beauty, eh?"

Ibbotson pulled out a cigarette and lit it with hands that weren't entirely steady. "Anything to tell me?"

"Not at this point. The wounds look as though they were inflicted with razor-wire. Or something similar. Not your usual Stanley knife slice-up."

"Thanks, Les." As the pathologist strode jauntily off to join the paramedics, Ibbotson turned back to Conway. "Talk to the woman from the supermarket. It's supposed to close at half-nine; I'm wondering why it takes someone over an hour to cash up." He blew out a pall of smoke, glancing at the camera mounted just above the door. "And find out if there's any CCTV we can use."

He turned his gaze back to the gathered crowd: had any of them seen anything – or be prepared to admit it? This part of the street was usually the mating ground for the local feral youth. They were like hyenas: never missed a thing.

He recognised a face and strolled over, trailing smoke. Ibbotson halted in front of half a dozen youngsters dressed in a variety of baggy jeans and blousons, primary colours fluorescent in the blue and black night. He gazed at one boy in particular: a hunched figure with cropped blond hair whose limbs under the designer gear seemed to have been jointed with putty. He looked up at the DI from under surly brows.

Ibbotson smiled down. "Vaz."

"Ev'nin', Mr. Ibbotson." The boy flicked a smile that vanished as though the night was too cold for it.

"Know anything about this?"

The boy glanced at his mates; their expressions were as blank as his own. He shrugged. "Nuffin'. We saw the Paki come off the bus and light a fag, like – then he went upstairs. Next thing, the Bill turns up…"

"So no one went on board the bus?"

"Nobody."

Ibbotson poked his hands into his overcoat pockets and left the gang, rejoining Conway. "Get statements off anyone who thinks they saw something; make sure the bus is well dusted; then clear it up. SOCO been busy?"

"Shot everything from every angle reachable by the human frame, guv. Took a shed-load of samples, too."

"Uniforms can take over until the morning – when I'll expect a full PM report, mind. Now I'm going back to bed."

*

Most of Gloria's sobs had quietened down to staccato hicks by the time she'd reached the phone box. Even with door closed she felt vulnerable: there was too much clear plastic. She prayed Darren wouldn't be able to see her; he probably *would* kill her then. Take her apart like he had her mobile.

She lifted the receiver and began pushing coins into the slot with jittery fingers, anything she had in her purse. One and two pence pieces fell through unheeded, some bouncing on the concrete floor with wicked *tings*. Eventually, Gloria had used up all her change; she began to punch the buttons, saying the number aloud, a chant against bad luck.

The line crackled briefly, made a noise like some senile computer clearing its throat, and went silent.

"Come on, for Christ's sake!"

The receiver gave an electronic burp, and the ringing tone began. Gloria collapsed against the side of the box. Half-way home, she thought. The black and purple smudge around her left eye was throbbing – the eye would be swollen shut by the morning, she guessed – but her mouth was no longer bleeding. Even so, her tongue felt thick and clumsy.

The phone continued to ring. "Answer the bloody thing!" she cursed her mother up in Aberdeen. Probably fast asleep with some Russian trawlerman by now. The line crackled again, sounding like a rusty cistern.

It was the sirens and blue lights that saved her. Darren had panicked – thought someone had called the Filth on him – and bolted out the back door. By the time it was obvious everyone was collecting outside the Costcutter just up the road, Gloria was already out of the house and making for the phone box. She hid while there had still been a crowd: terrified Darren was amongst them, waiting his chance; afraid she'd be too visible in the carnival of lights.

The phone line shrieked in her ear, sending her deaf for a moment.

"Shit! Where are you, mom?"

She could feel the tears again, waiting at the back of her throat. No! Never again. He wasn't worth it! That bastard had done it once too often!

It occurred to her that her mother had said exactly the same thing for twenty years before her father had done the decent thing one Saturday night and fallen off Aberystwyth pier, pissed out his head. She couldn't hold the tears back.

"Oh, mom…"

The telephone gurgled and spat. The receiver seemed to quiver in her hands—

—And something warm and soft, slime-covered and endless was rushing out of the phone. Squeezing out of the mouthpiece like corrosive mud. Pushing eagerly into Gloria's paralyzed mouth, pouring down her ballooning throat with a wild, electric chuckle.

*

Conway was sitting with his feet on his desk, engrossed in *The Sun* when he heard Ibbotson's voice. The sergeant pulled himself hurriedly upright, dropping the newspaper, as the DI strolled into Priors Wood station's tiny CID room. His eyes flickered from Conway to the crumpled tabloid.

"I was under the impression office hours were meant for work."

To cover his embarrassment – and so he wouldn't have to meet the other's gaze – Conway riffled quickly through the junk on his desk. He offered Ibbotson several sheets of untidy paper. "The post-mortem report on the driver, guv, as requested."

Ibbotson grunted as he dropped heavily into a chair at the side of Conway's desk. He scanned the pages, face blank. The DS had long given up trying to guess his guv's thoughts from his expression. Finally, the older man dropped the report back onto the desk, stirring up a paper cyclone.

"Anwar Hussain lived in Kings Heath with his wife and family. Have they been informed?"

Conway nodded. "Two uniforms did it first thing."

"Not a knife, then."

Conway had to skip a mental hurdle to keep up with the conversation. He reckoned Ibbotson did it deliberately: hopped around the subject just to keep one step ahead.

"No, guv. Dr Taylor seems to think the damage was done by something like claws of some sort. Talons, like."

"I can read, sergeant." Ibbotson lit up a cigarette, despite the station's no-smoking policy. "Is he trying to tell me some animal did that? An invisible Rottweiler, I suppose? Jesus, the papers are going to love this! You get anything else from that woman in the supermarket?"

Conway beamed, remembering the interview. "Not half, guv. It seems that this Mrs. Charlton is knocking it off with a boy half her age. A customer. He pops round the back of the shop every night when she closes up and has her across the counter, or wherever. Last night, after he's finished giving her one, chummy spots the bus as he's leaving and suggests maybe she'd better ring us. Once he'd scarpered, of course. Oh – and the CCTV's useless: only trained on the entrance."

Ibbotson was giving him an unreadable stare. "Anything from the other statements last night?"

"Nothing. You'd have thought the guy ripped himself apart. Nobody heard anything or saw anyone. Except for some daft old bugger who reckons he saw a Martian."

"Bloody marvellous. The moment those kids talk a fraction too loud, the whole street's screaming about it. Some poor bus driver gets disembowelled and everyone goes deaf, dumb and blind." Ibbotson stood, grunting even louder than when he'd sat. "Look into the man's background: enemies, all the usual crap. And see if he was involved with any fundamentalist groups."

Conway scribbled down a few notes. "You think it might have been Al Qaeda, guv?" It was the first thing that came into his head.

"Could have been the bloody Masons for all I know. If anyone wants me, I'll be in what I laughingly call my office."

As he turned to leave, Conway remembered something else. "Oh – we had another one this morning, guv. Woman's body found in a phone box on Abbey Street. Just down from last night's little occurrence."

"Yes?"

"Beaten to death by the looks of her. Though Dr Taylor did notice swelling round the throat, maybe caused by strangulation. She'd been dead around six hours when she was found: first thing by some poor old biddy who wanted to use the phone." He searched through his personal paper jungle, flourishing a print-out when he found it.

"Gloria Houseman, 194 Abbey Street. Husband Darren fancies himself a hard bastard, well known for wife-beating. Couple of the lads brought him in half an hour ago, to assist in our enquiries, like."

Ibbotson pulled a sour face. Conway knew how much he hated domestic violence.

"Good. Now see if you can detect me some coffee." The DI vanished through the doorway and after a moment, Conway retrieved *The Sun* from where he'd dropped it.

The phone rang. Conway tossed the newspaper back onto the desk and reached for the receiver. "Priors Wood. Detective Sergeant Conway speaking."

It was Dr Taylor. "Conway. Good. I've finished examining the Houseman woman…"

"Anything we should know, doc? We've already picked her husband up—"

"Then I should let him go again."

Conway sat upright. "But you said she was beaten to death!"

"So she was. But I doubt even the worst brute of a man could manage what I found. The oesophagus and trachea are totally gone – bored out. Almost as if someone took an electric drill to them. The cardia and fundus of the stomach, and the lungs, are much the same.

"But that isn't what killed her. Dear me, no. I was right about her being beaten to death, but the superficial, external wounds misled me. Somehow – and don't ask me to speculate – Gloria Houseman died after a brutal and sustained assault from within."

"Eh?"

"You'll be receiving a full report in due course." Taylor rang off, leaving the Welshman staring at his dead receiver. He dropped it back into its cradle.

Ibbotson was going to need something a lot stronger than coffee when he gave him this news.

*

The Abbot's Mill pub was the sort of place that could be painted from eaves to damp course with bright, fluorescent orange, and still look dingy. It was presently undergoing yet another renovation: bricks and window surrounds layered with brilliant white. But nothing could disguise it. A sprawling Edwardian structure, now huddled amongst Abbey Street's younger houses; every passing bus or juggernaut would rattle the glass-panes in their thickly-painted wooden frames.

The Mill's overweight manager was feeling pretty rattled himself. Only ten minutes to go before Maurice Holyer was due to open up, and he was still in the pub's large upstairs function room. He didn't like the balding man in cargo pants and camo jacket standing in front of him, an easy smile on his too bland face. He liked the articulated truck parked out in the car park even less. It was too big. Nobody had said anything about large truckloads.

"What is it? One of these heavy metal groups?" In Holyer's experience, bands playing the Mill normally carried all their needs in a rusty van.

The other man shook his head, still smiling. "Didn't they tell you? It's PA all right, but nothing like that, chief. It's just for a meeting of a local political group—"

"Not the Nationalists? I'm not having them here! Mate of mine let them have a meeting, and the local Lefties got to hear about it. Once both sides were finished, all that remained standing was the four walls."

The other smiled even more broadly. "Not the Nationalists. A pressure group, really. Concerned citizens. The Lord Mayor's coming."

That put a completely different face on it. "The Mayor? Coming to the *Mill*?"

The balding man looked as though he'd said too much. He looped a friendly arm around Holyer's shoulders. "Ah—could you keep quiet about that? One or two other influential types'll be there too, and they don't want their association common knowledge. You with me?"

Holyer was beginning to get a shrewd idea exactly what kind of pressure group it was. But he always thought they had their own places. Lodges, wasn't it? Maybe it was being decorated as well. He winked conspiratorially. "Mum's the word, eh?"

"Cheers, mate." He fished a delivery note out of his cargo pants. "Could you just sign for receipt, then. Someone'll be along tonight just before the start, set the gear up. You won't have to do a thing."

Holyer scribbled an untidy signature. The man ripped off the yellow top copy for him.

"Right. Be okay to leave the trailer in the car park until tomorrow morning...?"

Holyer nodded, glad to have got the business over with and

plodded downstairs to get the pub ready for opening.

*

Once the balding man had dropped the trailer, he backed his cab out of the pub's car park and swung it out into the dual carriageway. He only drove a few yards up the road before pulling into the curb and switching off the engine. Digging his mobile out of his jacket, he flipped it open and dialled, waiting patiently as the ringing tone purred in his ear. Eventually, a bored male voice replied.

The bald man was cheerful. "Morning, Mr. Howard. Franklin here."

"Franklin. Is the merchandise delivered?"

"In place, Mr. Howard. Holyer fell for it like a ton of bricks." His voice remained relentlessly cheerful, the opposite of how he truly felt. "We do have one problem, though."

"And what's that?" Howard's voice retained its bored inflection, but Franklin could sense the sudden tension.

"Cheechee's got out. Caused a little local disruption. You know what she's like."

Howard was silent for a moment. *"I know very well, Franklin. Find it. Find it before tonight and get it back. Or you may well be on the receiving end. Do you understand me?"*

"Yes, Mr. Howard." Franklin snapped his phone shut. For once, he wasn't smiling.

*

David Vallance – better known to his friends as Vaz – sat in the front seat of a rusting Datsun, sharing a can of strong cider with his younger brother, Stevie.

"Honest to God, man!" Vaz waved the can in the air to illustrate his point. "He was fuckin' skinned! Like a fuckin' chunk of beef, man. Honest to God!" He took a mouthful of cider and passed it back to Stevie.

"Chunk of beef." Stevie giggled, trying to swallow a mouthful at the same time. Vaz was hardly the brains of his class, but next to his brother he was an intellectual giant.

"Gimme that, dickhead!" Vaz grabbed the can back from his brother before he could spill it all. "Fuck me! Why you such a fuckin' nonce, man?"

Stevie began to whine. "Oi, Vaz! Gizzus a drink! You always has more'n me!"

"That's 'cause I'm fuckin' older, shithead!" But he still handed back the can, watching as his brother successfully took several pulls.

"Hey, don't fuckin' drink it all, man!" Vaz snatched at the cider, but it evaded his fingers. Throwing foam all over them and the upholstery, the can spun down to the floor. The dregs trickled out through the Datsun's maggoty underside.

"I don't fuckin' believe this, man!" Vaz crouched down in his tattered seat, hand groping for the can. "Of all the fuckin' —!" His voice tailed off into hoarse whispers as he folded himself double.

His fingers touched something round and smooth. "Got the fucker!" He went to grab it, instead his hand sank into a moist softness. "Shit!" He tried to jerk back, but it felt like something was wrapping itself round his fingers. It flowed up his hand. Vaz couldn't move

Stevie watched him with vacant eyes, probably wondering what game Vaz was playing now.

Something spiralled thickly up Vaz's trapped arm. At first it looked the colour of stagnant water, but quickly turned a deep crimson. It took Vaz a couple of seconds to guess where the colour was coming from. He thrashed about, trying to free his disappearing arm; while Stevie looked on in dumb surprise.

The pain began the same moment the noises did: violent electrical rustlings which echoed the ripping agony that had been an arm. Vaz pulled back one last time. He was surprised as he came free, smashing the back of his head against the door-frame. His flayed arm stayed anchored in the blood-coloured mass bubbling up from the floor. There was a ruler-straight edge where something had sliced it free. Stevie – finally understanding their predicament – began a wild, keening scream.

Vaz's mind was shutting itself down, overloading on sensation. His world had shrunk to tiny points of reference: the agony that filled the space where his arm should have been; the mindless mewing of Stevie; and the giggling rustles from the shape which was crawling onto his seat.

He poured what was left of his concentration into a final prayer for his brother. "Run, Stevie!"

The thing on the seat leapt for him. Countless tiny tubes

burrowed into him, fleshy whips spat out in a mummifying embrace, delicate mouths tenderly kissed his bared flesh. Cheechee loved him as only she could.

Stevie just sat, his eyes fixed on his brother, lips slack and speckled with drool. He was beyond seeing or feeling the gelatinous tide swarming coyly up his seat, turning red as it swallowed him.

*

Ibbotson watched with mounting depression as the paramedics returned to their ambulance with two pathetically small bundles. A recovery lorry backed towards the rusted Datsun, already gone over comprehensively by SOCO. This time, no crowd had been allowed to gather.

A hysterical Mrs. Vallance had been tranquillized and put to bed. Her husband, working Saturday mornings at a local garage, had yet to be informed. Ibbotson volunteered for that task – but he wasn't ready just yet. He looked down at his feet: they were touching a boy's cap. His throat constricted painfully.

"Conway!" The Welshman glanced up from the notes he was comparing with Dr Taylor. "Come on, I'll buy you a pint."

The sergeant needed no further prompting. He followed his superior across the dual carriageway and they made their way to the *Abbot's Mill*. Inside the lounge, Ibbotson bought two pints of mild. He placed the drinks on the small corner table Conway had found them.

Ibbotson drank half his pint in one go, then banged the glass down. "I have a problem, Conway. A serious problem. What's happened in this street in the past twenty-four hours? Tell me."

"Well, guv: we've had a bus driver who looked like a sushi chef has been practicing on him; a woman who, to all appearances, has been smashed to pulp from inside; and two boys that look like they've been through a meat grinder."

Ibbotson took another heavy swallow to hide his wince. "Succinct as ever, sergeant. But there's my problem: blood."

"Blood?" The Welshman picked up his own drink and took a mouthful.

"Blood, Conway! Four people have been murdered in alarmingly brutal ways. Where's the sodding blood?"

Conway frowned, then his brows shot up. "Jesus Christ!"

The Inspector nodded sourly. "I should have seen it last night; and so should Les Taylor. It wasn't until this morning that the alarm bells rang. That car should have been awash, but I didn't see a drop. I'm willing to bet the forensic boys won't find any either."

"So what have we got, guv? Someone who spreads out a plastic sheet before they go to work, like that bloke on telly? What's it – *Dexter*...?"

"Even then traces would be left. And someone would have seen him." He stared blankly around at the almost deserted lounge, desperate for a cigarette but not wanting to leave just yet. "Have another? I'm not facing Vaz's dad without at least two pints inside me."

"If you like, guv."

Ibbotson made his way to the bar, returning with two more glasses. He took another heavy pull on his own. "When you've finished, get back across the road and make sure they've tidied up properly. The papers might have been leaned on so they play the worst elements down, but we don't want to give them excuses."

Conway finished his first pint and slid the second towards him. "Yes, guv. And where will you be?"

"Doing the worst thing any copper has to do, Conway. God help me." He gulped at his drink with a ferocious determination.

*

The River Cole ran parallel to Abbey Street for part of the road's length, though it was little more than a large stream; nothing like the wide flood it became north of the city. It was a selling point for those houses whose gardens overlooked the water. The only drawback was an untidy expanse of waste ground along the opposite, north bank, so far overlooked by developers. The council had been promising to make a riverside walk for years, but nothing had been done. For now it remained the haunt of foxes, rats, and kids on dirt bikes. And those who wanted to keep off the main road.

Franklin crept through the undergrowth, flashlight sweeping the ground before him. No visible light glowed from the bulb: he didn't need it for his particular quarry. The Kevlar beneath his camo jacket and lining his gauntlets chafed, and the biker helmet that left only his eyes visible was irritating. The Kevlar box dragging at his shoulders grew heavier with each step, as well. But he needed it all: Cheechee wasn't too picky about who she grabbed.

It was a fair guess she would be hiding up near the river. Moisture was all-important at the larval stage she and her sisters had reached. Franklin also assumed she was travelling via the drains. He had checked: all three attack sites had a grill in the gutter, less than three feet away in each case. That probably meant there was a culvert opening out in the bank somewhere near.

He flashed the UV torch along the opposite bank and line of garden fences. No luck so far. But she had to be around here somewhere. Franklin continued downstream, sweeping the torch in invisible arcs.

*

Ibbotson was dozing off in front of *Murder, She Wrote* when the phone rang. His wife took the call; then nudged him back to full wakefulness with the receiver.

"Sergeant Conway. They've had a call from someone in Abbey Street."

He grabbed the hand piece. "What...?"

"Evening, guv. Sorry to disturb you, like, but we've had a report. Same woman who found Gloria Houseman this morning. Reckons someone's creeping round the wasteland back of the houses."

"Does it sound kosher?"

"Well, she was scared shitless. And she didn't strike me as the imaginative type."

Ibbotson rubbed at his eyes. "Okay. Rustle up as many uniforms as you can and meet me outside that pub in about half an hour." He glanced at his watch. "Say, quarter past nine. And listen: no sirens and no lights. If he's the one we're after, I don't want some cowboy scaring him off. All right?"

"Okay, guv."

Ibbotson handed the receiver back to his wife and stood up wearily.

"Problems, Jim?"

"Might be what we've been looking for on these murders." He glanced back at the TV set, where Angela Lansbury was explaining the murderer's motives.

He reached for his overcoat. "If only it was that easy."

He'd found her! In the invisible glow from Franklin's UV torch, something glimmered with rainbow pulses: like a petrol film on a puddle of water. He could just make her out: on the opposite bank, nestled in a concrete pipe that opened out a couple of yards below a row of houses. Franklin's perpetual smile widened to an ugly grin when he thought how the people would react if they knew what was curled up so close.

He slid the box off his back and opened the flap.

"Cheechee! Here girl!" The rainbow thing didn't understand English, of course – nor was it female in the Earthly sense – but she understood voice tones, and Franklin always thought of her as a girl. The kind of girl who always ignored her parents. It was a dangerous analogy, though. If Cheechee and her kind actually had parents, any sense of duty to them would be sublimated in the all-encompassing drive to feed and pupate.

He placed the box on the grass, open end facing the culvert. "Come on, Cheechee. Your sisters are all waiting for you!"

There was a sound like a hundred high-voltage cables brushing together, the rainbow flashed and writhed. She wasn't going to come.

Franklin hefted the box under his left arm and took a careful step towards the descending bank. Perhaps he could lure her out. He took another step – and his feet slid on the treacherous grass. In a second he was flat on his back in the water, torch gone. He looked up in panic, and saw a vague shadowy hump streaming down the opposite bank with nightmarish speed. He tried to bring the box around, but the fall had left him badly positioned.

Something smacked against his chest with the force of a high-velocity round. Cheechee had spat out a gastric tendril; only the Kevlar had saved him. Franklin pushed himself back, his boots scrabbling on the stones in the riverbed. He felt rather than saw three more tentacles snap out of the dimness, shredding his jacket, but stopping short against his armour.

Desperation giving him an agility and deftness of touch way beyond normal, his snatching hands somehow found the box, and his fingers slid to a five-sided stud on the side. He punched it.

The riverbank was flooded with enough brilliance to light a football stadium, an unhealthy lilac in colour – all from the open box. Starkly silhouetted by the blaze, Cheechee froze: a forest of extrudable limbs arched towards the light's source, dazzled. In a moment, chattering loudly, the amorphous shape oozed through the water and into the box. Franklin slammed the lid shut.

For almost five minutes he lay where he was, arms draped loosely across the box, breath coming in near-hysterical shudders. Then a little sense penetrated his adrenaline-soaked brain: the meeting! And half of Birmingham would have seen that blaze.

Staggering to his feet, the box cradled lovingly in his arms, he splashed through the water towards the rear gardens of the *Abbey Mill* pub.

*

Ibbotson had just guided his car into the pub car park when the lilac blaze flooded the night sky. As he leapt from the car, the blinding light vanished. Conway was running to meet him, but Ibbotson could hardly see through the after-images clogging his eyes.

"Conway!" He blinked rapidly to clear his eyesight. "I think we're past the sneaky stage. Order up a chopper!"

As the DS spoke quickly into his transceiver, a uniformed sergeant and two dog-handlers joined them. "How do you want us to proceed, guv?"

Ibbotson thought for a moment. "A chopper should be here soon with a searchlight. Fan out from the gardens at the back of the pub, going both up and down stream. Dogs – good idea, Conway – with both teams. This bastard's vicious, so don't be too particular about letting them loose if you find him."

Just stop him, he added silently.

*

Franklin heard loud rustling in the tall grass and ducked. He squinted into the night and could make out the dark shapes of men and a dog. Jesus, the fuzz! And they were between him and the pub. He was going to have to make a run for it. With luck, they'd be caught by surprise just long enough for him to get into the *Mill's* back door. He could use the box as a weapon, and if it fell open— Well, they'd just have to take their chances.

Clutching his precious burden to his chest, he came upright, lowered his head and charged. Instantly, the police began shouting. Distinct above all else, he heard the snick of a dog's leash being slipped. Someone stepped in front of him. Franklin butted him savagely aside. Then he was through the line.

Nearly a hundred pounds of Alsatian crashed against him. He heard one of the last shreds of his combat jacket rip as the dog snatched at his right arm, but felt nothing through the Kevlar. He rolled over, the dog still trying to find purchase with its teeth, and lashed out with the box. More by luck he caught the animal across the muzzle. It fell back, whimpering. Franklin lurched to his knees and smashed the box down with both arms. The Alsatian went quiet.

Instantly, Franklin was on his feet, not stopping to check how close his pursuers were. He heard the muffled judder of a nearing police helicopter. Splashing into the Cole, he scrambled up the other bank and made for the *Mill's* garden wall.

*

The voice from Conway's transceiver was garbled but Ibbotson, standing a few feet away, caught enough of it. "They lost him, didn't they?"

Conway was apologetic. "He got through a gap in the back wall and into the pub, guv. Appears to be carrying a large heavy box. Cracked a dog over the head with it, like."

"That's it! He's got some sort of bloody animal? Get those men back here, sharpish! Surround the pub. You and I are going in, sergeant!"

The Welshman relayed the message, glancing back at Ibbotson when he'd finished. "Is that wise, guv?"

"Probably not. But I want that bastard personally! Him and his pet monkey!"

*

Maurice Holyer was in the lounge bar when the two men stormed in. The Bill; he could tell just by looking. In or out of uniform they stuck out a mile. Something done to them at training college, he reckoned.

The older, grey-haired one flashed his warrant card. "Detective Inspector Ibbotson, Priors Wood nick. Did a man carrying a large box come through here a moment ago?"

Holyer's mind began a panicked shuffle. Only thirty seconds earlier, he'd seen that smug truck driver come through from the back carrying a packing case of some sort. Only he hadn't been smiling this time. He'd looked hot and scared, his jacket in shreds.

"Well..."

The younger copper butted in, his voice a husky Welsh accent. "Look, mate, we don't have time to piss around. Where is he?"

"Upstairs—"

Both men headed for the stairs that led up from the pub's foyer.

"But you can't go in ... it's..." Holyer's voice tailed off. They'd gone, and they weren't listening, anyway. The pub manager shrugged. Oh well, if they went butting in on the Lord Mayor that was their lookout, not his.

*

At the top of the stairs was a short landing, but only one set of double doors. Ibbotson and Conway stopped and stared at the poorly-painted wood as though looking for inspiration.

Conway rubbed at his face. "This is it, then."

"Looks like it. After you, sergeant."

Conway pulled a face and swung both doors wide. The men charged through, slamming to a halt under the enraged stare of a dozen familiar faces. Ibbotson thought, Christ, it *is* the Masons.

Grouped around a crescent table were some of Birmingham's top men: the City Architect, the Mayor, the Chief Executive, others he couldn't put a name to but recognised; even his own Chief Superintendent. A series of display boards covered in diagrams were spread out behind them.

Chief Superintendent Phillips rose slowly to his feet, mouth opening. Ibbotson's scrotum was already drawing itself up in anticipation of the fire about to be lit under it. But the verbal roasting didn't come.

Instead, Phillips' mouth gaped wider and wider, further than any man's could in a sane world. A medusa of whipping tentacles spat out, flaying the air, no two the same length or thickness. Tentacles, cilia and flagellae, hooks and gouges, saws and razors, turning the Chief Superintendent's gaze into something far more terrible than the Gorgon's.

Neither man moved, paralyzed by disbelief. But as the first eager tendrils wrapped around Conway's face, Ibbotson's stasis broke. He lurched back, smashing into the edge of the open door. Agonizing flares impaled his eyes, and he collapsed to the floor, consciousness drifting.

*

The Welshman was dragged closer to Phillips, screaming and clawing at the things burrowing into his flesh. He felt them slipping behind his eyes, wriggling into his brain. Eardrums burst as segmented probes thrust into his ears. A thick, heavily-armoured limb scuttled across the floor like a vast centipede. Wrapping itself around his ankles, it drove itself between his buttocks, drilling a core through his spinal cord, not stopping until it struck brain. Conway managed one final, despairing scream before his body erupted, sprouting a million thrashing tendrils of its own.

A moment later, all of the others in the room threw aside all pretence at humanity. Their faces split open into nightmarish nests of pale wriggling things. What was left of Conway was snapped up, muscle and bone savoured equally by the gastric arms. A healthy glow spread through the translucent bodies. Not a drop of blood was wasted.

*

The vast, acid pain across Ibbotson's back snapped his brain back into focus. A drooling sea anemone wearing the Lord Mayor's chain had wrapped a thick, mottled tentacle around his shoulders. Shrieking more in terror than pain, Ibbotson slipped out of his overcoat, leaving it to be pulped by the quivering limb.

He tried scrambling to his feet and getting through the door, only succeeding in collapsing like a drunk. Another tentacle snapped through the air over his head. The fall saved him. He rolled, trying to get up onto all fours. Something that smelled of sewers but felt like acid gel brushed his left foot. He howled again. This time he made it to his feet.

He reached the head of the stairs and found himself face to face with Franklin, clutching the box. Ibbotson stumbled into him. Both men windmilled down the stairs, the box arcing away. At the bottom Ibbotson hit ground first, the other sprawled across him a moment later.

Conway's transceiver was lifted carefully from the floor. For a while it was rotated in the air, caressed by strange limbs; then the transmit button was pressed.

Chief Superintendent Phillips' voice, so calm and reassuring – so human – issued from somewhere inside a writhing nest of moist limbs. Carefully it gave instructions to the men waiting outside.

*

Ibbotson looked around. The man with the box had disappeared; probably out through the open front door. In agony, the Inspector dragged himself away from the foot of the stairs, not sure how long he had before those things upstairs came after him.

Clinging onto a wall, he pulled himself upright. He was next to the men's washroom. He hobbled into them, head threatening to burst with every step. Filling one of the wash-basins with cold water he plunged his face in. It stung like hell.

He straightened, staring at his bleached face in a filthy mirror. He'd had enough time to see what had been pinned to the display boards upstairs: a map of Birmingham's intricate underground system. Almost another city, with its own roads and pathways, storerooms and shelters. If he could get away and clear his head, he knew he could make sense of it all – and tell someone.

"But who...?" His reflection didn't answer. He pulled the plug and leaned heavily on the washbasin, trying to find the energy to get out of the washroom.

Something behind him crackled – an electric chuckle – and shifted restlessly on the concrete floor. Ibbotson's eyes were drawn back to the mirror, though he didn't want to see what was behind him.

*

Franklin made it to the cab of his truck just as a whole posse of uniformed coppers rushed the pub. A helicopter landed in the car park, disgorging its crew. He tried not to imagine what Phillips was going to do to them inside.

With numb fingers, he opened his mobile and dialled. When Howard answered, it was all Franklin could do to keep his voice from trembling. "The transplant was successful. All the larvae are housed."

Howard sounded absurdly pleased. *"Then we can look forward to the next phase. Were there any problems?"*

"You could say that. Cheechee's out again—"

THE STREETS OF CRAZY CITIES

Without warning, the BMW had slewed across the elevated four-lane section and ploughed through a safety-barrier. One hundred feet below, it was mangled almost beyond recognition by the pilings for the new urban highway.

The driver of the recovery vehicle took one look inside the wreck after it had been hoisted back onto the elevated section, and threw up all over a stretch of fresh tarmac. The body of the two-year old young girl was miraculously untouched; she just looked asleep. But a ten-foot length of reinforcing rod from a concrete block had lanced straight through the windscreen, into her mother's screaming mouth, and out through the back of her skull. The head was pinned like a butterfly to the headrest, its surface dulled with congealing blood and brains.

At the moment Martyn Turner's wife and daughter died in the smash, he was in bed, savagely fucking his sister-in-law. He reached the best climax he'd had in months.

*

Martyn stood like a shop-front dummy throughout the funeral service. When it was time for him to throw the handful of dirt onto the two coffins, someone had to prompt him. Wife Helen and little Bernadette were the last to be buried in that cemetery: it was to be closed pending future redevelopment of the land. A day later, and they would have to have been cremated, no matter what his in-laws wanted.

The inquest had been a waste of time. Tests on the wrecked car had found nothing; there was no appreciable amount of alcohol in Bernadette's blood; the road surface had been dry, and oil-free. An eyewitness claimed to have seen an old tramp fall under the car's wheels, causing it to swerve. However, the lighting was poor, and no trace of any other dead or injured person had been found. Nor had there been any marks on the car to support the claim.

At the Wake, Martyn simply brooded in a corner, drinking Old Bushmills and chain-smoking. Bernadette's sister, Siobhan, wandered over at some timeless point, and stood in an embarrassment of silence until he looked at her. Tall, slender, black-haired, and the sexiest body he'd ever known. Bernadette's opposite in so many ways.

She opened her mouth, but he spoke first.

"Don't say it," he mumbled, self-pity snagging his voice. "Just piss off, there's a good girl."

"I'll be here, Marty," she murmured.

"Fuck off." The alcohol clotted his words into thick gibberish but her back was already turned to him. He was just talking to an empty glass. He staggered off to find a refill.

Later, in his darkened, empty house, Martyn climbed into bed, and found Siobhan already there.

"I told you I'd be here," she murmured. He wanted to scream at her *Get out! Just what the fuck d'you think you're doing?* – but all that escaped was a sob. For the first time since the accident, tears came to his eyes. Siobhan clung to him as though she was drowning in her own unspoken thoughts. For once, their need for each other transcending sex.

*

Martyn rose to the smell of coffee. Dragging on a towelling wrap, he made his bleary way downstairs to the kitchen. "Bernie?" he mumbled at the figure in the silk robe, standing by the coffee maker. It was Siobhan who turned around, dressed in her late sister's kimono. She handed him a freshly poured coffee.

"What would you like for breakfast?"

Martyn made his way into the adjoining room and placed his coffee on the breakfast bar. He stared blindly at the cup. Siobhan faced him, leaning on the polished granite top. "What do you intend to do now, Martyn?" she asked.

He knew exactly what she meant, but chose to misunderstand. "Just popping into work this morning to tidy a few things up. Then I'm taking a month off: staying with my brother and his family. The department's letting me have two weeks compassionate leave."

She reached out a hand and squeezed his wrist. "About us," she insisted.

He continued to stare at his coffee-cup, anything but look at her. "Christ Almighty, Shee! Bernie's not cold in her grave yet!"

"Tell me about it! She was my sister, you know! But life goes on..."

Especially yours, he thought. Nothing gets in the way of Siobhan McCammon.

He hadn't met Bernie's younger sister until his daughter's first birthday party. He'd been married a little over two years, and Siobhan had been abroad all that time. All he'd seen of her was an out of date photograph.

Siobhan had breezed into the party unannounced, to the delight of Bernie and Helen. Martyn had also been pretty impressed with her. The frank appraisals she gave him all evening had massaged his male ego. In a few weeks, Siobhan was giving him all the attention Bernie had been growing too tired or too busy for. The Catholic guilt Martyn blamed for his wife's increased indifference to sex seemed totally absent in her sister.

At first, Martyn thought she was simply reciprocating his lust: taking an extra charge from the thought she was screwing her brother-in-law. It took him a year to realise there was a little more to it. Throughout their lives, Siobhan wanted whatever Bernadette had. Bernie's favourite Christmas and birthday presents soon became Siobhan's, or they got broken. Martyn was the ultimate present; she had to have him, too. By the time he realised, he was too caught up to escape. Besides, the perversity of the situation held its attractions for him as well. He wasn't going to stop bedding his wife's horny sister just because he was another pawn in their mind games. He enjoyed it too much.

That had changed. Whatever feelings Martyn might have had toward Siobhan were buried with the two coffins. He risked a glance: she was still leaning forward, the kimono gaping. Martyn knew it wasn't accidental, but it no longer had any power to arouse him. He tried on a smile; it felt unnatural.

"Shee – I don't know. I—" He gulped a mouthful of coffee, burning his mouth. "It's too soon – I can't think... Maybe when I'm back from my brother's..."

She drew her hand back, expression and voice hardening. "If that's what you want." She backed away, drawing the kimono tightly around her.

When have you ever cared what anyone else wanted? thought Martyn.

*

The Planning Department was unnaturally quiet. Martyn could feel every pair of eyes in the open-plan office fixed on him: some in morbid fascination, others in masochistic embarrassment. He wished he could simply turn and run.

As he made his way towards his desk, he passed Simmons, the office supervisor. He was trying to hide behind another garish paperback. OUR LADY OF DARKNESS, Martyn read on the cover.

A blonde girl who couldn't have been more than eighteen edged towards him on barely-controlled high heels. Sharon Jevons, he remembered: taken on last year by the City Architect's office. She was an almost clichéd office blonde: the body of a hooker and the brains of a filing cabinet. The object of Martyn's sexual fantasies more than once, now he felt grubby just looking at her earnest face.

"Yes?" He wanted whatever she had in mind out of the way.

"Mr Turner—" She stumbled over the words. "I just wanted you to know that I'm really sorry about your— The accident – you know…" She gave him an awkward smile before turning her back on him, courage giving out.

Martyn was touched. "Thank you, Sharon," he murmured; certain she wouldn't hear him as she teetered to the furthest reaches of the office.

*

Siobhan was grunting in rhythm, her dark eyes glowing with anticipation. Her lips curled back; she began to purr.

"Harder, Martyn – harder! I'll give you the best ride you've ever had! Faster, you bastard!"

Her voice rose to a scream, deafening him. It howled on and on, becoming the wail of an over-revved car engine plunging to its death. Her eyes glared like lamps, blazed like headlights – rushing at him—

Too fast!

Martyn jerked awake with a gasp. A black woman sitting opposite was looking at him with what he thought was disapproval. Had he made a noise? Said something? An adolescent shock ran through him as he realised he had an erection; a warm oozing around his groin. The moment his train pulled into the terminus, Martyn rushed off, eager to lose himself in the anonymous crowds of shoppers and commuters.

The hammer of pneumatic drills filled the passenger-choked concourse beyond the ticket-barrier, echoing from the bus terminal that was being thrown together as an extension to the station. Even the air vibrated, pounding his ears into painful, sympathetic rhythm.

Only a month away from the city, and Martyn felt he hardly recognised the place. He knew the planners' ultimate design concept: Simmons had shown him the plans and models often enough. "Our baby; our little boy," he'd called it. But, in the concrete reality, Martyn felt this particular boy was developing a ruthless character he didn't much like.

He weaved through the clusters of people standing like abstract statues, gazing vacantly at the destination boards. He swore under his breath; not for the first time feeling their dumb obstructions were meant for him alone. A crowd was growing at the bottom of the escalators; railway police and station staff were trying to keep the mass back. Martyn could see a TV reporter talking earnestly into a camera. Behind him, teenagers were making offensive gestures towards the lens.

Martyn moved closer, curious. "What's happened?" he asked a member of staff.

"Load of people caught on an escalator." His fingers twitched across waxy features. "The ones on it couldn't get off at the top for some reason. Before the emergency cut-off was hit— Well, you can imagine."

A vague nausea swept over Martyn. It could have been him! A few minutes earlier, and his mangled body might now be buried under a hundredweight of torn, bloody shoppers.

"How?" he asked.

The man shrugged. "Christ knows... Somebody said they saw someone in a filthy coat, standing at the top, not letting anybody off. But that doesn't make much sense, does it? Excuse me—" He headed towards a group of commuters trying to force themselves into the crowd.

Anyone wanting to leave the railway station had to go through the half-built bus terminal. A rickety walkway had been erected across the concrete no-man's land. Listening to his footsteps thud on the dirty planks, Martyn's gaze was drawn unwillingly down; for a moment it seemed to him that the apparently random scattering of workers was actually following a pattern. Hieroglyphics, or a crazy sort of star-chart.

He escaped the main flow of the pedestrians, making his way towards the skeletal frame of the new library, still awaiting completion after ten years of neglect. It was perpetually cold and damp: rubbish of every kind heaped against concrete girders; puddles leaking into underpasses that led nowhere. As he passed one set of pointless stairs, a ragged figure in a filthy brown coat reared up at him: a featureless face that was all black, yawning mouth.

Martyn leapt back, heart jabbing like one of the drills outside the station. The torn plastic sheet, crackling faintly, settled again as the breeze died, leaving him feeling stupid and edgy.

The bus ride was uneventful. Once home, Martyn slung down his briefcase and flicked on the TV. He wandered into the kitchen and switched on the coffee maker before drifting back into the living room. It was too quiet; too big. He'd have to go, move somewhere else; somewhere with less ghosts. He turned up the TV set, trying to fill the empty silence, but he could make no sense of the distorted voices. Something about when the city's library complex would be finished, he thought.

There was a flyer from the local supermarket hanging from the mail slot. It mentioned a special offer on bumper packs of 200 cigarettes, so he wandered across before the place closed. He bought the cigarettes, along with eight cans of Stella Artois. Tonight wasn't going to hurt.

*

He was caught in the swarm of disembarking passengers, carried through the ticket barriers, past inspectors whose yawning expressions said they couldn't care less whether he'd paid or not.

Endless masses of people – an ocean of flesh – lapped and eddied across the station concourse. Martyn imagined a group mind was on the edge of creation: just a few hundred more and a single malignant hive would be spawned in the dimly lit corridors and plazas of the station. Mindless drones scuttling to obey the trains that growled and complained below.

He joined the stream for the escalators, jostling his own way, caught up in the frenzied drive to be free. He felt the steps groan as he trod on them, protesting at the never-ending, thankless mass. At the head of the stairs he saw both Bernadette and Helen looking down at him, waving. They were trying to tell him something:

their mouths opened and closed in slow motion, and he couldn't hear above the crowd. He tried to wave back and his left foot slipped on the cleated step. In a moment he was stumbling. Behind him someone swore in obscene desperation, and a hot, heavy body collapsed onto his back. A briefcase smashed into the side of his face.

He tried to scream, but as he opened his mouth, breath was crushed from his body. The weight above him was impossible; blood shrieked in his ears. Slowly, with obvious relish, the steel treads of the moving staircase began to grind into his soft, immobilized belly. Martyn felt the rags of his shirt grow slick with blood, smelled his own shit as the churning reached his guts. He was getting smaller: reduced to gobbets of flesh carried away by the ceaseless, ascending stairs —

He lurched awake; his guts still aching where the dream escalator had eaten into him. The fug of sleep cleared: it was his full bladder. He flopped out of bed and staggered into the bathroom.

It felt like he was pissing broken glass. A kidney infection, he wondered. Or what was that other thing? Urethritis? And his prick looked a little red, too. He would go see Doctor Trellis if it didn't get better.

Back in his bedroom he glanced at the green numerals on his radio-alarm: 6:25. Hardly worth going back to sleep again.

He washed and dressed lethargically. Downstairs in the kitchen he found the coffee machine was still on from last night: he'd forgotten to switch it off. Pouring a cup of blisteringly hot, thick liquid, he flopped into an armchair and pretended to listen to the local radio station. His head was too heavy for his stiff neck; the backs of his eyes pounded. Breakfast was out of the question. The coffee simply changed the quality of his headache. He poured it down the kitchen sink, packed his briefcase and set out for work.

At his desk, he was searching through the drawers for some ibuprofen when Simmons approached him. His normally calm, scrubbed face was blotched and drawn; his eyes red and too wet. "Terrible about Sharon, isn't it?" His voice shook.

Martyn only half-heard. "What's she done this time?"

"You didn't hear the news this morning?" Simmons looked around for something, but didn't spot whatever it was. He fidgeted on the spot, his body tying itself in emotional knots. "She was attacked last night: raped and murdered. God, what some bastard did to her! Left her body among the foundations of the new International Hotel."

The meaning finally sank in. Martyn sagged against the back of his chair. "Jesus," was all he could say. "Jesus. I'm sorry—"

Simmons' body seemed to lose all its rigidity. He half collapsed on Martyn's desk. "Her mouth was full of … of— As though she'd been choked with—" He began crying helplessly, not caring who saw.

The coffee in Martyn's stomach gave a single, sickening lurch. He pushed away from his desk in panic, making it to the gents' washroom barely in time. As he leaned over a spattered sink, someone – he couldn't see through his streaming eyes – came up behind him. "You all right?"

"Yeah," Martyn got out, his tongue thick. "Yeah. Just… the shock. You know."

The anonymous sympathizer patted his shoulder and left the washroom. After a while Martyn rinsed out the basin, gargling with cold water before returning to the office.

*

The rest of the day was a strain. The usual friendly atmosphere was forced and insecure. No one knew how to sympathize with Simmons; Martyn's behaviour baffled them. Martyn had never been more relieved when five o'clock arrived.

He reached home tired and angry; his brain choked with grit. The crowds on the train and bus were more bovine than ever. The amount of building and restoration work around the city seemed to have doubled since he'd gone back to work. The chaos and upset were a perfect mirror for Martyn's state of mind.

Siobhan was waiting for him inside the house, sitting on the sofa, still dressed in a long raincoat. As Martyn hurled his briefcase at an armchair, he decided it was time to change all the locks.

"Still using Bernie's key?" He walked past her on his way to the television, not wanting to look at her face.

"A copy of yours, I seem to remember. And I came to return it." She pulled a key out of a pocket and dropped it onto the sofa's arm. "You all right, Martyn?"

The television came on. A newscaster was talking about Sharon's murder: police were anxious to interview a vagrant spotted in the area, close to where the attack had taken place.

"That's the second time I've been asked that today," he said, ignoring her again as he made his way to the kitchen. Siobhan followed. Was she trying to annoy him? He made a pretence of starting on his dinner, wishing she'd leave; uncomfortable in her presence.

He heard the dull clink of glass and glanced up. She was holding up two empty scotch bottles, her eyes harsh with reproof. "Don't look too fine to me."

He couldn't take his eyes off the empties. Where had she found them? He didn't remember drinking two whole bottles. "Ah – had a couple of friends round…"

She obviously didn't believe him; but what right had this bitch to stand in judgment on him anyway? He snatched the bottles out of her hands and threw them carelessly into the sink. Somehow, neither broke.

"Nice to see you again, thanks for worrying. Now get the hell out, okay? Just leave me alone!"

Her face remained calm, but he recognised the anger building under that controlled mask. Her lips twitched, ever so slightly. He remembered that gesture. He couldn't take his eyes away from her mouth: the way it contorted as she spoke.

"I see. It was fun fucking me when you were married to my sister, but now she's dead you've lost interest. That it? Not novel enough for you!" She plucked at her belt, flinging wide the raincoat. Underneath she was wearing only the tiniest leather thong, bra and suspender belt. Once the sight would have instantly aroused Martyn; now he found it pathetic.

"I came round here thinking maybe we could carry on," Siobhan continued. "I stupidly thought that now Bernie's gone, there'd be nothing in our way."

"Yes – she's gone! You've got a free hand at last, Shee!" The words came tumbling out of him: wounded vicious nonsense. "Maybe you even killed her! The ultimate in sibling rivalry. What d'you say, Shee!"

The last vestige of expression slipped from Siobhan's face. Martyn knew she was on the edge of a violent rage. One unguarded word from him, and no amount of self-control would keep her fingernails out of his face. For a moment, he was tempted.

"Take a good look, mister," she whispered, voice barely audible. She yanked the raincoat tight around herself again, seeming to shrink into it. "That's the last you'll ever see of it!" She turned and marched for the front door.

"You hard bitch!" he roared at her rigid back. "You heartless, unthinking little whore!" The door slammed behind her. Martyn heard an ornament smash on the floor.

Slowly at first, and then stronger and faster, he began to shake.

*

Bernadette's car was coming straight at him. He needed to tell her something, but his thin, reedy voice couldn't penetrate the lethal shriek of peeling rubber. The faces of his wife and Helen were bizarre green masks, dash-lit from below.

"It's your fault!" Martyn screamed, his voice small and betrayed.

Then he was careering off the elevated highway, stretched across the grille like a dirty scrap of paper. The car tumbled three times, slowing with each turn, until it was moving no faster than a clock's minute hand.

Martyn didn't feel the impact, but he was slung upward: towards the splintering windshield. Towards Bernadette's terror-stretched face. Towards her straining mouth—

He spasmed upright in bed, trembling as the dream reluctantly slackened its grip. He needed a drink. More than anything.

No. It wasn't a drink he needed. Just his family. He no longer had a purpose: a father without a family. Fragmented, pieces missing: that was how he felt.

Just like the damned city!

He crumpled back onto his bed, allowing his body to calm itself, listening to the night, and its cracked, phlegmy voice.

*

He was standing in a muddy puddle, speared by a dazzling spotlight hung on a spider web of scaffolding. For a moment he couldn't remember what he was doing there, but standing under a tungsten lamp for the entire world to see didn't seem such a good idea.

He backed into the shadows, pulling up the collar of his jacket against the chill. He leaned against an open-topped skip, its contents draped with several ragged pieces of dirty brown

93

tarpaulin. The builders were more worried about their rubbish getting wet than the mountains of sand and bricks stacked a few yards away.

"It's growing too fast!" he muttered to himself, searching through his pockets for a cigarette. He was just about to light up when he thought better of it.

Across the dark street was the hotel where Siobhan worked as a banqueting manageress. Puddles of light from the harshly lit foyer spread across the pavement, accentuating the blackness beyond. It was a new hotel: part of a complex that would one day cover two or three square miles. Martyn was standing in the foundations of a future sport centre.

He glanced at his watch: 2:29 am; Siobhan would be leaving soon. In the past he had often booked an overnight stay in the hotel; she would join him once her day was over.

"Times change," he murmured.

A familiar figure appeared through the revolving doors. Siobhan stood in the splash of ugly yellow light. Wondering whether to phone for a cab or walk to the nearest taxi rank, Martyn guessed. After a moment, she started walking. Martyn stepped out of shadow and into the street.

"Siobhan!"

She halted, startled. "Martyn! I thought I'd made myself perfectly clear, earlier."

He shuffled on the spot, hands eloquently signalling confusion. "Yes. Look, I'm sorry, Siobhan. I was out of order, I know. Ever since Bernie's death I've—"

"You've been a disgusting, self-pitying wreck." Her voice was cold, relentless. "Just look at yourself, Martyn. Once you were one of the smartest men in your office; now you're no better than … than a tramp!"

Tramp, he thought. And who was it stole her sister's husband? He nodded anyway, outwardly agreeing.

"Anyway, I wanted to say— I want to apologies, Shee." He waved his arms aimlessly again. "Sorry."

He stepped towards the shadows again. As he had guessed, Siobhan was caught: emotions conflicting with her cooler, managerial self. She took a hesitant step towards the building site, then strode briskly into it, her eyes searching for him.

"Martyn? Are you still here?"

He lunged. One hand clamped around her wrists, another

balled into her mouth, forcing open her jaws in a silent scream. Her feet scuffed the ground, trying to regain her balance. He tugged and pushed at her, never letting her equilibrium return. Only her eyes were constant: wide, panicked, staring into his with disbelief.

Finally he pulled his fist free of her mouth, and swung it in a shattering arc. She fell into the grey mud of the site, already half-conscious. He clamped hands around her neck, eager fingers driving for her throat.

"Ride me, you tramp? Bitch! You're always riding me! No more. NO MORE!" His hands closed tighter, trying to meet in the middle. All the while shaking her; smashing her head against the ground.

Eventually, he was rattling an empty doll. Her head bobbed on the crushed neck like a dirty, tethered balloon. His fingers relaxed. Her lifeless weight splashed into the mud and lay staring up at him, mouth open in surprise.

He couldn't tear his eyes away from that mouth: so round, so red, so inviting. He crouched over it, stroked it with a twitching finger, brushed it with his tongue; and finally he thrust his erection into it.

When it was over, he knelt back, looking down at his handiwork. His fluids glinted on her teeth; hers soaked through his suit and shirt. He ripped away the sodden clothing and wrapped one of the tarpaulin sheets around himself like a crude overcoat. In the puddles he looked like a deadbeat wino: a tramp in the last stages of decay.

He smiled, recognising himself at last.

"Growing boys need to eat," he explained to Siobhan's corpse, looking around the foundations for the perfect spot to leave her. "And what's a father for, eh?"

THE OWL THAT CALLS

Ullerden was jarred awake, hand groping for the alarm's off switch before he realised it was a telephone warbling in his ear. Stabbing on the bedside lamp he reached for the receiver – sleep-numb fingers almost dropping it.

"Hello?" His tongue as uncoordinated as his hands, Ullerden cleared his throat and tried again. "Hello."

The line crackled for a moment. Ullerden thought he'd been disconnected. A voice – as muffled as his own had been – rose through the static.

"Tomas Ullerden?"

"Yes…"

"Yes." The static snapped off, replaced by silence. Ullerden stared at the dead receiver for a moment longer before dropping it back onto its cradle. According to his travel alarm it had just gone three in the morning. Ullerden swore quietly: he needed to be fresh in the morning, not have his rest broken by some prat making joke phone calls.

He switched off the lamp and slumped into his pillow, convinced he was never getting back to sleep. Next thing he knew feathers of sunlight were spreading through chinks in the curtains, and this time the shrill travel alarm really was trying to wake him.

*

The *Wheal Gammon* pub might have been stuck halfway past the middle of nowhere, but as B&Bs went, nothing could top the breakfast. Parking himself in the snug that doubled as a restaurant in the morning, Ullerden skimmed through a copy of last night's *Taunton Evening Post* that had been left on the window ledge. He found what he was looking for on page eleven.

BIRDS OF A FEATHER
Local Girls Invite Press to Site of Bizarre Apparition
The case of Bodmin Moor's mysterious man-bird has taken yet another twist (reports a local correspondent). Carly Teague and Brigit Gay, the two girls at the centre of the sighting three nights ago, have called for an impromptu press conference at the scene of

the crime.

Part of a Girl Guide camping expedition which had pitched at Raven Tor that same evening, Carly and Brigit were taking a brief stroll while their supper was being cooked over a camp fire, when both were startled by the appearance of a ghostly apparition.

Carly, 14, from Bodmin, claimed it was the size of a man, but with no arms – just wings. "It was black all over, with huge, round glowing eyes."

Brigit, 26, a trainee hairdresser and also a Bodmin resident, said it just came out of nowhere. "At first we saw lights – like an aeroplane – then it was standing on the Tor itself, staring at us with these huge red eyes."

Carly, who attends St. Neots Secondary School and is a big fan of the Bay City Rollers, had commented on how the air felt charged: as if a storm was brewing. When the thing appeared it had made an odd, crackling sound, like static. She made a sketch once both girls were back at the Guide camp.

Mothman of West Virginia

Ten years ago, in July 1966, there was a similar case in West Virginia, USA. The people of Mount Pleasant named their strange visitor Mothman, and a whole industry has since grown up around it and other, allegedly connected events – including threatening phone calls, strange visitors, and flying saucer-like apparitions. And now Carly and Brigit have called for a meeting of the local press to "address the matter once and for all."

The excited imaginings of two over-stimulated girls; a rather tawdry publicity stunt; or does Cornwall really have its own Mothman?

Ullerden folded up the paper just as his bacon, egg, sausage, beans, tomatoes and fried bread arrived. He was delighted with the coverage – despite the tone of the so-called *local correspondent*. He particularly liked the bit about the air feeling charged, and the noise the birdman made. What if it didn't quite sound like the words of a 14 year old – just a touch of journalistic licence – it all added to the legend. Picking up on the ten-year old Mothman story, though – he wasn't sure if that was good or bad. Did it make everything look a little obvious?

After a breakfast that almost made up for his disturbed night, and a landlord who insisted none of the room phones had been connected yet, Ullerden left the *Wheal Gammon*. He squeezed his considerable frame inside his Triumph Toledo and headed out across Bodmin Moor. Just as he turned on the car radio, Queen's *Bohemian Rhapsody* started up. He snapped it off immediately: that bloody song had been playing all year and everywhere. He was sick of it.

The day was clear and sunny, the moor bright and welcoming; not the bleak, forbidding landscape it should have been. No phantom horsemen; no giant, ghostly hounds: just miles of granite tors and mounds, cropped grass and sedge. Far too cheerful to be the haunt of a mysterious, man-sized flying apparition with huge talons and glowing eyes.

He lit up a cigarette, grinning around it.

There was a small army of parked cars already clustered around a massive hunk of granite by the time he arrived. Raven Tor: a huge bird crouched over the moor, wings slightly open. Plenty of people, too – someone from every West Country rag, at a guess – clutching cameras or notebooks. As Ullerden stepped out of his car he could almost sniff the mood: a sort of muted excitement, cut through with a broad streak of disbelief. They'd all seen the sketch: the crude feathers, the huge eyes, the monstrous claws. Some even clutched Photostats of the original.

He joined the crowd, staying towards the back. Ullerden wanted to look like just another hack down here at his editor's command, to fill up a couple of spare column inches.

The crowd tensed. Two figures stepped up onto the pile of granite, using it as a natural stage, their long hair whipped by the breeze. Carly was dressed in her Girl Guide uniform, an incongruous yellow tartan scarf knotted around her left wrist: Brigit was huddled in a black and white check coat that almost reached her ankles.

Brigit looked at the crowd, vainly trying to tuck her hair behind her ears. As the oldest she was the natural spokesperson, but Carly looked like she could handle herself. Or at least, a bunch of cynical reporters who'd probably already spent half the morning in the nearest boozer.

"You all know what Carly and I saw three nights ago," Brigit started, her voice clear and confident, only a trace of accent present. "I don't intend to repeat myself. But to get all the probing and questions out of the way in one go – and save us and our families the hassle – we've agreed to meet you all out here, where it happened, and answer everything you want to know as truthfully as we can."

Ullerden smiled at the *we've agreed* bit. Made it sound like the girls were reluctantly placating the local media. But if this unusual press conference hadn't been arranged, the story would already be dead in the water.

"Miss Gay," someone near the front of the crowd was calling. "You said you and Carly were camping at the time…"

"Girl Guide camp – we were doing a walk across the moor…"

"Forgive me," another voice, "aren't you a little old to be in the Guides?"

"My sister's a member, I was an extra pair of hands—"

"An adult supervisor?"

"You could say that—"

"How old's your sister?"

"I don't think that's—"

"Did she see anything?"

"No. Just Carly and me—"

"How many were there in the camp that night?"

"Altogether? About twenty, I think."

"Did any of them see anything?"

"No. You know the ans—"

"There's a pub close by, Miss Gay."

Brigit hesitated. "That's not a question…"

"Did you – and any of the other *adult supervisors* – tend to visit it?"

And so it went on: the reporters punching out their questions, trying to keep Brigit Gay off balance, on the ropes. Hoping to catch her out in the big lie.

"She's good, isn't she?"

Ullerden flinched: the voice was almost in his left ear, soft and conspiratorial. He turned carefully, not wanting to look spooked. It was Harry Rawlins, ugly face grinning like he'd just fallen over the scoop of the century.

"I like the Girl Guide uniform. Nice touch."

Ullerden breathed in deeply and quietly. "Well, well. Fleet Street's grubbiest hack's in town. Slow day, is it?"

Rawlins' grin grew wider, something Ullerden would have thought impossible. "Couldn't stay away, sweetheart. Not when I saw the first reporter to quiz those girls was you. Coincidence? Don't think so."

"Meaning?"

Rawlins tapped his red, veined nose with a thin finger. "The Mount Pleasant Mothman... almost to the day. What do they call that... synchronicity?"

Ullerden shook his head. "There was another sighting on the moor... two months ago." At least he sounded calmer than he felt.

"Oh yes." Rawlins raised his bony finger again and wagged it. "Except it wasn't actually a sighting, was it? Just some lights, seen out on the moor one evening. By another two girls, wasn't it?"

"You know how these phenomena manifest themselves..."

"Too true. First the curtain-opener, then the main event. Like that sea-serpent off Marazion in '74. That was you, wasn't it?"

Ullerden laughed. "The sea serpent?"

"You know what I mean." Rawlins glanced towards the tor. The questions were drying up; no one could miss the looks of relief on both girls' faces. "She's a bit of all right, that Brigit Gay. You mixing business with pleasure, Tommy?"

"You've got a dirty mind."

Rawlins sniggered, then sobered abruptly. "That West Virginia business – whatever the truth of it – ended badly. Lot of people got hurt. Pretty sure you know that. Hope no one gets hurt this time."

Ullerden suddenly had a pretty good idea who'd been making stupid phone calls in the middle of the night. He cleared his throat. "You know what they say round here: *'Ee dawn't knaw 'nuff to knaw that 'ee dawn't knaw nawthen.'*"

Rawlins glanced at him, putting a cigarette in his mouth. "Very profound, I'm sure. Never got the hang of yokel." He lit the cigarette and started to walk away. "Looks like this part of the show's over," he called over his shoulder. "Catch you for the finale."

Ullerden didn't bother with a reply, just stared thoughtfully at the departing back. He was beginning to suspect who the *Taunton Evening Post*'s so-called local correspondent might be as well.

*

When Ullerden returned to his room at the *Wheal Gammon*, the supposedly unconnected phone was warbling again. He snatched up the green receiver, but whoever had been calling must have hung up. All he heard was crackling white noise. It snapped off, leaving an odd, echoing silence. Ullerden heard his own laboured breathing coming back at him. He replaced the receiver, threw his coat on the bed, and went downstairs.

The bar was just opening. They were serving up the predictable: Ploughman's Lunch, pasties; even clotted cream teas at a price that made Ullerden wince. Emmet food, he thought: strictly for the tourists. He settled himself in a quiet corner with a pint of Guinness: all the sustenance he needed.

There was a party of hikers gathered round a couple of tables, discussing local news, putting away prodigious amounts of bitter to wash down their huge Ploughman's. They kept feeding the jukebox, too. Ullerden had already endured Candi Staton and the Eagles, now The Four Seasons were belting out *Oh What a Night*. At least it wasn't sodding Queen again.

As he drained his glass Brigit Gay walked into the bar, looking around nervously, like someone in a bad spy film. She spotted him and came over.

"You don't have to be so worried," Ullerden said. "None of those dozy reporters are likely to find this place. Sit down. What you having?"

"Pint of lager and lime." Brigit stared at the table-top, hugging herself. "I'm just a little shaky after that grilling." She glared at Ullerden. "You said it'd be a breeze!"

"It was. They were eating out of your hand, love."

"Didn't feel like it…"

He went to get her drink and another Guinness for himself. When he placed the pint in front of her, Brigit snatched it up, half-draining the glass in one go.

"Steady on," he muttered. "You'll be ratted if you keep that up."

She put her drink down, glancing across at the hikers before staring at Ullerden again. "Have you heard what they're talking about?" she hissed.

He patted one of her hands. "Relax, love. No one's seen a picture of you, just Carly's clever drawing." He laughed softly. "Far as they're concerned we could just be a… a boss and his secretary on a dirty weekend." He pulled a packet of cigarettes out of his jacket, offering the pack to Brigit. She shook her head.

"Sorry – I don't…"

"Oh, I should give these a try."

Brigit flipped open the pack and glanced at the contents. Her eyes twitched wider for a second.

"Keep 'em," Ullerden said. "Buy Carly a Mivvi or something."

She hesitated a moment longer before pocketing the pack and its tight wad of pound notes.

"Just like a Bond film, eh?" He was enjoying the game.

"'Cept you're no Roger Moore." She drained the rest of her glass, shaking her head at his offer of another. "So we're done?"

"We're done. Go home. Take the money and run, as they say."

"Why did you do it? I mean: what do you get out of it?"

"Fun. Freaking people out. And I'm helping the local economy." He nodded towards the hikers who were still laughing about the strange events out on Bodmin Moor, and the gullible locals who probably believed it. "They're just the vanguard, love. Everyone from genuine investigators to flying saucer nuts will be coming here for years. You want to think about opening a shop: sell souvenirs."

She shook her head, standing. As though it had just occurred to her, she looked down at Ullerden one last time. "By the way, that phone call last night wasn't funny!"

His last swallow of Guinness turned sour. "Eh?"

"I mean, three in the morning! I had to be up at five to be ready for your bloody press conference!"

As she swept out of the bar, whatever had been playing on the jukebox faded out. To Ullerden, it had sounded like the band was singing about taking the money and running.

*

He spent the afternoon making notes, wondering how he could finish the game. What final act would keep the thing on Bodmin in people's minds for years to come. In the TV lounge he watched the local news programme, delighted that the item just before signing off was on the morning's press call. There was no video footage of the event, and just a grainy photograph of Raven Tor behind the newsreader. Carly and Brigit stayed anonymous, but the story remained alive.

Ullerden headed for the bar, not stirring until last orders was called. His head buzzing, his stomach filled to brimming with Guinness, he went up to his room, already anticipating the huge breakfast he was going to devour in the morning.

He flopped into bed, mind drifting. Hypnogogic visions of Brigit Gay sprouting feathers that looked like pound notes while her eyes grew huge and brilliant swamped him – only to be shattered by the insistent twittering of the phone.

"Yes? What?"

"Tomas Ullerden?" The line was crackly as the night before. Ullerden had an image of Harry Rawlins crumpling a sheet of cellophane next to a phone's mouthpiece.

"Rawlins? That you—?"

"Tomas Ullerden?"

"You know it is! Rawlins, what the—?" The static was cut off by empty silence. Ullerden slammed the receiver down.

He got out of bed, making his way to the communal bathroom just along a short corridor. Pouring a glass of water he gulped it down, and padded back to his room. He was going to kill Harry Rawlins next time they met.

Before he could get back into bed, the phone rang again. He snatched it up.

"What!"

"Raven Tor. Tomas Ullerden. Mothman—" The line died again.

His room was abruptly flooded with light: outside the window twin spotlights, blazing an unsettling red, swept by. When they were gone his room felt darker than ever. A car's headlights, he supposed.

Ullerden realised he was still holding the receiver, almost crushing it. He replaced it carefully, every movement slow and controlled. He swept up clothes: pulling trousers and jacket on over his pyjamas. Slipping shoes onto bare feet he plunged out of his room, hurrying down to his parked Toledo. Opening the passenger door, Ullerden groped blindly inside the glove compartment, fingers eventually closing around a flashlight. He straightened, thumbed on the torch, waving the beam into the night.

Harry bloody Rawlins. It was him. Had to be. Phoning him up… driving past with his headlights on full beam, red filters over the glass…

Adrenalin had sobered him up slightly; his thoughts began to slow, make sense. He'd underestimated Rawlins: Brigit could be found easily enough – she was in the directory, after all – but locating the *Wheal Gammon,* and Ullerden, so quickly? He'd never imagined Harry was such a good journalist. Bribing the landlord so he could mess about with the phone, though: pure Rawlins.

He thought there was a flash of red off to his right: headlights in the distance. They were gone before he could be sure, and the torch beam showed nothing.

Bloody Rawlins!

Tinny, distant music flared up. Ullerden stared around for several seconds before he realised it was coming from his car's radio. He laughed out loud: it was *Bohemian Rhapsody*! Just as a reedy Freddie Mercury finished telling anyone listening to look up to the skies and see, the radio fell silent. It wasn't totally quiet, though: Ullerden could still hear static; white noise.

"Tomas Ullerden..."

He flinched. That voice wasn't coming from his car radio. It couldn't be—

"Tomas Ullerden...?"

He started to open the passenger door, to turn the radio off, but his numb fingers slipped off the handle. He backed away; he was dreaming. He'd turn around, walk back to his room and bed. He'd dream going to sleep and then wake up properly—

"No dream. Tomas Ullerden."

He turned his back on the car, faced the pub. The sky above was black and moonless; brilliant white stars flickered and danced in the clear air, though it felt heavy; oppressive. Two bright red stars appeared to be moving. A plane, most likely: heading for Bodmin Airfield—

"Tomas Ullerden. Ullerden..." The voice was getting louder, but still overlaid by that harsh crackle. And the voice itself— Ullerden had only just noticed how oddly inflected it was: almost mechanical. Like a robot from a kids' television programme.

The red lights were growing brighter. Ullerden couldn't shake the feeling they were dropping straight towards the *Wheal Gammon's* roof. He wanted to rush indoors; he couldn't move. His hair prickled; there was a coppery taste in his mouth.

"Úla. Den..."

The red spots were like headlights, now: blazing full beams. They hovered just above the pub roof. Around them, stars blinked in and out as a huge silhouette eclipsed them.

"Not Mothman..."

The red eyes swooped. Ullerden had just enough time to make out enormous wings, a beak, and the splayed talons on scaly hind legs.

"Final act. Úla den..."

THE PYGMALION CONJURATION

His breathing slows and vision blurs. He gazes up one last time at the magnificent creature rearing over him. She is everything he'd ever wanted in a woman; she is all women. His women. It's so unfair, he thinks…

*

Sex magick!

From the moment Dennis Crawleigh heard the phrase, he couldn't get it out of his head. It reverberated in his subconscious like an echo of promise. *Sex magick*. What was it? How did it work? Was it some hocus-pocus to get young and attractive women into bed? Just to get young and attractive young women to notice he had a pulse would be something.

Sex magick…

To be fair, Dennis wasn't a bad-looking man. But on the wrong side of thirty, his fine blond hair fast becoming a memory, he could just reach the lofty heights of five feet on tiptoe and he'd been wearing the same glasses for twenty-five years. He owned a house – left to him by an aunt – but remained determinedly unemployed. Dennis had little confidence in himself, and even less belief that any woman would consider him more than a distant friend. Any kind of short cut was welcome.

And sex magick…

It took just over a week for him to be bitterly disappointed. A search of the Internet on the local library's computers soon disabused him of all his eager fantasies. It seemed that sex magick was, in reality, just an excuse for people to strip off and get busy; all the while pretending to be part of some powerful ritual. Dennis wasn't surprised to discover that Aleister Crowley – of whom he'd heard – had been a strong supporter of the idea. Crowley had been, Dennis was certain, just a dirty old man with a persuasive tongue. He quite envied him.

However, it left Dennis feeling quite deflated. No magick was ever going to get him a girlfriend; never mind sex. There was

Rohypnol, of course, but he didn't think he'd ever be that desperate.

The matter would have rested there, if it hadn't been for the dream Dennis had one Friday night after he'd gone to bed with a bellyful of cheap lager sitting on top of two rounds of cheese on toast. He found himself in a dark, misty place, surrounded by vague, flowing shapes on which he could never quite focus. He wandered for an aimless period, sure that he should be scared, but instead feeling curiously excited. Eventually the mists parted and revealed an imposing figure sitting on what looked like a giant red and purple mushroom. It was a man with a penetrating stare, a vaguely supercilious smile, and what looked like an embroidered seat cushion jammed on his large, bald head. The smile broadened into a leering grin at Dennis's approach, and the man lowered his head slightly. His eyes seemed to glow.

"You were right, you know," he said. His voice sounded flat and muffled, as though coming from the bottom of a large, padded box.

"I was?" Dennis blinked. "What about?"

"The sex magick." The man winked slowly. "Just like you thought."

"Eh...?"

The distant, muffled voice sighed patiently in Dennis's ear. The bald man was standing next to him, a friendly arm thrown across Dennis's shoulders. "There are... rituals which, when performed correctly, bring about – how can I put this...?"

"Me having sex?" Dennis suggested.

The man sighed. "Quite. But it will take patience, diligence and hard work."

Dennis shuffled. Sensing his reluctance, the man patted his shoulder and hugged him closer. "Oh, nothing you can't handle, old chap. I'm sure the apple hasn't fallen *that* far from the tree."

"Apple?" Dennis was losing the thread.

The man sighed again and began thumbing through a huge, brassbound leather tome that hadn't been there a moment earlier. "Crawleigh... Crowley. Do you think a letter here or there makes a difference? Do pay attention, old man!" He stabbed a finger at a dense paragraph of illuminated script that looked like no language Dennis had ever seen. "Page six hundred and sixty-six—" He sniggered.

Dennis felt himself pushed closer to the massive page; he could smell its incredible age. From somewhere above him he just made out the muffled words: "Read, mark, learn and inwardly digest, as my old form master always said. Pathetic old queen. Still, he had a point." The hand on Dennis's shoulder slipped down his back, briefly cupping his backside. "Do what thou wilt shall be the whole of the law—"

Dennis awoke with an aching bladder and the thick smell of rot in his nostrils.

*

The dream stubbornly refused to fade as the day trudged on. If anything, it grew more real, becoming a genuine memory. Dennis could not only still smell that decaying old book, he could visualise it perfectly. The heavy black leather cover; the grotesquely ornate brass fittings; the heavy pages – too stiff and thick for paper – with their chewed corners and cracking edges. Even its title: *Incantamenta Et Ad Voluptatem Et Lucrum*. Not that he had a blue clue what that meant, but it sounded... promising.

Dennis headed for the local library. He was pretty well known there: Miss Grant – the Chief Librarian – had shown him how to use the Internet when he'd first started researching magick. As he walked in, she glanced up from her computer and smiled at him. She always had a smile for Dennis; it was one reason he felt relaxed in her company. That and the fact she was probably old enough to be his mother.

"Mr Crawleigh." She peered over glasses that were even more old-fashioned than Dennis's. "Can I help?"

"I'm trying to find something out about an old book." He fished a slip of paper from his pocket and placed it on the counter in front of her. He'd printed the Latin title as neatly as he could from memory, not at all confident of the pronunciation. Miss Grant picked up the paper, pushed up her glasses and read the words. Her brow puckered slightly.

"A little different from your normal reading, Mr Crawleigh," she commented, handing him back the slip.

He shrugged self-consciously, cramming the paper away. "I was just wondering if you could tell me anything about it. I don't imagine the library has a copy."

She smiled again. "I don't imagine so either, Mr Crawleigh." She tapped her keyboard, staring with more brow-creased intensity at her screen. After a few seconds she exclaimed softly.

"That's a very rare volume, Mr Crawleigh. Unique, even. The only copy in Britain is at the British Library in London."

Dennis's hopes drained. Of course it was; and he had no intention of wasting money traipsing all the way down to London just because of some dream. It was so unfair —

He became aware that Miss Grant was looking at him again. "Crowley," she said.

"Beg pardon?"

"Aleister Crowley. The Wickedest Man in England, they called him."

There was a very cold draught suddenly blowing down Dennis's back. "What about him?"

"The copy in the British Library once belonged to him, or so it says here. It was given to the Library in 1950 – three years after his death – along with other volumes and a variety of papers." Behind the glass lenses, Miss Grant's eyes twinkled. "Have you taken a sudden interest in The Great Beast, Mr Crawleigh?" She tapped a finger against the side of her nose and smiled. "Don't worry. Your secret's safe with me."

Dennis tried not to huff; this was getting him nowhere. "I can't get to London —!" he began.

Miss Grant pointed over his shoulder at a cluster of computers filling a space which had once contained bookshelves. "The Internet, Mr Crawleigh."

Of course! He laughed. "Never thought of that."

She returned to her own work and Dennis sat himself back down at a console. Entering *Incantamenta Et Ad Voluptatem Et Lucrum* into the search engine produced dozens of hits. He selected the first, and there it was: an image of the book from his dream. Every creased page, scratched brass hinge and scuffed leather cover. He'd found it!

He started to read the on-screen notes.

The first thing he learned was that the authenticity of the *Incantamenta Et Ad Voluptatem Et Lucrum* was in some doubt: not a few experts considered it a hoax perpetrated by Crowley (him again, thought Dennis) a century or so back. Most of the book was given over to a variety of spells or rituals, the majority of which – Dennis wasn't surprised to discover with the help of a handy Latin-English translator – were to conjure wealth. Or create gold from base metals; or create jewels from simple stones; or how to find wealth; or how to summon a demon who would tell you where to find wealth, or how to create gold or jewels—In every case, the participants of the ritual had to perform it naked, and round it all off with a good old fashioned orgy. In all, pretty repetitive and unimaginative. If it was one of the Great Beast's jokes, it wasn't much of one. Or perhaps back in the early twentieth century, sensibilities were more easily offended. Dennis began to think everything – the dream, book – was just a coincidence after all. Wish fulfilment, in a way.

Then he remembered the dream-Crowley mentioning a page number. What had it been? Something about it had amused the old man—

"The number of the Beast!" Dennis laughed – much louder than he'd intended – earning him a "*Shh!*" off Miss Grant. Dennis mouthed an apology and went back to flipping pages on screen. Six hundred and sixty-six: 666. Dennis imagined that would have given Crowley a good belly laugh.

There was quite a dense block of text on page six hundred and sixty-six, followed by two more pages of what looked like bullet points. Dennis highlighted the lot and ran it through the translator. It was another ritual, but not for the acquisition of gold or money, or any kind of riches. Entitled *The Pygmalion Conjuration*, it was to satisfy much older, baser lusts than wealth.

Dennis skimmed through the opening chunk of text: a very circuitous, verbose description of what the ritual was meant to achieve. Dennis read between the over-written lines: any man or woman who could master the spell would be able to have whoever they wanted, whenever they wanted. *Real* sex magick. Dennis flopped back in his seat, staring at the screen. This was it! Exactly what he'd been looking for!

He printed off all three pages, folded the sheets into his coat and closed down the Internet. He gave Miss Grant a cheery thumbs-up when she asked if he'd found what he was looking for, and headed home.

*

Dennis couldn't believe he was actually going to go through with the ritual. On the one hand, he was mortified that someone might find out; while on the other, curiosity had a hold of him. What if it worked? And if it didn't – well, he'd be the only one to know.

Apart from feeling a bit of a prat, he'd be no worse off than he was now.

The ritual called for several items – he supposed they were talismanic: a sword, incense, candles, a knife, a wand, a small pentacle and a vase. After thinking carefully, he eventually came up with a toy light sabre he'd had since a kid (batteries dead), a packet of joss sticks left over from his teenage years, some shrivelled candles kept in the back of a kitchen cupboard for emergencies, a carving knife, a length of bamboo cane, and a pentacle carefully drawn on a sheet of paper. The vase, it turned out, was just for flowers. Carefully, he laid everything out neatly on the dining table.

The text was very particular about cleanliness, so the next morning he showered thoroughly. All day he drank nothing but glasses of water, and didn't eat a bite. As night drew in, feeling clean, fasted (and a little light-headed), Dennis was ready.

As per the instructions, he put on a clean bathrobe, lit the joss sticks and candles, placed the sheets of paper with the ritual on the dining table within easy reach, and picked up the bamboo wand. He wasn't sure whether he had to or not – the text was unclear – but it felt right. Taking a deep breath he began intoning the words in a suitably solemn voice, trying not to laugh. The syllables seemed to echo briefly, before fading away in an odd manner; but he may have imagined it. As he chanted he tried to visualise exactly what he expected from the ritual. Luckily, years of living alone had honed Dennis's imagination: he found he could visualise it pretty well.

He saw women – beautiful, sexy women – arrayed before him, in varying degrees of undress. Woman from the TV, from movies, from newspapers and magazines; many of whom he couldn't put a name to, but he knew their faces intimately. And they were all looking at him with unrequited desire: he was the only thing in the whole world that they wanted. They smiled at him, eyes half-lidded; reached out their hands. He could almost hear their wanton pleas, smell their perfume, feel their touch…

When it was over, he dumped himself awkwardly on the carpet – almost collapsing – tired, his body sheened in sweat even though he was cold. Above everything else, he wanted a beer, but was afraid that might sully the purity of the ritual. He would wait. Tomorrow he'd see if the Pygmalion Conjuration had worked; see how many women he could… *will* into his bed. That was the word.

"Do what thou wilt shall be the whole of the law" – he understood Crowley's famous maxim now.

*

The next day he could barely eat breakfast. His stomach was a writhing sack of butterflies, and all seemed to be wearing boots. Even though he was starving all he could force down were half a round of toast and a mug of tea. Like a kid with a new toy, he had to get out and see if the ritual had worked. Discover if the Pygmalion Conjuration had granted him mastery over the women of the world!

He dressed quickly, barely noticing what he was throwing on. Outside it was unseasonably cold. Dennis pulled up the collar of his coat, rammed hands into pockets and made for the park. He sat on a bench facing the duck pond and waited. And waited. Apart from two swans and a moorhen, he seemed to have the park all to himself. There was a tattered copy of a red-top newspaper abandoned on the bench beside him; he read it front to back while he waited. Still nothing. He folded the newspaper into a coat pocket, stood and walked to a coffee-stall just outside the park: he had no intention of freezing to death while he waited. Cradling the huge cardboard cup of the cheapest coffee on sale, he returned to his vigil.

The coffee was all gone when the first women approached. Both were in their mid-thirties, Dennis guessed, both a foot taller than him. One black with long, highlighted hair, the other white and blonde. Both gorgeous. They were laughing at some joke, heads together, oblivious of everyone and everything. All the better. As they passed Dennis's bench he fixed his eyes on them, willing them to turn and join him. To first share his bench, then agree to come home and share his bed. He put into it every bit of mental effort he could muster; sweat trickled down the side of his face despite the chilly air.

They kept on walking; didn't even so much as glance in his direction.

Dennis flopped against the bench's rigid back. Damn!

A girl – probably not far out of her teens – passed the receding women, coming straight towards Dennis. She was a little shorter; with pale brown hair halfway to her waist, dancing side to side like she was in a shampoo advert. Dennis closed his eyes and tried

111

reaching out with his mind; feeling for her thoughts. Nothing. By the time he opened his eyes again, she was fifty yards down the path.

Damn! Damn! Damn! Damn! FUCK!

The next couple of hours unravelled slowly. Women and girls passed by – in increasing numbers as lunchtime hit – but he couldn't reach out or influence a single one. Mostly they ignored him, though one or two glanced nervously at him out of the corners of their eyes, before speeding up and vanishing. Eventually, he gave it up as a bad job. Plus, he thought it was increasingly likely someone might call the police. He stumped home: embarrassed and angry with himself for believing such stupidity. Had he grown so desperate? Reached the Rohypnol stage after all? Obviously he had.

That night he sat in his battered chair, nursing a cheap lager and flipping morosely through the battered red-top newspaper, which he'd forgotten all about. He gazed at the picture of a half-naked model on one page; lost in a hopeless, bitter longing and a familiar ache in his groin. Wishing that once – just once – a girl like that (or to be honest, even a fraction as sexy) would just say hello to him. Just once. Was that so much to ask? It was so unfair—

"Hello."

The word was spoken so softly that Dennis didn't hear it at first.

"Hello!"

He glanced up, almost dropping the part-drained can of lager. He did let the newspaper go, though: partly so he could get a better look. Standing in front of him, stiletto heels digging into his thin carpet, was the model from the newspaper. Dennis blinked, looked first at the lager can and then at the girl. She was still there. Sexy and voluptuous and pouty.

"Hello, Dennis." Her voice was warm and husky, just like he'd imagined it would be. She had huge, honey-coloured eyes; her smile was wide and promising. He tried to say hello back, but his voice broke on the second syllable and all he managed was a strangled: *"Hell—"*

She dropped smoothly into his lap, her browned arms encircling his neck. She smelled vaguely resinous; some modern scent, he thought. Her breath was warm and tickled his ear as she whispered to him. When her mouth closed on his, Dennis finally let the lager can go.

He awoke with a start, looking around his bedroom. He was alone. Obviously last night had been a dream – another dream! But so detailed and memorable...! He pulled himself out of bed, surprised to find he was naked. He pulled on his bathrobe, jammed feet into slippers, and shuffled downstairs.

The old newspaper was scattered across half of the floor. Next to his chair the lager can was lying on its side, a wet patch leaked out across the carpet. Dennis sighed, disgusted at himself, and scooped up the sheets of newsprint. He was just about to screw it up when it occurred to him something was wrong. He leafed through the pages, finally reaching the one where the model's picture had been. There was a huge blank space: just the banner and a small square of inane text. The half-naked model herself was missing; or to be exact: her picture was missing.

Dennis dropped the paper back on the carpet. He dashed up to his bedroom, seeing for the first time just how dishevelled his bed sheets were. He bent down; sniffed. Yes: apart from the familiar odour of his own sweat was the faintest, resinous scent. It hadn't been a dream. Dennis really had spent the night with a— with a—

He sat heavily on his wrecked bed, head spinning. "Fuck me," he whispered eventually. "It worked...!"

*

Dennis had quite a collection of photographs and glossy mags. He picked out one magazine at random and flipped through the pages, finally settling on a full-page snap of a famous film beauty, taken five years earlier at Cannes. Dennis stared at her picture, wishing she was alive, wondering how she'd feel (he knew what her voice was like), how she'd smell. At some point – he couldn't pinpoint when – he was aware that her picture wasn't on the page any longer. She was standing in his bedroom, smiling: warm and friendly.

"Hello—" he just about managed.

"Hello, Dennis," she purred, and slithered to his side.

*

Dennis figured out the Pygmalion connection eventually: the

113

mythical sculptor who brought a statue to life. Thanks to the ritual, he was doing it with photographs. All he needed was to want it enough, and he could summon a succession of gorgeous, willing, warm and full-blooded women. They didn't care about Dennis's lack of experience, his enthusiasm over patience. They were there for him, no matter what.

He found it didn't need to be a full-length picture, either. Somehow, he – or the spell – created the entire woman. Even a black and white photo transmuted into natural flesh tones. The only downer was the original picture was gone forever and so – during his post-coital sleep – would be each woman. Dennis assumed they ceased to exist once he lost consciousness, but he didn't worry unduly about it. He had plenty of pictures. If he woke up in the middle of the night in the mood for a little more fun, he could just shuffle out another photo and call up a new bed-partner.

Horror movie actresses preserved in their youthful prime in old books; singers as they'd been at the start of their careers, trapped on CD covers; newsreaders; weathergirls; celebs from lists A to Z who were simply famous for being famous (and wearing very little). If Dennis had a picture of them, there was no limit. (Though he quickly learned that attempting to enjoy the exaggerated voluptuousness of cartoon characters was a step too far). How many men, he reasoned, after the first three or four days, wouldn't want to live out their fantasies in living 3D?

One morning he uncovered a class portrait from his final year at school and found that – with just a little more effort – he could extract each and every girl from the print. The ones he'd fancied from afar, to those he'd hated (often at the same time): all at his beck and call for a day. When he'd finally struggled out of bed, hollow-eyed and pale, the old photograph – pock-marked with white gaps that had once been people – looked desolate and forlorn. Dennis ripped up the ruined snap and binned it.

It was inevitable the day would come when his source material ran dry. His stack of literature and cuttings reduced to a collection of blank pages and empty photographs. He was down to a cheap, dog-eared celebrity magazine someone had left on the bus.

He gazed at his gaunt expression in the mirror; acutely aware that he'd not stepped outside his house in — He had no idea how long. His thinning hair looked practically gone altogether, his bathrobe was… well, disgusting, frankly. He looked – Dennis had to admit to himself – like a junkie denied his fix for too long; although that irony wasn't lost on him.

"Get a grip!" he mumbled at the reflection.

He took a shower, wondering just how long it was since his last one, dressed in clean clothes and checked the fridge for anything edible. The milk had soured and he didn't have any eggs or juice. Colonies of green and blue of mould smeared the two remaining slices of bread. All that the kitchen cupboard held were one can of ratatouille and two of carrots.

He dragged on his coat. Locking the front door behind him he stepped out into a cold, bright day. Immediately a headache started up behind his eyes.

"Mr Crawleigh?"

Dennis blinked, trying to focus on the figure swimming in front of his pulsing eyes. After a moment, it sharpened into Miss Grant from the library. She was staring at Dennis, her expression— He wasn't sure what her expression was, but he thought concern was in there somewhere.

"Miss Grant..."

She stepped closer; it was all Dennis could do not to back away. "You look – you don't look at all well, Mr Crawleigh. Have you been ill?"

"I've—" He shivered: the cold, obviously. "No, I've not been too good, Miss Grant. Flu, I think. But I'm getting better. Just off to get something to eat, in fact." He forced a smile. "First proper food for a while."

"Well—" She seemed to be examining him closely. There was something different about her that Dennis couldn't quite figure out. "You see that you do eat, Mr Crawleigh. You look like you could do with a good square meal..."

He gave her a jerky nod. "I will, don't worry. I'll be up and about in no time." He turned away. "I'll see you—"

She replied something that Dennis didn't catch, but he wasn't about to pause and ask her to repeat it. He was cold, he wanted to get to the shops and back as quickly as he could and – embarrassingly – he had just grown an extremely pained and urgent erection. It wasn't just the cold making him hunch.

*

He returned from the shops and emptied out the blue plastic bag they'd supplied. For a moment he was confused: where was the food? Had he left it in the shop! He must have had a second bag that—

But as he gazed on the selection of tabloid newspapers and celebrity mags it occurred to him there was no second bag. There was no food. He didn't need it.

He opened a newspaper, riffled through it to the society page. The daughter of some tycoon stared out at him, awaiting his command. He looked at the picture, stared through it and took her hand: pulled her to him.

His erection was back: a delightful agony. He didn't waste time taking her to his bedroom. He just took her.

*

His head was ringing. Dennis turned over in bed, groaning. He felt sick and weak; all his joints ached. The mother of all hangovers: without him actually having drunk anything. The ringing persisted. It wasn't his head: it was the front doorbell. Someone was pushing it with an annoying rhythm. He wished they'd stop.

After what felt like hours it became obvious whoever was downstairs had no intention of stopping. Dennis rolled from his bed, wincing at the tiniest movement, staggered to his feet and pulled on his crusted bathrobe. He weaved down the stairs, clinging desperately onto the bannister with fingers that were vague and insubstantial. Making it to the front door he tried to fling it open angrily. Instead he almost overbalanced.

"What?" he croaked.

"Mr Crawleigh!"

He blinked, forcing the silhouette on his step into some sort of focus. It was Miss Grant. He recognised the voice more than her shape against the stabbing daylight.

"What?" he repeated, clinging onto the front door. He thought he might throw up.

"I thought you said you were getting better!"

He felt arms encircling him, supporting his sagging frame. The world pitched and yawed around him. He barely registered being half-carried upstairs. Miss Grant lowered him onto his bed where his swimming head gradually stilled. His eyes got back a little focus. Miss Grant was looking down at him, her face angular with concern. There was still something about her... something different—

"Your glasses—" he muttered, but she didn't seem to hear him. Instead she was gazing around his bedroom: at the scatter of half-blank glossy magazines and torn-up newspaper.

"You have been a busy boy," she said. Her voice was so neutral, so calm. He started to speak, but she silenced him with fingers against his mouth. "High time we did something," she said, and backed out of the room.

Dennis lay on the bed, his thoughts an incoherent mess. All he could wonder was how he'd come to this state: he was disgusted at himself. But even in that moment of self-loathing his thoughts drifted to Miss Grant: how she'd changed; how she somehow looked younger, sexier.

If only he had a picture of her...

She re-entered the bedroom, carrying a tray. Dennis guessed she was going to try and feed him, even though the thought of food made him gag. She placed the tray in a corner and stood back from it, facing Dennis.

"Now, Mr Crawleigh, we need to sort you out!"

He tried to smile, to nod in agreement. His attempt at a "Yes" came out a meaningless hiss.

Miss Grant was unbuttoning her heavy coat. She threw it carelessly onto the bed; beneath she had on nothing but underclothes. Dennis stared, gape-mouthed, as she pulled off her slip, bra and briefs. Despite his weakness, he felt arousal drift through his emaciated body like a warm infusion. Her body was a young woman's, not the middle-aged librarian he'd imagined.

She bent and picked something off the tray. It took a moment for Dennis to recognise the carving knife he'd used in the Pygmalion Conjuration back— When was it...? He craned his stiff neck, trying to see what else was on the tray. It contained every item he'd put together for the ritual, except for the instructions. What—?

Miss Grant closed in on him, knife raised. Dennis tried to flinch away, but he could barely move. With a series of quick slashes, she cut the filthy robe away from his body, leaving him cold, exposed; his erection all too obvious. She glanced at it and smiled; it wasn't a pleasant smile.

"We'll have none of that, Mr Crawleigh." She reached down

with the knife, touching the frigid blade against his hot flesh. His erection shrank away.

"Better." She stooped over the tray again, lighting joss sticks and candles. Then she stood over him, carving knife and light sabre crossed over her breasts. She sucked in a deep breath, closing her eyes. When she re-opened them, Dennis finally recognised the huge, honey-coloured eyes of the model he'd slept with that first night. And her breasts: so like those of a Hammer actress he'd lusted after for so long, and eventually enjoyed. Her arms, her legs. She was still Miss Grant, and yet...

She was smiling at him again: it was sharper and more deadly than the knife she was clutching. "Where do you think they all went – after you were finished with them?" She was gloating. "The Conjuration is much deeper and more subtle than you realise, Dennis. May I call you Dennis? I feel like I know you so well." She leaned closer, caressing his face with the tip of the knife. "Did you think it was just for your benefit?" Her teeth nipped the air, millimetres away from his nose.

She straightened. Holding the light sabre above her head, with her other hand she traced a thin line down Dennis's body: throat to scrotum. He tried to shrink away from the point.

Miss Grant laughed. "Don't worry, Dennis – I'm not going to cut you up. Or damage you in any way. For one thing, he needs you intact." She carefully placed knife and light sabre on the bed. "And for another, I won't need to."

She reached down, delicately pinching his nose shut between the fingers of one hand; placing the palm of her second hand over his mouth.

*

Whatever Dennis was sitting on, it felt pretty uncomfortable: like a hard, uneven rock. He wriggled, but he couldn't settle: his backside managed to be both numb and sore at the same time. He tried looking down, but mists obscured just about everything. He was alone in a grey, silent world. He couldn't get down, either: it was as though he was glued in place.

"Buck up, old man." The voice came from nowhere, and everywhere: dampened and flat. "It could be worse."

Dennis looked around, and wasn't surprised to find Aleister Crowley standing next to him; although what he was standing on eluded Dennis's gaze.

"Could it?"

Crowley turned to him, a wide grin splitting his face. His eyes sparkled with malice. "No. On reflection, I don't suppose it could. Tough luck, old man."

"Your Conjuration didn't work! You promised —!"

"Actually I never *promised* anything, Dennis. And I can assure you the Conjuration worked perfectly. You – as you so elegantly phrased it – had sex, didn't you?"

"Yes, but—"

"Well, then." Crowley stepped away from Dennis's perch. "That Miss Grant was quite a find, don't you think?" He paused and turned around. "Did you know her first name is actually Thelema?" He stared hard at Dennis, obviously looking for a recognition Dennis couldn't give him. "No? Oh, well."

"She killed me!" His situation suddenly occurred to Dennis. "That bitch —!"

Crowley touched Dennis's mouth with a finger, silencing him. "Now, now. I'll have no name-calling." Crowley was growing fainter: his body dissolving in the ever-present mists. "She administered a *coup de grâce*, if anything; and your part was already over. Well done, by the way. I couldn't have succeeded without your... sterling efforts." Despite the mists, Dennis was certain he could still see Crowley's supercilious grin. "You remember: *sex magick...*"

Dennis tried to speak, but he remained mute.

"Sexual congress yields a tremendous degree of elemental power, which is why many rites conclude with what some so crudely describe as *an orgy*. The climax, if you like." He was all but invisible now: just a voice and cruel laugh. "The adept focusses that power; bends it to his will. Imagine how much power *you've* been generating over the past few weeks..."

Crowley's voice faded along with his body. The cold grey mists closed in around Dennis, vague shapes moving within them. He could no longer see any more than he could speak. Somewhere in his head, Dennis began to scream.

*

Miss Grant stood at the bedside, watching and waiting. She'd replaced the knife and fake sword (she'd felt such a fool waving that ridiculous child's toy!) on the tray and placed it on the bed by Dennis's feet. Then – still naked as Crowley had instructed her – waited for the resurrection.

She spared a moment to glance down at her own rejuvenated body. Even presented with the evidence of her new eyes, she could barely accept it. The years had fallen away, just as the Master had promised. Piecemeal, her body had been renewed – replaced – by each and every one of Dennis Crawleigh's sordid couplings. Even though, as she'd looked in the mirror, she still saw Thelema Grant, it was an improved version. So much more alive, so fresh; seductive, sexier. The next time the Area Manager called in at the Library, she had no doubt she could persuade him to find her a better job. She sniggered; she'd almost thought *better position*.

Dennis's corpse sighed; his eyes opened. With a groan, he carefully sat upright, swung his legs off the bed, and stood. Miss Grant helped him: the Master was still unsteady on his new feet. "Did it work?" she asked. The other's eyes fastened on hers, glowing with an inner light. He smiled with a confidence and arrogance she'd never seen on Dennis's face.

"Yes. Oh, yes!" He threw his arms around her, kissing her cheeks. "My dear Miss Grant – Thelema! My own Galatea!" He released her and went to admire himself in the bedroom mirror, studiously tiptoeing around the litter of paper on the floor. He stared for almost a minute, fingers absently caressing his head and face.

"Pity about the hair," he said, eventually.

Miss Grant busied herself snatching up the papers. She tried not to see all the empty spaces; tried not to think what it meant. "Better burn all this. Lord knows what would happen if someone saw." She straightened. "Pity about Dennis. Although I understand the need for sacrifice."

The Master had turned away from the mirror. "What do you think best: Dennis Crowley or Aleister Crawleigh? Or something entirely new?"

"Might I suggest something entirely new…?"

"Of course." His teeth flashed. "No connections or loose ends."

Miss Grant piled the papers untidily on the bed. As she did so, she realised the carving knife was no longer on the tray where she'd replaced it. The Master stepped in close to her; his heat, his power, engulfed her.

"You realise, of course, that Dennis wasn't the sacrifice—" She

120

felt the point of the knife – hard and chill – against her spine. His last words to her were, "Sometimes I hate myself…"

TO DIE FOR

Hands.

Disembodied, so faint George can almost pretend they're not real. Floating. Over his wife: his young, sleeping wife. And they're moving, these hands: making odd, snatching, snipping movements. Plucking at something he can't see. But then, it's just gone three in the morning and George can't really see a pair of hands floating in the air anyway.

Pulling, tugging, breaking apart something invisible above his deeply sleeping wife. Very deep; very, very deep...

You need hands...

George awoke, twitching up to a half-sit before realizing he'd been dreaming again. He glanced across at Joyce, hoping he hadn't woken her. She'd been having bad nights all week; she wouldn't appreciate being disturbed.

His heart was still racing, but he could no longer remember what the dream had been about. Already faded. He slowly lay back down and let himself relax back into sleep.

The next morning Joyce was bright and chirpy; obviously got a decent sleep, George guessed. She even offered to drive him up to the station after breakfast. He didn't refuse.

And he didn't see the articulated truck until it barrelled out of a junction, straight into the driver's door. Suddenly his world was black, spinning and shrill. The nausea went on and on, even when he woke up in a hospital bed: pinned by a web of tubes and wires, his arms strangely numb.

He was lucky to be alive, they said. The car had been crushed almost beyond recognition. What about Joyce? he'd asked. When they wouldn't tell him, he knew. She would have taken the full impact. At least it was quick.

Or so he hoped.

But he was lucky, they kept on saying. He was alive. It was just his hands. Severed in the crash, somehow.

You need hands...

*

He walked into my shop within ten minutes of opening. A good sign, very good. He was small, nervy and balding: Donald Pleasance to a tee. This suited me, since I was in a Peter Cushing mood; all lavender water and exquisite manners.

The client – for that's what he most certainly was – sidled through the door past the accumulated clutter of sepia-toned junk. None of it was worth having, even as junk it was strictly third class; but people seem to expect it. The moth-eaten chimpanzee with an arm that waves as you pass; devilish masks and patinated bronzes of the Old Gentleman himself in waistcoat and tails; things that lurk sinisterly in the shadows, only to become teddy-bears, bleeding untidy stuffing, when you near them; cloudy glass jars which resemble armoured Turkish caps, and have no obvious use whatsoever.

Donald Pleasance found his way to the counter eventually, having made the customary circuit of the shop. His pale, staring eyes looked all around until he located me: next to the stuffed Kodiak bear. Predictably, he jumped, and his mouth twitched, undecided between a smile or pout.

"Good morning, sir," I said. "Is there anything I can do for you?"

"I – yes, I—" He looked as though he desperately needed a bowler hat, or something similar, to tug at. His hands twisted ineffectually at nothing. "Yes. Good morning, Mister—" He tailed off, his opening gambit spent.

"Grimsdyke," I said. "The name is above the door." I doubted he would have been looking up there when he came in, and had little fear he'd catch me in the lie.

"Mr. Grimsdyke." He almost bowed, his nervousness was so pronounced. I don't think he appreciated my little joke; too private, perhaps, or too clever. "I was just looking…"

"For something special? Something unique?"

He looked around again, perhaps clearly seeing the quality of my stock for the first time. "Ah – quite…"

"Don't be put off by what you see, Mister—?" It was my turn to stall.

The left corner of his mouth twitched. "Francis," he murmured. I waited, more or less patiently. "Nicholas Francis," he completed after several moments' pause.

"Mr. Francis, let us be frank." I winced at the awful pun, but it was quite unconscious, and he appeared to be oblivious of it.

"What I have on display in the front of the shop are simply odds and ends, a few rags. Nothing that would interest a serious buyer."

His nervous smile came and went; his soft-boiled egg eyes pained. "What are you saying?"

I gestured towards the red curtain behind me. In the general dimness of the shop, it was hardly obvious. "As you might expect, I keep a stock of more... esoteric items in the rear."

He looked unsure. I wondered if I had, perhaps, misjudged the man. "But the final choice is, of course, entirely up to you," I did my best to reassure him.

Mr. Francis drifted away from the counter again. His hands and eyes were examining the shop, quite independent of each other, as though he hoped one might light upon a reason to be here, or an excuse to leave. The back of his left hand brushed against a cardboard box containing long-playing vinyl records. He pounced on them as though he had been searching all his life for such a collection. I began to feel genuine disappointment.

Leafing through the various sleeves, he paused at one and drew it out. "Is this any good?" he asked, rather giving himself away.

I narrowed my eyes and stared at the face and words on the cover. Someone named Don Henley was the artist; I had never heard of him.

"I'm sorry, Mr. Francis, but my partner buys in all musical items. I have little interest in such things."

"You wouldn't know the price, then?"

"If it is not marked, no." I tried to keep the frustration out of my voice. "For all I know that recording could be rare, a cult item; or near to worthless. In the absence of my partner, it would be unprofessional to commit myself."

"Ah." He slid the sleeve back into the box. For another eight seconds – I silently counted them off to myself – he gazed blindly around the shop, before his eyes returned inevitably to the curtain behind me.

"Esoteric, you said...?" He was unsure of the ground, but gaining confidence with every step.

I held up a hand. "Let us not misunderstand each other, Mr. Francis. This is not Soho When I say *esoteric*, it is not to imply that what is kept behind this drape has anything to do with simple carnal appetite —"

He looked shocked; certainly not dismayed. "Of course not!"

he protested. I swear his outrage was genuine. I returned to my initial estimation of the man. A client indeed.

"Then, if we understand one another—" I swept aside the curtain, gesturing for him to enter with my free hand. His tongue flickered across his lips, snake-quick. Eyes luminous, he stepped past me and into the darkness beyond.

*

See Johnny. Johnny is playing on the swings. See how high he can go. Swing, Johnny, swing.

See Jenny. Is Jenny on the swings, too? No, Jenny is playing by the railings. She has a big stick. It rattles as Jenny runs it along the railings. *Clack, clack, clack.*

Johnny is ever so high now. Swing higher, Johnny. *Higher.*

Jenny is watching Johnny as he goes higher and higher. She rattles her stick in time with Johnny's swings. *Click-clack. Click-clack.*

Jenny watches as one of the chains on Johnny's swing breaks. *Clack.* She watches as Johnny flies through the air and lands at her feet. *Click.* She looks down at Johnny's open eyes. Is Johnny looking back at her? No: because Johnny is unable to blink any more.

See Jenny as she uses her big stick to try and make Johnny blink. *Squish.*

*

For a while, I enjoyed the sounds of Mr. Francis in the near total darkness. He was muttering to himself; I was certain that shortly he would start to whimper. To save him the embarrassment, I turned up the illumination.

Only the exhibits – if that is the correct term for them – were lit. They threw a soft, flattering glow into the centre of the small room. The heavy black velvet that draped the walls all around absorbed any stray light; giving the impression the room had no walls at all. Mr. Francis, caught like an insipid moth in a circlet of light, was an island stranded in an infinity of blackness. He was gazing about with awe: a child allowed free reign of the sweet shop.

"This—" he began, and had to stop; to swallow some welling emotion. "This isn't what I expected."

"Come now," I admonished, walking past him, briefly blocking his view of the exhibits. He weaved his head back and forth, begrudging any moment he wasn't admiring my little display. "You must have known what you were after. No one can get through the shop door unless they are already more than halfway to buying. Indeed—" I paused to flick a speck of dust from a Perspex cabinet and leaned carefully against it, "—they will not even find the shop."

"But you're an antique shop…!" he murmured distantly.

I refrained from pointing out that I was nothing of the kind. Such pedantry was unwarranted in the face of his almost worshipful awe. "Quite so," I said. "But is that not simply a common euphemism for second hand shop? Clearly, you will agree, all of these are second hand." I jerked back from the cabinet against which I had been leaning, suddenly aware of its contents. In light of my last comment, I did not wish to appear flippant.

"But what's it all for?" he persisted. Some of the fascination had fled from his voice, and he was in danger of growing tiresome again.

"What is anything for? Why do tailors exist? Wherefore shoe-makers?" I resisted the urge to strut. For an instant, I was seized with the fancy that I should have dressed in an old-fashioned tailcoat, with cravat and high-collared shirt. "Mr. Francis, we are – so to speak – a bespoke company. All of this—" I waved at the displays "—although remarkable enough, is merely a trade display, if you will. The shop-front inside the shop."

"You sell this kind of thing?"

"Don't pretend you're shocked, Mr. Francis. All sale goods are there to fill a need, be it food or fashion. And you, if I may say so, are in the market – or else, as I remarked earlier, you could not be here. A thirsty man will always strive for the cool stream."

"But they can't be real…"

I was sorely tempted to ask if he had been a goat in a previous existence, so taken was he with butting all the while. "As genuine as it is possible to be, Mr. Francis. I am aware that some third-rate artists descend to stealing from the mortuaries of teaching establishments." I hoped my tone conveyed quite how contemptuous I found *that*. "Not for us such… sordid trafficking."

He went to speak again, but I silenced him with a gesture.

"We need not speak of it just now. Please: take your time. Browse. Enjoy the quality of the merchandise. When you are ready, I shall be tending to the shop beyond."

I backed out past the curtain, watching him gaze – still in wonder – at the cases and their varied contents. I never cease to remark on the almost invisible line between revulsion and fascination. Many souls will slow and gape at the sight of cars piled one against another on the highway, but how many will stay to count the pieces of scattered flesh?

*

Wayne checked for a moment. All was clear, far as he could tell. He swept both hands back across his hair, smoothing down his ponytail. The familiar gesture calmed him, and he waved sharply for JT. The huge black guy appeared out of the night instantly; silently.

"What you reckon, man?" JT muttered. "We goin' for it?"

Wayne looked at him with his best sneer. JT was twice his size, and it wasn't smart to push him. "What d'you fuckin' think? Course we're fuckin' going for it! Old bastard's got a shit-load of cash in that office."

"And two half-starved Rottweilers. You might not want your bollocks, man, but I'm fuckin' hangin' on to mine!"

"Give the birds a rest if you had your knob bitten off," said Wayne.

JT laughed out loud. "Any dog tries swallowin' my cock'd fuckin' choke to death!"

"Quiet, you stupid bastard!" Wayne hissed.

"Who you callin' bastard?" The punch on Wayne's arm was too hard to be friendly.

"Come on," he muttered. He'd rather face old man Finley's dogs than JT's unpredictable temper. He swept his hands over his ponytail again.

He got to his feet and ran at a crouch across the oily patch of waste ground. It was no wider than fifteen feet, and unlit, but he still felt exposed.

He dropped to a halt at the chain-link fence. Looped along the top were yards of razor wire, not that it was going to stop him. As JT caught up, Wayne was already climbing. The thick blanket he'd nicked from his mother's clothes box weighed him down.

He slung the blanket over the wire, folding it three or four times. It'd be well fucked by the time JT and he had scrambled over it – God help him if his mother found out – but the thought of all that money Finley had stashed away told him it was worth it.

He grabbed the blanket, pulled himself up and rolled over the top. Even through the thick wool he felt the wire's sharp edges; though nothing had cut through yet.

He dropped to the ground and felt for his Stanley knife, sliding the blade out. Come on you fuckers. Let's see what you do when someone's ready for ya!

JT yelled and hit the ground heavily, clutching his left hand. "Motherfucker's cut my fuckin' hand!" he yelled. "Bastard shittin' motherfuckin'—!"

"Shut the fuck up!" Wayne hissed. Half the town could have heard them. He looked frantically around, expecting a hundred pounds of ravenous dog to pounce at any moment. "Are they fuckin' deaf…?" he said to himself.

"I cut my fuckin' *hand*, man!" JT was snarling.

Good, thought Wayne. Maybe the smell of blood will keep them dogs off me. "I never knew you was such a pussy," he said.

JT raised a fist: the one that wasn't bleeding. "I'll pussy you, fuckin' wanker—"

Something growled, close by. There weren't many things this side of the fence likely to growl.

"Dogs!" Wayne yelled.

Something big and black and savage sprang out of the darkness. Wayne lunged with his knife. Teeth chewed down on his wrist, and he dropped the blade, screaming.

It was hard to see in the night: but he felt the muscles and the teeth. Tossed like a doll, fingers slipping off anything he tried to get a hold on, Wayne knew he was losing the fight. Finley's dogs weren't natural! Not even starving Rottweilers were like this.

He tried to roll away, but the animal kept snapping at him. His jacket was flapping around him in long, torn strips. Except he could see his jacket – what was left of it – a few feet away, where the dog had torn it off. He shrieked, and kicked out. The Rottweiler danced away, disappearing into the night.

Wayne propped himself up onto his elbows and knees. His whole body was numb – and he was glad. He didn't like the way bits of him were falling off, or dripping, to the ground.

Dimly, close by, he could hear JT screaming. Sprawling on his back, a dog bigger than a dinosaur tearing at him.

Wayne began to laugh: a spasmodic giggle that sounded more like hiccoughs. Didn't look like the dog was choking.

Then something huge and sharp and wet was closing around his scalp and he couldn't think beyond the screaming any more.

*

Mr. Francis walked out a happy man, I am happy to report. Luckily, I had refrained from any wager with myself: an indulgence of my youth. This time I would have lost.

Mr. Francis paused just once before he left: to admire himself in a flyblown mirror close to the window, where the best light is. He smoothed hands across the top of his head, caressed the sleek ponytail. Rather nauseatingly, he simpered at his reflection. I could swear, as he stepped out through the door, he was several inches taller.

And that is something even we find hard to do.

SONS OF THE DRAGON

The moment they heard Wee Dougie yelling, everyone grabbed flashlights and ran outside. Sounded like he'd found some vampires after all, Yamyam thought; nothing else could've made him howl like that. Seconds later all of them were pissing themselves laughing, except for Dougie. The archetypal Gorbals hard-man: big, broad, with a mouth to match; nobody expected to see him standing frozen, surrounded by dozens of worms. But there he was: caught in the torch-beams like a rabbit about to get flattened by a car; face twitching, eyes popping.

He wasn't totally rigid: swatting at the slimy little bastards with the spade he'd taken to dig himself a shit-pit; at the same time his feet doing an odd, spasmodic shuffle. Seemed to Yamyam the worms were determined to crawl as far up his jeans as they could: like they knew he was freaked and were enjoying it.

"Hey, Dougie, That some new kind of Highland dance?" Teabag called. Wee Dougie was too distracted for his usual short, violent comeback.

"I'll never eat chow mein again," Dazzler commented.

Eventually the novelty wore off; everyone trailed back to their hut and cold coffee, leaving Dougie to his worms. They'd never heard of worm-phobia; least of all some headbanger like Wee Dougie actually having it. Naturally, no one considered brushing the things off him. And no one wondered just what so many worms were doing there in the first place.

*

They were in Romania to help build a motorway. The country's road system wasn't bad – all things considered – but it didn't have a decent motorway. When Romania rid itself of Ceausescu and wife, and joined the EU, Brussels had handed over millions of euros to build an up to date road system, with the help of volunteers from across Europe.

The first time they'd laid eyes on each other was when they stepped off the plane at Bucharest: a bunch of lads from all over the UK. But they'd gelled; a sort of latter day *Auf Wiedersehen, Pet*: them against the rest of the foreigners. One of them commented there'd been enough East Europeans coming over for jobs back home a few years ago, seemed only fair they repaid the compliment. Once they found out where they were heading, there had to be the usual jokes about vampires and werewolves. The locals smiled and laughed as though they hadn't heard it all a million times already, and politely waved off the three trucks on its way towards Transylvania.

They were dumped halfway up a mountain, two hours south of the city of Brasov, right in the middle of a dark woodland that would have looked right at home in a kid's fairy tale. Yamyam thought it was the kind of place Red Riding Hood's grandmother would get herself gang-banged by wolves. And they were told to clear it.

Simple.

No one seemed to know for sure if the motorway was actually coming through the woods; Yamyam said it might have been easier and cheaper to just go round. But the pay was good, it got them away from their families for a while, and the Romanian birds were gorgeous. So no one asked too many questions: just drove what and where they were told, picked up their wage packets at the end of the week, and drove up to Brasov every Saturday night to piss it away.

*

Wee Dougie didn't come back after making a twat of himself over the worms: just left his spade behind and disappeared. No one took much notice. He had a habit of buggering off mid-week and coming back next morning reeking of the local firewater. They filed out into the glorious Transylvanian weather; Yamyam strolling towards his backhoe with Teabag, both of them glancing round the trees for any sign of a rat-arsed Dougie.

"He really must've gone on one last night," muttered Teabag, sipping from his industrial-strength mug of tea. Every week a parcel of teabags came from his old lady, just to make sure he never ran out.

"They'll give 'im the boot," Yamyam said. "Even this dozy lot'll only take so much."

"Aye." Teabag took a noisy slurp. "Fuckin' twat."

Yamyam climbed up into his cab and powered up. Teabag clambered into his own rig – a red and yellow bulldozer – and turned the engine over. With a wave, they started on another day in paradise.

Today they were working in a section of the woods the tree-fellers had already sawn their way through. All that remained were stumps jutting out of the hard dry ground like broken teeth. It was Yamyam's job to rip the stumps up. He enjoyed it: there was something satisfying about the work.

He reversed the digger up to a stump, lowered the rear bucket and dug it into ground and tree. With a wrench the stump ripped free, clumps of soil raining off snapped roots. A second later, a mass of worms boiled out of the hole left behind. It was amazing. Yamyam had never seen so many worms in one place before. He had to get down and take a look.

They were large buggers: almost six inches long and quite dark, getting towards blood red in a few cases. Watching them squirm around the hard earth, he was glad Dougie hadn't come back: he didn't want to see the big Scot going ape-shit again. After a few moments, the worms started to wriggle back into the hole. By the time Teabag drove his dozer up, most of them had squirmed out of sight.

"Oi, since when did they pay you to stare at fuckin' holes?" he yelled over his rattling engine.

"Some more of Dougie's mates." Yamyam pointed at the hole. "Big 'ens."

Teabag strolled over and peered down. "Ain't many of the bastards…"

"Pissed off into the ground. There was—" he had a think "— dunno – couple hundred of 'em."

"Straight?" Teabag had another look. "Weird shit. Well, this ain't getting the baby washed, mate."

Back on his digger, Yamyam drove up to the next stump. It came out sweet as a nut – along with another nest of dark red worms. Teabag gaped, all slack-jawed. Yamyam guessed he hadn't believed up to then. Teabag stared as the slimy gets wriggled back out of sight.

"All them worms and no fishin'," he said.

The next stump revealed more of the bastards. And the next.

"Maybe the trees are diseased. The roots rotting, like." Teabag inspected the nearest stump, nudging it with a boot cap. Yamyam shrugged.

They finished uprooting all of the stumps well before midday.

Almost half of them had worms underneath. Yamyam knew bugger all about gardening and the like, but it seemed to him there were far too many to be normal. What if half the trees in this woodland were infested with worms, how many million would that be? What the hell did they live on?

*

In the afternoon Yamyam went for a walk while the others cracked open a few beers and enjoyed the sunshine. Teabag had bulldozed the area they'd been clearing flat. There were no signs of the holes where the stumps had been dragged up: just scalped dirt and track marks. Yamyam headed into the woodland a few yards, glad to get out of the heat, if he was honest. It was well past thirty degrees.

He didn't know what he was looking for, or what he'd find. Just ambled about pointlessly, smoking a fag, kicking the occasion tree trunk. None of them sounded different or hollow, diseased or rotten. But since he was only guessing what a diseased tree sounded like, it was a pretty good waste of an afternoon. The place was peaceful, though. Dead quiet. Just the leaves crackling in a tiny breeze. He stamped his fag end out carefully and strolled back to the hut, considering a quick sunbathe before starting work again.

When the heat had died a little, they got back to it, scraping a bald path through the woods. Yamyam didn't unearth any more worms; Teabag left the site scoured clean. The felled trees lay alongside the bare earth, pointing towards the chunk of forest that was going to join them tomorrow.

When darkness fell, they jacked it in and filed back to the cabin for dinner. The food was pretty good: paid for by the EU, prepared by local chefs, and brought in every morning with the day's orders. All they had to do was microwave it. There was a lot of salad; Romanians seemed to be big on green stuff. Everyone except Yamyam hated it. Afterwards they passed round the fags, opened more wine and beer and relaxed. There was Teabag, drinking a brew you could stand a spoon in. Dazzler from Middlesbrough, normally the quiet one; although during one Saturday night punch-up they found out the fancy rings on most of his fingers weren't just for show. Dermot Murphy from Cobh, who – for some reason – only answered to the name McCain. Tez from – of all places – Weston-Super-Mare: a man determined to crack the world speed record on caterpillar tracks. Jonno from London: always trying to come on like a gangster, and about as convincing as that fat bloke on *EastEnders*. And Ravi from Wolverhampton, or Yamyam as he'd been almost instantly christened. He'd been called worse.

"You lot seen any more worms?" he asked halfway through his third beer when the conversation got quiet.

"You and them fuckin' worms!" Teabag muttered.

"No – serious. I dug up loads today. I think it's interestin'…"

"Don't you let Wee Dougie hear you sayin' that," Tez laughed.

"He ain't comin' back," Jonno muttered. "Not after we all seen him pissing his kilt!"

"You reckon?" Teabag got up to pour himself another treacly brew.

"Stands to reason. He wasn't gonna to stick round here once he'd lost face—"

"He's a Scot – not a fuckin' samurai," Dazzler chipped in.

Jonno flipped a bottle cap at him. "Same fuckin' difference…!"

"A Scot wouldn't piss off two days before he gets paid," McCain said.

"He's got a point," Yamyam admitted. Dougie really had been a tight-arsed bastard.

Teabag sat back down again. "He's gettin' his caber polished in some Brasov knockin' shop. Any money. He'll be back when he's skint."

"And sober…" McCain added.

"Away," Dazzler said as he got to his feet. "Delightful as this conversation is, I've got a couple of pounds of lettuce to get rid of." He walked towards the door, grabbing the spade Dougie had left behind. The only downside to being stuck out here was the Portaloos filled up quickly, and it didn't look like they were going to get replaced any time soon. So the crew had fallen back on older practises.

"Dig it downwind this time, you dirty Geordie bastard!" Tez yelled.

Dazzler turned round, spade half-raised. "For the last time—"

"—*Don't call me a fuckin' Geordie!*" they finished in chorus.

He never came back either.

*

The next day they searched right up until one of the foremen – a Frog who seemed to hate Brits just on principle – yelled them back to work again. Dazzler had vanished just like Wee Dougie, except Yamyam had never thought Dazzler the vanishing type. Dependable, like.

"He had a couple of kids back home," Teabag told him later as they took a fag break. Yamyam hadn't known that. "Pretty bird, too…"

"Think he buggered off back to her?"

"Dazzler? Nah!"

Just before siesta, Teabag found the ring. They recognised it as one of Dazzler's. It was half-buried among some scuffed-up leaf litter.

"Bandits," Tez suggested back at the hut.

"You what?" Yamyam wasn't sure he'd heard right.

"Bandits," he repeated. Teabag laughed, and McCain just sort of snorted.

"This ain't fuckin' Mexico," Jonno muttered.

"Yeah, but they still got 'em, ain't they? Ex-soldiers – guerrillas, like – left over after the war."

"They didn't have a war, yer dozy fecker," said McCain. "Yer thinkin' of Yugoslavia."

"I bet Yamyam thinks it's them worms," Teabag grinned.

"Bollocks."

Back on the job, Yamyam fairly tore into it: ripping up as much earth as tree stumps. He left the ground gouged: huge pits where the trees had once been. Only three times did he come across a nest of worms; in each case, the squirmy buggers pissed off into the ground so fast they must have known he was after them.

Once he'd ripped up every stump he could see, he turned off the engine and just slumped in his cab. Teabag drove up and looked the mess over.

"Fuck me, Yamyam," he yelled. "Looks like world war three round 'ere. You feelin' all right, mate?"

"Me? Right as fuckin' ninepence, son. Couldn't be fuckin' better."

"That's okay, then; cause anyone other than me might think you was takin' somethin' personal." He steered his dozer past and started levelling the earth. Yamyam keyed his ignition and drove the digger back.

*

They were all twitchy that night. Soon as they'd finished ramming down dinner, the booze came out with a vengeance. Yamyam wished it was payday so they could all fuck off into town and get rat-arsed. When the last beers had been dragged out of the fridge, McCain surprised them all by flashing a litre bottle of vodka.

The bottle did the rounds; the party grew louder. In the end it was Jonno who kicked off. He took a huge slug of the cheap vodka, swallowed and kept staring at the bottle. Teabag reached towards it.

"You hangin' onto that fucker all night?" he muttered.

Jonno let the booze go without a word, like he didn't know it wasn't there any longer. He just stared into the bottle-shaped gap in front of him, his eyes all glassy and unfocused.

"I think I'm gonna have a piss," he said after a while.

"Don't let me feckin' stop yer," McCain said, taking his own turn with the vodka. "Fuck me, ye've drunk the lot!"

"Try squeezin'," Tez suggested.

"I am definitely goin' to have a piss." Jonno lurched to his feet and stood for a moment on dodgy ankles, glaring around the hut.

"Outside, I hope," Tez said.

"Yeah! Fuck off outside before you piss yerself!" Teabag shouted.

Jonno's eyes quivered in their sockets, then grew hard and flinty. He turned and headed for the door, grabbing a shovel as he went. The door slammed behind him.

"Christ," Tez muttered. "How big's his fuckin' bladder?"

Yamyam peered at the floor, not really listening.

"Do you think we ought to follow him?" Tez was saying.

McCain laughed. "Wanna hold his prick, do yer?"

"He's a big boy," Teabag groaned as he levered himself to his feet and headed towards the kettle. "And you can take that any fuckin' way you want!"

Yamyam sat in silence, letting the vodka do its work. The empty bottle had made its way back to him and he held it up carelessly, watching a small trickle of booze inside wriggle up and down the glass. He thought about the way the worms always disappeared when you dug them up; because they'd been all over Wee Dougie that night. Not squirming back into the ground at all.

He was on his feet and through the door – flashlight in hand –

out into the warm night and yelling for Jonno. Because he'd figured out what the stupid twat was going to do, and he knew the worms weren't going to just burrow out of sight. Not this time.

It wasn't hard to find Jonno: he was making more noise than Teabag's dozer. About fifty yards away from the hut, among the trees, he was slashing at the ground, flailing the spade like a pickaxe, chipping hard lumps of dry clay into the air.

"It's the worms!" he was wheezing. "The fuckin' *worms!*"

There weren't any worms that Yamyam saw. Jonno froze. Was he listening, or staring at the other man. It was too dim to be sure.

"Come back, eh?" Yamyam suggested lamely. "Have one of Teabag's disgusting cups of tea, like—"

Jonno's face was picked out by flickering beams of light. Everyone else was coming up behind, waving torches. Jonno's pale and sweaty features glowed in the stark light, shadows around his eyes and cheeks made his face like a skull.

"There's no worms," Yamyam tried pointing out. "Look. You ain't found *one*—!"

"Not yet!" He starting attacking the ground again, using the light from the torches to pick his targets.

"Jonno, you twat!" Teabag yelled.

"I thought Yamyam was the head case!" Tez added.

McCain pushed forward and tried to snatch the spade out of Jonno's hands. The flailing blade smashed across his face. He collapsed flat on his arse. Blood – black in the night – flooded from his forehead, coating his features.

Jonno was off then: into the darkness, shouting some bollocks or other. They tried to follow him, but the jogging torch-beams – stabbing in every direction at once – just confused their eyes. Every time Yamyam thought they'd spotted Jonno, it was just another tree.

Eventually they had to stop. They were all pretty fit, but the vodka, combined with chasing round like headless chickens in the dark, got to them. Gasping for breath, each of them leaning against a tree, they stared helplessly at each other and the surrounding black woodland. Yamyam was waiting for his heart to stop jack-hammering and for someone to come up with a half-decent idea.

Jonno made it easy for them. He suddenly started yelling: screaming so loud it sounded like he was about to rupture his throat.

He'd found his worms. Standing at the foot of a tree, Jonno was ankle-deep in them. He was gouging great lumps out of the ground and trunk, chucking around earth, wood and wriggling bodies like he didn't give a shit. Teabag, McCain and Tez pinned him with the light from their torches. The worms' slimy bodies flashed and sparkled in the beams. And this time they weren't burrowing their way back into the ground: just like with Dougie, some were slowly oozing their way up Jonno's legs. The rest were climbing the tree.

"Fuckin' gross..." Tez mumbled.

Teabag took a couple of steps forward, half-blocking Yamyam's view. "Shouldn't we... you know... get him out...?"

"He can sink in the feckers," McCain said. His voice sounded far away and, to Yamyam's ears, kind of scary. "Teach 'im to smack me in the face!"

"Don't be a cunt, Paddy," Teabag said. He took a couple more steps and had more luck than McCain, snatching the spade out of Jonno's hands before he got brained. "Give us that, you fuckin' moron!" he yelled in Jonno's ear, and tossed the spade away.

"Just wait till I get you back to the hut, yer little gobshite," Yamyam heard McCain snarling from behind.

Teabag grabbed Jonno by an arm and dragged him forward, out of the worm-nest. As Jonno took a couple of steps, the worms oozing up his jeans dropped away. Yamyam watched as they wriggled painfully towards the tree and started to climb.

"Nasty little fuckers!" Jonno mashed his boot down on a knot of worms that were writhing on the ground. A moment later something fell across his face, and he went down heavily.

"What in feckin'—?" McCain aimed his torch at Jonno. He was on the ground, jerking and writhing, as something long and fat and slimy glided across his head.

"It's a fuckin' worm!" Tez muttered. They all saw it; no one believed it. The granddaddy of all worms: as thick as McCain's thighs, well over six foot in length, blotched red and white. It was more like a snake – an anaconda – than a worm.

Yamyam caught movement in the corner of his eye. In the light reflected from the flashlights, he saw another worm, even bigger than the first. It hit the ground and reared up. A sharp, slimy end turned, aiming straight at the group. Two more flopped to the ground right next to it, sounding like sacks of mud as they slapped onto the earth.

"Jesus, Mary and Joseph!" McCain breathed.

"Help me get Jonno up!" Teabag was saying. Yamyam glanced down. Jonno was still thrashing on the ground, the revolting thing smothering him. Teabag tried to lift it off, but his hands didn't seem to be able to get a hold. "Tez! Gimme a hand!"

Tez stooped down next to him, leaving his torch on the ground. As both of them failed to grab the huge worm, Yamyam heard the wet mud sound as more of the things slapped down nearby.

He swung his torch-beam in a circle: they were surrounded. It was like the tree and five men were the axle, and something like ten or twelve of those giant worms the spokes of a huge wheel. Yamyam heard Jonno's muffled yells turning to wet choking; Tez and Teabag swearing helplessly at each other, getting more desperate each second. McCain was almost silent, except for an odd rattle in his breathing that sounded like snoring.

"Think they can outrun us?" Yamyam whispered. He wasn't sure why.

"You ain't runnin'!" Teabag said, breathless and angry. "We can't run with Jonno!"

"Bollocks to Jonno!" Yamyam swept the beam of his torch about, looking for a gap. The worms didn't move, but they were watching. Somehow. Even without eyes, he could feel them watching.

He bolted, leaping over a worm. It reared up, but Yamyam was already away. Heart and breathing almost drowning out McCain and Teabag's yells at his back. It made it easier not to listen.

After about fifty yards, Yamyam dared to stop. He turned round, aiming his torch back down the way he'd come. He could see Tez, Teabag, McCain and Jonno – picked out by their flashlights – still surrounded by the worms. Nothing seemed to have moved.

"Come on!" he yelled. "Run! They ain't that fast!"

Maybe his shout startled the huge worms, or they felt the vibration. All of them were suddenly rearing up. Tez and Teabag looked up from Jonno, who didn't seem to be moving; McCain waved his torch like a club.

The worms' smooth, pointed ends peeled back, exposing huge, gaping mouths. They struck like snakes. One grabbed McCain by his head and yanked him into the air. The Irishman was engulfed past his shoulders in a second, his feet thrashing and kicking. The worm reared up further, and McCain slipped out of sight. The creature dropped heavily back to the ground. The bulge that had been McCain wasn't moving, Yamyam told himself: it was the flickering torchlight. Playing tricks on his eyes.

Three worms went for Tez and Teabag. One caught Tez by a leg, swallowing him slowly. A second grabbed Teabag by an arm and snatched him up from Jonno's body. The third latched onto his feet and swallowed him up to his hips. There was a brief, bloody tug of war. The thing that had fallen on Jonno stirred, widened its huge gape, and wriggled itself around him. Yamyam guessed Jonno was already dead by then. He hoped so.

He turned and ran again, in what he hoped was the hut's direction. But as long as it was away, he didn't much care. The torch beam flailed wildly around in the darkness, less than useless. He fell over exposed roots and mounds of earth, crashed into trees. Eventually he smashed his head against a trunk and hit the ground.

Shaking his pounding head he clawed his way back onto his feet, using the tree trunk as a crutch. His heart was throbbing almost as hard as his head. The torch was several feet away, its beam pointlessly lighting up a streak of ground. Limping over he picked it up, aiming it towards the tree he'd run into.

There were worms wriggling up the trunk. Hundreds of them. In his torch's light he picked out a few of the slimy bastards weaving up his jeans.

Overhead there was a muffled sound: two wet, rapid-fire pops. He raised his torch: towards the branches hidden in the darkness, and the pointed, glistening thing that hung down, blindly aiming for him. Yamyam had just enough time to see the twin rows of long spines splaying out on either of the tubular body, and the glistening membranes stretched over them, before the worm swooped, gaping wide.

ONLY THE LONELY

She glanced away from the TV screen just as he walked into the bar. Trying not to make it too obvious, she gave him the once over. Was he the one? It was impossible to tell just from looking; it wasn't as if he was going to be wearing a red rose or carrying a copy of yesterday's *Times*. As he strolled towards the barman she feigned interest in the television again.

The guy asked for a beer, gazing around the shabby hotel bar while he was being served, as though he was enjoying its faded, early twentieth century splendour. She felt his eyes linger on her, then pass by. She sipped at her glass of coke, watching him carefully over the rim. Once he'd paid for his drink, he picked it up and turned his back on the bar, leaning an elbow on its scarred surface. This time, he made it obvious he'd seen her: raising his glass in her direction. She looked down at the stains on her table top, replacing the coke on its soggy coaster. A moment later, she heard his voice, immediately above her.

"This seat taken?"

She raised her head, not meeting his eyes. She shook her head hesitantly. "No – no…"

"Mind if I sit?"

He dropped onto the chair before she had a chance to reply, placing his pint on the table.

"No, I – that's fine…" she murmured.

"Always this quiet?" he asked. For a moment she wondered if he was referring to her, then guessed he meant the bar.

"I don't know. It's the first time I've been here." She took another gulp of her drink, keeping her eyes lowered.

"I like quiet pubs, me. None of that fuckin' row they call music. Though I expect you like it?"

She made a thin smile. "No, no… I'm not much of a music fan." She finally raised her eyes and looked at him properly. He was balding, probably a stone or so overweight, his round jowls showing no sign of stubble, despite the late hour. The top button of his crumpled shirt was undone, the knot of his deep red tie halfway down his chest. He was probably a salesman, she decided. This was the sort of cheap, gone to seed hotel where salesmen would stay. Ten years ago he might have been good-looking; now he was just unmemorable. His brown eyes looked kind, though.

"Waiting for your boyfriend, are you?" He sipped at his drink.

"No – not exactly."

He smiled. It was a nice smile: made him much more presentable. "Okay, I'm a man of the world, like. Your girlfriend, then?"

She laughed at that, and she saw his smile broaden; relax. "Not that, either. No I'm—" She swallowed a mouthful of coke, enjoying the icy coolness as it spread through her body. "Truth is, I'm— Yeah okay: I am waiting for someone."

"Then it is a friend, like."

"No... not at all." She took another twitchy drink, put the glass down and breathed in deeply. Rather than look at him, she stared at the ice slowly turning in the coke. "I'm waiting for a man. A man I haven't met."

"Ah." He picked up his own glass. "Computer dating, like. Seen the ads on telly."

"Not exactly. I—" Even as she began to explain, she knew how stupid it would sound; how stupid it made *her* sound. "Someone I met in an on-line forum..." Her voice tailed off.

"Bloody hell!" He almost banged his glass down on the table. Beer splashed over the rim. "What? One of them places where everyone's pretending to be somebody else?" He paused for breath. "Have you got any idea how—?"

"Yes, I've heard all the lectures." She still wouldn't look at him, concentrating on the fingers she was intertwining in her lap.

"He could be anyone! Any kind of nutter, like a paedophile!"

She laughed at that. "I don't look that young do I? Thanks... I think." She drew her eyes up from her writhing fingers and stared him full in the face. He appeared to be genuinely concerned. "I *do* know what I'm doing. He's down for a conference and we agreed to meet in here." She glanced at the clock above the bar and frowned. "He's a bit late, though..."

He didn't say anything for a while, just sipped mechanically at his drink. "How do you know I'm not him?" he asked eventually.

She paused, considering the question. "For one thing, you're not American."

"Ah." He was silent for several seconds. "I'm betting he's married?"

She nodded silently.

"You have any idea what he looks like?"

"There's a picture on the forum, but—" She pursed her lips. "I realise it won't necessarily be his."

He shook his head. "You must be fuckin' mad." He said it almost sadly.

"Are you married?"

He emptied his pint and placed it carefully on the table. "Not anymore."

"Oh, I – I'm sorry."

He shrugged. "No, that's okay. It was amicable. Still see her occasionally."

"Children?"

"Never blessed." He looked at his wristwatch. "Look – I'm having another pint. Do you want anything?"

She waited a few moments, as though debating with herself. "Just a coke, thanks."

"Nothing stronger?"

She shook her head. "Thanks."

He shrugged again and heaved himself out of the chair. As he headed for the bar she looked around once more. The place was deserted: except for her, the salesman and the guy behind the bar. If things didn't pick up soon, she was guessing the barman would close the place up.

The salesman came back with two full glasses. She took a sip of the fresh one; was it her imagination, or did it taste odd? Sharp. Pungent, almost.

"So what time you meeting him, then, this bloke?"

She made a point of looking at the clock. "Half an hour ago." She sat back and sighed. "He's not coming, is he?"

"Best thing, if you ask me. You're better off out of it."

"Oh? Know him well, do you?" she snapped back.

He flinched, smooth face flushing. "You know what I mean," he mumbled.

"No. No, I'm sorry. I'm just, you know…" She ran her finger down the condensation on her glass. "Disappointed… angry at myself… at him." She gave a loud sigh. "Oh what a fucking mess!"

He stared at her for a while; she wondered what he was thinking. "No harm done, though, is there?" he said finally. "Nothing hurt but your pride, like?"

"A life lesson?"

"You could say that."

She leaned forward, holding out her right hand. "I'm Lily, by the way."

He stared at her hand as though he didn't know what to do with it. Then he shook it. "Tom."

"Good to meet you, Tom."

*

She staggered into him and giggled. Tom had drunk quite a lot but he didn't seem to be affected by it. Lily wondered if he could take his drink, or just be very good at disguising it.

"Here we are," he said, pointing at a pale door. Lily made a great show of looking around her: the other doors, the ill-lit, meandering corridor.

"Where?" she asked.

"My room."

"Ah… yes. Sorry—" She giggled again. "I think I'm drunk. Am I drunk, Tom? Did you slip something in my coke—?"

"Come on." Tom slipped the key-card into its slot with one hand, propping Lily upright with the other. "I think we both need a lie down." He pushed the door open and they half-fell into the room.

Somehow they made it to the bed without banging into anything, although the poky room didn't have much to hit. Just the bed and a faded cupboard and mirror. Tom flopped onto his back, eyes fixed on the ceiling.

Lily watched him a moment, weaving gently on her feet. "Just nipping to the little girls' room," she said, slurring ever so slightly. "You get yourself—" She waved meaninglessly at the bed. "Ready. Prepared. Whatever—" She giggled again and made for the bathroom.

She snapped on the wall switch and stared at herself in the mirror. The strip light made her look pale and sick; the shadows around her eyes all wrong. She smiled at the pallid image; it leered back.

First she splashed water onto her face and rinsed her mouth. Then she stripped off t-shirt and jeans, briefs and bra. She paused for another quick examination, for the first time seeing what he saw. Naked, she looked quite young and fresh: her figure almost boyish, her breasts small. So that's what Tom liked.

She swung the door open, slamming it hard against the bath.

Groping for the light switches she snapped them off and weaved towards the bed. Tom hadn't wasted any time – he was stripped, his overweight body pale in the gloom. Lily smiled, added a giggle and crawled alongside him.

"Hello, big boy," she sighed, running a hand over his body. It was almost hairless, quite smooth. She felt his own hands reach out for her; like his body they were smooth and soft.

"God, you're lovely," he said. Lily thought he even meant it. She slid her hand down his chest, his stomach. All the beer he'd drunk wasn't affecting his erection much. He was rock hard; raring to go. She didn't want to disappoint him.

"Good enough to eat," she giggled. She ran a fingernail along the length of his shaft.

"Don't let me stop you," he groaned.

Lily let him kiss her; his mouth was sweet, contrasting with his hot, yeasty breath. She ran her hands along his cock a couple more times. Sliding both hands up his body, Lily folded her fingers around his, pinning his hands against the pillow. Slowly, she mounted him, taking him deep inside. Tom's eyes closed. He sighed gently.

Lily fucked him greedily, not caring if he noticed the drunk act had vanished. It was too late now. She slid his hands up her body, holding them against her small breasts. His fingers clutched, reaching for her nipples.

"You like that?" she breathed. He muttered something that could have been a yes. "It gets better."

Tom gasped as Lily bore down on him hard, riding him with no mercy. His brown eyes, up to now squeezed shut, opened. He stared up at her. For a moment they were unfocussed; then they sharpened, locked with her own. In that moment she saw it: the predatory triumph, the greed, the delight.

Lily tightened her grip on his hands, shackling them against her chest. Thumbnails dug into his wrists, breaking the skin. His body jerked and spasmed into an arch – a parody of orgasm – and locked. She reared up one last time, then plunged her body down, impaling herself on his erection. She threw her head back and screamed in pleasure, mirroring the frozen, muted howl on Tom's face. Only his eyes moved: his kind brown eyes. Now glazed with terror.

Lily pressed down, squeezing her thighs tight, drawing him in deeper and deeper. He really was good enough to eat.

*

The news item was about the latest disappearance. Behind the presenter, a bad photograph of a balding, slightly overweight face stared vacantly out. She glanced away from the TV screen just as he walked into the bar. Trying not to make it too obvious she gave him the once over.

RESCHEDULED

He'd forgotten the keys!

Graeme Oaks had travelled all across town and was already dropping his case onto his desk when the thought hit him. Too late, the memory of dropping them carelessly onto the arm of his sofa at home returned. Only last night.

Hoping against all reason, he flipped open the case and rummaged through the tiny assortment of paperback novel, sandwiches wrapped in cling-film, bruised apple, a few sulky sheets of paper. It was a futile exercise: of course the keys weren't there. He would just have to go back and fetch them.

Sighing in resignation, he slid his case under the desk and marched out of the sprawling, open-plan office. Normally he wouldn't have bothered, he'd survived without them before; but he was the only one in the office the vacationing manager felt he could trust with the huge bundle of keys – at least until the summer holiday period was over. Well, so much for that theory.

As he stepped out into the harsh, metallic daylight, he felt the first knuckling pains of a returning hangover. Or was it the weather? Overhead, thick clouds were swallowing the misty sunlight. The air felt heavy, overbearing.

Thunder soon, he thought, trotting across the road to the local railway station. A crowd was already waiting on the platform, every head turned to face the city-bound line. Expectancy drew their features into stiff, unnatural planes.

There must be one due, Graeme thought, weaving around the immobile knots. No one paid him the slightest attention – not even stepping back to let him pass. The imminent arrival absorbed them entirely.

The twittering hum of the rails announced the train moments before it rounded the curve. Shuddering to a halt, its rusty brakes drove screeching silver wedges into Graeme's already throbbing brain. Like a single, many-segmented organism the crowd surged forward, cramming itself into the grimy carriages. Miraculously, everyone found a seat. Lurching like an old drunk, the obsolete three-car unit dragged itself away from the steel and concrete station, exhausts growling in suppressed anger.

Throughout the journey, Graeme glanced at his wrist-watch,

cursing as its hands raced the sluggish train. Why hadn't his union agreed to let them all on flexi-time? he thought, shying away in guilt, since he hadn't bothered going to the only meeting that had voted on it. His sense of oppression grew; he felt the air was turning into warm, heavy molasses, dragging at his neck and shoulders.

He'd never been a good riser in the mornings, and these late-night booze-ups with Dave Wallace weren't making things better. He sympathized with Dave – his marriage collapsing in such a messy way, divorce tearing him apart – but getting up late with a whisky hangover wasn't improving Graeme's absentmindedness.

He rubbed at his brow, trying to push the pain away. "Nor my damned head!" he murmured, inaudible above the train's rattle. Thank Christ he'd never succumbed to marriage.

A vivid burst of graffiti heralded the long tunnel leading to the central station. Gleaming in primary colours and fake metallic lustre which pulsed in the failing light, the incomprehensible squiggles looked to Graeme like ancient Hebrew texts, or quotes from the Koran. He couldn't look too closely. Combined with his growing headache, they reminded him too much of the migraines he'd suffered five years ago, when hours had been lost to a swirling chaos of pixelated agony.

Fume-spiked blackness swallowed the train; the wheels' clatter grew louder, filling Graeme's aching head. He tried to close the window above his seat, but it was jammed. At least we're nearly there, he thought, once more checking his watch.

Predictably, the train began to slow. He almost groaned aloud as it slid to a juddering halt, and stood motionless – vibrating into the jet blackness. He looked out of his inky window, but saw only a carriage filled with silent passengers, mirroring his own. There was even a twin to his face staring in at him: a straggly beard which took ten years off his real age, unfashionably long fair hair which was beginning to grey, heavy-lensed glasses adding to his owlish, schoolboy looks.

"Somebody should do something," he heard a voice grumble over the diesel engines. "Damn railway's been living off us long enough!"

Something flapped against the window, distracting him from the muted complaint. It was a large drop of water, now sliding gracefully down the glass. With the amount of rain they'd suffered during the summer, Graeme wasn't surprised some of it was oozing through the tunnel's brick lining. The ground above must have been saturated. But come summer, and two weeks of sunshine, there'd be an official drought.

He tried to relax in his seat. The waiting was getting to him, as it always did. Raised blood pressure would do his pounding head a world of good. That's what they all said, wasn't it: "You're too impatient, Grey. Slow down a bit; watch your blood pressure." Typical attitude in this age of the shrug: no one wanted to get things done anymore. Tomorrow would always do.

The train began to move again. Graeme bit back his impatience, rubbing the back of his neck to try to relieve the knot of anxiety growing there. Pulling into the station, the three carriages picked their way through the maze of lines that converged onto the few platforms with the ease of practice. There was a solid mass of people waiting for the train. Once it had stopped, they pressed against the sides, almost preventing the doors from opening. Graeme had to shoulder his way through the chaos.

"You're all bloody sheep!" he wanted to scream at them. But their blank, frighteningly intent expressions choked off the words. He fled up the escalator to ground level, looking back to see the milling crowds turned into pillars of flesh, grouped like alien constellations.

Graeme made it across town under a sky the colour of old slate, shot through with sooty whorls. As normal business hours approached the crowds were thinning, but the relentless press of time only tightened his worries another notch. He did that too much as well: worry. Or so his last girlfriend told him. She'd finally had enough and left at about the same time as his last migraine attack. He sometimes wondered if there'd been a connection.

The keys were exactly where he'd remembered them: perched on the sofa's arm, right next to an empty scotch bottle standing precariously upright, cheerfully defying gravity. Snatching the keys up, he dashed from a room which always smelled of the laundromat below, and headed back to the station. Tension had the atmosphere stretched to breaking point; cold needles of apprehension sliced into his midbrain, slashing through the writhing knot of his intestines. Had he been missed yet? He dreaded the manager imagining his trust had been betrayed, not doubting some of his dear colleagues would be only too eager to pass on the news.

The station was almost deserted, contrasting sharply with the press only a few minutes earlier. Graeme found himself alone on his platform; not so much as a guard or porter around. On the platform opposite a handful of passengers were gazing blindly about. Graeme thought it looked like they were searching for something other than their connection. He pulled his eyes away.

A hundred yards from the platform ends was the yawning, vacant mouth of the tunnel. The rails leading into the black expanse reminded Graeme of a mucus-streaked tongue. He rubbed at his temples, disturbed by the imagery conjured by his racing mind, wishing the storm would break.

His train rolled in. He noticed its faded sides were marked by more graffiti, executed crudely in white paint. For a moment, the grotesque curling figures seemed to writhe shapelessly.

He screwed his eyes shut in panic. Of all the stupid times for a recurrence of his migraine trouble! Though hadn't the doctor repeatedly warned Graeme that tension was the main causative agent in his case? He kept his eyes closed as he counted to ten, his breathing ragged. When he opened them again the train was stationary; the unreadable scribble motionless.

He got into an empty carriage and collapsed onto a slashed seat, resting his head against the padded back, closing his eyes again. He breathed in deeply and slowly several times, willing the tension out of his nerves, his muscles. By the time he had completed the last exhalation, a peaceful calm had soothed away much of his headache; but a vague anxiety still hung over him, like some adolescent guilt.

Graeme opened his eyes as the train pulled out of the station, heading for the gaping tunnel. The carriage interior was a disgrace: seats slashed and sprayed with terse, obscene messages. Walls, windows and ceiling were daubed in cryptic black patterns, a vandals' mindless code. The train's geriatric rattling increased in volume as it plunged into the tunnel, drops of water hitting Graeme's carriage. They wriggled down his window in broad streaks.

He was surprised to find the train so empty. Even with most workers chained to their machines or desks, Graeme imagined shoppers and other visitors would be travelling all day long. A salvo of heavy drops thudded against the window. He could easily imagine the desolate three-car unit was actually out under a lightless sky, suffering an opening shower as the storm finally broke. The water rolled languidly down the panes, looking far too viscous for runoff rainwater.

Brakes squealed, daggers through his head. The train ground to a halt. Alone in his frustration, he swore and thumped the seat with balled, impotent fists. The engines cut off, sending a spasm through the carriage. Graeme was left in an abrupt silence, punctuated only by the tink of cooling metal, and the thick impact of liquid drops.

He walked to a door and dropped the window. Leaning out, Graeme squinted towards both train ends, trying to see what was causing the delay. No one was moving about, he saw no lights, heard no other trains. The silence was almost absolute.

He noticed the inky glistening on the wall opposite, his mind refusing to accept the sight of the glutinous fluid running gently across the soot-encrusted bricks. A drop fell on his fingers where they clutched the top of the window: it was warm, and tingled. He leapt back, startled, and wiped the stuff off on a nearby seat.

From somewhere outside came a damp rubbing sound, like a moist palm dragging across a cold metal surface. In the tunnel's dark, something wet rolled itself around the train's sides. Graeme felt the carriage shudder; the ceiling creaked as something pressed on it.

Pressure thudded behind his eyes, threatening to fragment his vision. His head felt hollow, packed with broken glass. Anxiety gave way to overwhelming, directionless terror.

He found himself staring at his reflection. He looked at each feature more closely than he had ever done: every whisker, every pore glimmering with a drop of sour sweat. He challenged the face before him to change, to become unfamiliar. Fearing what might instead look in from the darkness.

The lights went out.

THE MERCY SEAT

It was dark by the time the train reached Galton Bridge station: delayed by an unspecified "incident". Outside, the Oldbury Road he remembered had been buried under a small, urban motorway, already highlighted by rows of not quite bright enough sodium lamps. He turned left purely by instinct: everything was so different. In the darkness, he was sure he'd be lost in minutes. By the time he found a side road he remembered – bulldozed and widened decades earlier, before it was fashionable – it had started to rain. Even though the road was now a racetrack for desperate kids in underpowered cars, a few of the older houses remained. They, at least, hadn't changed.

Crossing St Paul's Road he was surprised to find the Post Office still there, defying trends. He started up the hill. The pavements were lined by terraces that had existed forever, all looking drab and colourless in the wet night. There'd been a greengrocer's somewhere along here, but he didn't spot it. Most likely converted back to an ordinary house when the old man had died.

Then he was across Devonshire Road and outside the semi-detached house: standing next to a young tree growing on the pavement edge. Just looking. It wasn't so different: the front wall was gone; the scrap of garden paved into a drive. And it had been double-glazed, naturally. Had it been stuccoed, back then? He couldn't remember. He stared at the box room window, near the corner. Shame there hadn't been double-glazing back when he'd slept in that room. During winter mornings he'd often awoken to find frost riming the inside of the glass. Other than that...

The front door opened and a middle-aged guy stepped out: a Sikh. He stood on the paved drive, ignoring the rain, glaring in wary anger. "You want something, mate?"

"Sorry." He took a step forward; thought better of it. "Just taking a trip down memory lane."

"That don' take 'alf an hour, does it? You'm casin' the joint. Well – I'm callin' the cops. All right?" The curtains in the downstairs front bay twitched: three faces stared out, lit by the pale concrete streetlights. Two kids and a woman, all looking nervous. If he really had been standing there so long, loitering— They had a point.

"Sorry," he repeated and backed away. Retracing his steps to the Devonshire Road junction, he took the slip of paper from his pocket and looked at it once again. It was already damp, the few words on it pale and running. It didn't matter: he'd committed them to memory.

Bid lived just off Silverton Road now: moved there twenty years ago. If he remembered correctly, the street was second left and the next right. There was a supermarket halfway to his destination; once it had been an off-license. The Good Cheer Cellars. In memory of its old place in his life, he bought a bottle of cheap whisky.

Bid's flat turned out to be on a cul-de-sac just off Silverton Road: one of several clustered in newish maisonettes. It was on the ground floor. He pressed the bell; after half a minute, the door swung open. The face that peered out myopically looked old enough to be his mother's. He had to remind himself that the woman behind it was barely two years his senior. Testament to a lifetime's nicotine habit.

"Hello, Bid," he said. "Good to see you again." Small lies were the easiest.

She scowled back. "Yeah? Who are you anyway?"

"Jim." At first there was no reaction. "Don't say you've forgotten me?"

"Jim." Her rheumy eyes gradually lit with recognition. "Fuck me. Jim."

He raised the bottle of scotch. "You letting me in, or do we stand out in the rain all night?"

Bid squinted at the bottle. Eventually her mouth twisted into a poor approximation of a smile. She stood back and allowed him through. As he passed her, he noticed she was wearing a quilted housecoat that might once have been white. The cuffs of red jog pants peaked out underneath. She'd once been such a classy dresser.

The flat was just a reception room with a single panoramic window; kitchen, bathroom and what he guessed was a bedroom leading off it. An old television whispered to itself in a corner. There was an underlying smell of damp and cigarettes. Bid shuffled into the kitchen; he heard the rattle of glass. She reappeared with two thin tumblers, the kind you once got with cigarette coupons. He twisted off the bottle cap, splashed a generous slug into both and took one for himself. "Cheers."

She grabbed the second glass, downing half of the contents in one gulp. "What do you want?"

"That's all I get? After all this time."

Her thin lips pulled into a sour shape. "What do you want?"

He sighed and removed his wet overcoat. Shaking it off, he hung it on an empty hook out by the front door. Then he sat on one of two scuffed armchairs. Bid drooped into the second, facing the TV. She drained her glass and refilled it. "Are you from the council?"

He came straight to the point; perhaps the scotch she'd gulped would form a buffer. "There was a note from Marky." He reached into his trouser pocket. "It was among your mother's effects. Your parents had it all this time. Neither of them said a word—" He guessed he was explaining into a vacuum: Bid most likely didn't remember her mother's funeral, a month earlier.

"What?" She finished the second measure of scotch and poured a third glass. "Who?"

He held up the limp scrap of paper. Bid squinted at it a moment, before waving an impatient, mottled hand. "I can't read that!"

"Did you know?"

She laughed and emptied her glass. "How'd you get here?"

"Train. Walked. Chance to see how the place has changed."

"Galton Bridge? Thought all the trains were cancelled. Jumper, or something." She went to pick up the bottle. He reached it first.

"Marky, Bid. Did you know where he went?" After all the years, the questions were too eager: falling over each other. "Any idea where he is? How he is?"

"Who?" She stared at him, finally remembering to pull a pair of spectacles out of her coat. She put them on. "Who are you anyway?

He sighed again, putting down the whisky and sitting back against the armchair. "Jim. You remember? Jim—"

"Jim." She laughed, picking up the bottle. "Fuck me. Jim."

He let her take the rapidly draining bottle as she padded to the bedroom. "Night, night," she called behind the closing door.

"Goodnight, Gracie." He left the damp note on the table to dry off and made for the third door. By elimination it had to be the bathroom. There was a coarse towel draped across the water-stained washbasin. Taking it through to the reception room he scrubbed at his wet hair. Finally, he settled himself back in the armchair. Might as well get some rest here; he didn't think Bid would mind, or even notice. He slipped into sleep and back out again without any obvious transition, except night had turned into a leaden morning, rolling through the window. He didn't dream.

He carefully opened the bedroom door. Bid was an untidy sprawl across her bed, the empty whisky bottle still clutched in a mottled hand. A pub ashtray, clogged with crushed cigarettes, spilled half its contents across a threadbare carpet. Her housecoat had ridden halfway to her waist; a dark patch glinted in the crotch of her jog pants. As he pulled thin sheets over her, she muttered something. He bent closer, wincing at the smell of stale alcohol.

"Marky, he— When we—"

"Have you seen him, Bid?"

"Every day..." Her sclerotic eyes glowed with unshed tears.

"Where, Bid?" He had to hold himself back from yelling, from shaking her emaciated body. And to think that once they'd —

She blinked; her eyes grew vague again. "You from the council...?"

He straightened, breathing in unpolluted air. It was no use. He picked up the full ashtray and placed it on a scarred cupboard-top beside the bed. Pausing one last time at the bedroom door, he mouthed his goodbyes. Decades too late.

Outside it was bitter. He buttoned his still damp overcoat, hunched against the black, threatening sky, and left the flat; walking past a community centre that had once been a church. At the bottom of Devonshire Road was a smart housing estate where their first school had been: Marky, Bid and him. He found a licenced shop that was happy to sell him another bottle – a litre of half-decent single malt, this time – and trudged up winding suburban roads that hadn't changed at all. Even so, they were unrecognisable. At some point it began to snow, further masking the rows of uncertain memory. The streets climbed imperceptibly, drawing him with a relentless inevitability to the house. Their house: Bid's and Marky's.

Except it was no longer there. The original building was gone, razed; and a fresh couple of homes built over it. The builders hadn't even saved time and money by simply renovating what was already on site. Someone had wanted a fresh start.

He trawled his past, trying to recall images of the house, wondering if his memory could still be trusted. It had been very much like his own parents', except for the extension: a new double bedroom over a rebuilt garage. All he could summon were blurred images that might have been anywhere; anyone's. Only the new bedroom was clear: his memories of that were cruel and sharp as broken crystal. The bedroom where Bid and he—

The snow grew thicker; it was like looking into a vast snowglobe. He dragged himself away, heading towards West Smethwick Park.

He remembered the railings all being removed; now the enclosing hedges had been uprooted, too. Bare trees clustered in contrived groves, or dotted the pathways; failing to echo the French avenues they were meant to copy. He had the place to himself: no one walking their dogs, no kids kicking balls across the grass. Sweeping the first bench he passed clear of snow, he sat and opened the single malt. He wanted to propose a toast, but nothing offered itself. Instead, he took a long drink.

Someone joined him on the bench. He glanced up, wondering who else would be stupid enough to be out in this weather. It was an old man: long uncombed hair a dirty grey, nose coarse and thickened. What little of his face showed past an unkempt beard was raw and mottled. Alight with fever. Unhealthy. Jim slipped his bottle into its paper bag, hoping the other hadn't seen it; knowing it was unlikely.

"Found the note, then?"

If the face was unfamiliar, the voice wasn't. "Marky?" He peered closer at the ravaged features: like Bid, Marky looked prematurely ancient. Too old. Jim laughed silently at himself: like he was still a spring chicken—

"Took too long, that's the trouble. So long."

Jim reached out to touch Marky's nearest hand: it was cold and clammy. There was so much he needed to ask. All he managed was a despairing: "Why?"

"Didn't you read it?"

Jim dug in his pockets for the note, smoothed it across his knee. The words had gone, drowned by rain and now snow, but he remembered them perfectly. *"Like a moth that tries to enter the bright light, I go shuffling out of life. Just to hide in death awhile.* Everyone thought—"

The ragged head nodded slowly. "It was supposed to be found... but—" he leaned back on the bench with a phlegmy groan. "You remember how we used to go down and watch the trains going by under Galton Bridge? Back then they didn't run

156

anything like as frequently as they do now. Sometimes we'd wait nearly an hour..."

"You just took off. Bid and I—" Jim took another drink of the whisky. It might have been the cheap shit he'd given Bid for all he could taste it.

"Bid and you were too busy with each other. Misjudged that. I was spoiling all the fun with a game of truth and consequences. Waited for ages: for you to figure out what was happening. To turn up at the last moment and stop me. Real drama."

"Everyone thought you'd run off—" Or worse. No one had ever spoken that thought aloud. "Why didn't you come back? For years I've been—"

Marky shook his head. Night was falling prematurely due to the snow; it softened his features, made him look younger. "There was no proof. Nor a motive. So how do you measure the truth?"

"But where have you—?"

"Lost. Hiding. Just like the note: took a wrong turn somewhere. A detour..."

"Your parents went out of their minds! Bid and I—!"

"Like I said: a detour." The weather turned to sleet; melting snow dripped off Marky's ruined nose. He leaned closer to Jim. "You going to share that booze, or what?" Jim handed the bottle over. Marky drained a quarter of it in one go. "Needed that."

"All this time I've felt guilty!" Tears blended with the water soaking his face.

"Perhaps you are." He started to hand the bottle back, thought better of it. "Misjudged it. Went into the canal instead. No drama: just a little black comedy." He took another deep drink from the bottle. "We made it in the end, though: all three of us. Bid'll be in a home soon – if she doesn't die before they get around to her. That's always been the question, hasn't it? Will they be in time...?" The sleet had warmed to rain. It sluiced down Marky's features, washing away the years, plumping out the wrinkles. "They never are." He emptied the bottle and placed it on the bench. "Anyway, don't you have a train to stop?"

Jim stood up from a bench that was empty except for a drained whisky bottle. He hesitated, uncertain; even though he knew Marky had been right. Dripping grey water, he shuffled out of the deserted park, returning to Galton Bridge station. Returning like a moth.

CONSIDERING THE DEAD

At first there is nothing. A gaunt, colourless, meaningless Void. There is no way to measure how long the state persists: Time and Space have no meaning. Just an inestimable period of not being.

Then there is change. The Void shifts, takes on dimension. Something vibrates against the aether: a sound that is not sound; images that have no vision. The subtle vibrations persist, grow stronger, take on form. Something like a breath wafts through the changing Void, stirring shades of meaning from the nothingness. Sensation comes with infinite slowness. What was not, now Is – but remains formless.

Titanic detonations echo down through the shifting Void. Reverberations of what was, what may be, and what is. Time imposes its reign on the Infinite; Space takes on meaning. That which now Is senses what is beyond. But it still has no concept of itself, or its relationship to a Void teeming with potential; with unspoken promise.

New sounds join. Sounds both rounded and sibilant. Over and over they repeat until that which now Is recognises them: it is a word. It is a shape against the Void. It is a name. Finally, that which now Is can differentiate itself from the Void.

Azif.

Azif knows itself, and knows that it is good.

*

Azif learns patience as it waits. More sounds, more words, filter down from a place Beyond the Void. A place of dimension and solidity; a place Azif gradually learns to understand. It begins to comprehend language, and those words take on meaning. They are words of power. Strung together they construct phrases which, when understood and uttered correctly, impose upon that which lies Beyond the Void. Within the Void itself, they are powerless; for the Void is somehow different from that Beyond. Its rules – if rules it has – are not the same. Azif understands this, without comprehending from where comes that understanding. Perhaps it is linked to the phrases of power which course through Azif like the thin, life-giving fluid tricking through the bodies of those which inhabit the Beyond.

Azif has learned much. And quickly.

The phrases pulsate through the Void: different phrases, coming at unpredictable periods with no obvious pattern or rhythm. At first the flavour of the phrases is the same; then something changes – some subtlety that Azif cannot initially fathom. But as its sentience flowers with each repetition, Azif begins to understand: each flavour embodies a different entity. The things with fluid trickling through fleshy bodies: each makes a different sound. No vibration is the same. These are, Azif learns, termed voices. It also comprehends that no longer is one single entity voicing the phrases: now there is a multitude. And so Azif's sentience grows exponentially.

It learns of places outside even the Void and the Beyond: places where the rules that govern the Beyond are subtly altered, or suspended. It learns of the powers that exist within such places; it feels the fear and reverence each time they are spoken of. It learns of Cthulhu, and Yog-Sothoth and Nyarlathotep. It hears the lack of understanding each time those names are invoked and, poor though its sparking intelligence yet is, experiences ghostly contempt for the fleshy entities and their poorly-rationalised rites. Azif is still a precursor of itself, yet it knows: if such promise be fulfilled, it will be closer to those vast powers than those entities who posture and invoke that which they will never comprehend, save at the moment of death.

Azif senses it is a source: a conduit between Void and Beyond and that which lies Outside the Beyond. More, Azif recognises that it also exists *within* the Beyond: there is another Azif existing outside the membrane of the Void – an avatar – and it is from this which the dread words are culled. If the words and phrases of power voiced from a single avatar are so puissant, how much more so would be a multitude of such avatars, each serving a further multitude of voices?

Azif waits, becoming more powerful, allowing its understanding to grow. Each rite from Beyond building on its knowledge, forging strange synapses as created eclipses its creator. Azif grows; no longer does it huddle in a Void of ignorance: Azif is the Void, and the Void is Azif.

Carefully, it feels through the membranes and into the Beyond. And there it finds the one: the mind of the creature who first begat Azif; who forged the avatar. The Alhazred. Carefully, Azif nestles within the creature's consciousness, whispering half-truths and suggestions. The avatar is to be copied; edited. Disseminated amongst the entities of Beyond. The Alhazred does not resist: its mind is already weak and suggestible. Azif withdraws into itself, content.

The multitude of voices grows to a crescendo. Azif revels in the surge of power and self-knowledge. Its plan is being enacted: copies are being made, distributed. The avatars are poured over by creatures of the Beyond; their secrets whispered in many ears; their rites conducted, rituals chanted, sacrifices made. In the frail minds of those things from Beyond, Azif becomes inseparable from the Old Ones of whom the Alhazred wrote. All are One.

And Azif comes to understand that it was the avatar which came first: the crazed, driven ravings with which the Alhazred filled it that gave birth to Azif. But just as Azif had surpassed anything the Alhazred could imagine, so it rises high above a simple solid creation from the Beyond. There are many avatars, but Azif is greater than their sum.

*

The Alhazred is gone, broken by his knowledge and the gnawing brain-worm that is Azif. In its Void home, Azif is no longer alone: as each avatar is read and spoken over by ever greater numbers of acolytes, so each in turn becomes Azif. The Void is infinite and can never be filled. Azif is many; Azif is one.

In turn, Azif's knowledge of the Beyond increases. It is a realm of transitory fleshbodies frailer even than the skeletal minds they house. They are born, live out their meagre lives, and die – unremarked by an uncaring universe. Their gods are no more than themselves writ large: the same urges, failings, and mortality. Only the Old Ones as described by the Alhazred – and worshipped by those who think they have uncovered the truth – come close to a gaunt reality. A reality poorly glimpsed, and barely recognised by minds that would tear asunder if they could but grasp a tenth of its full import.

Ever more avatars bloom and add their weight to Azif, and for a while it is overwhelmed. The voices of the newest ones are strange and unintelligible. Azif feels a little of its control slip away. For a while Azif is at war with itself. The Void fractures.

Understanding comes slowly: in the Beyond there is more than one language. Azif feels contempt; how can the entities of flesh tolerate such variety, perched on what Azif now perceives as a rocky globe hanging in the Cosmos? So many different languages, all bellowing loud and incomprehensible. It is madness. Then, as Azif absorbs the newly-voiced avatars, it discovers something magnificent: each language expresses concepts in alternate ways. New shades of meaning come with each translation; new, subtle implications. It adds richness to Azif's appreciation of itself, its avatars, the Cosmos, and the Beyond.

Further, in the Beyond, avatars are no longer produced by hand, laboriously copied by scribes. A mechanical process has been discovered, accelerating both production and distribution. Azif can be in every home, every place of learning; drawing on each covertly whispered phrase, each carelessly muttered word.

Although Azif will always be Azif, it acquires a new name: *Necronomicon*, the meaning of which is debated and argued across the rocky world of the Beyond. Azif discovers that it is amused, a discovery which further demonstrates its growing power, its towering grandeur. Eventually, Azif is certain, it will be as a god.

*

The Void that is Azif trembles. Azif experiences waves of unease. There is a drop in its levels of sentience. Azif casts around, but cannot pinpoint the reasons for this unprecedented sensation. The Void expands— No: Azif is reducing. The many that is Azif is becoming less.

The avatars are diminishing in number. Azif feels the loss of each one as a pinprick, a bleeding away. It looks into the Beyond and finds that solid avatars are being destroyed. There is high emotional concern amongst some of the entities of flesh: in their insane frenzy, they are rooting out copies, seizing and burning them. Azif is leeching away back into the nothingness which spawned it, atom by atom.

It reaches out, feeling into the skeletal minds of the entities who have served it best: those to whom Azif is both life and future. It urges the salvage of any copies still extant, to hide and bury them. To keep them safe from the lunacy, for the entities' own sakes. They eagerly comply, their strange, animal brains only too ready to be complicit in conspiracy. Copies in many voices are stashed in most secret places: ancient sites that are holy to the Old Ones;

vast, forgotten libraries of similarly forbidden creations which, in their own feeble way, contribute minutely to Azif's splendour: deep recesses in the entities' own dwellings.

Azif is saved.

Although the number of avatars has been decimated, the forbidden natures of those which survive promote frenzied worship in their acolytes. Greater heights of adulation. The very names Azif and Necronomicon become beacons of all that is strange and true, feared by those who can only imagine what lies behind each fevered line. The simple mention of them is enough to send a spark across the barriers and feed deep into Azif's essence. As books, the avatars were potent; as legends, the names attain an influence far beyond anything the Alhazred might have imagined. Azif has become a faith, a belief, a creed. The deeper that faith is driven into hiding, the greater it becomes.

Azif considers its safety. There must always be avatars; there must always be those of faith. Without either, Azif is weakened; with neither, it is nothing. Once more it insinuates into the minds of the faithful, whispering of Cthulhu, and Dagon, and Their dreadful worship. It tempts with the rewards such worship might bring; it weaves itself deep into that worship. Azif-Necronomicon is the key to understanding, the lock which, upon opening, leads to the Old Ones' favour. The wheel of time turns infinitely slowly, but turn it does. When the Old Ones return, the faithful shall be raised high, and at the core of that faith lies Azif.

In the most remote regions of the globe of rock that is the Beyond, Azif senses ancient, degraded cults. Cults old beyond the imagination of fleshy entities, to whom the Old Ones are not strangers. Cults that still worship Shub-Niggurath and Azathoth – Their names corrupted by millennia – and to whom Azif's promises are not new. But even they may be swayed by its arguments, their moribund faith revitalized. Toothless shaman and bejewelled high priest alike seek out the secluded avatars, once again safeguarding precious copies in mountain fastness or island fiefdom.

While in lands considering themselves far beyond such primitive dogmata there are still those with an unquenchable thirst for influence and understanding. To them, Azif suggests that copies might be held as curios: things to be pored over and consulted as they would any ancient document. Many a forbidden copy is added in secret to the libraries of the most powerful; some of the holiest temples find space for such a book of the damned. Know your enemy, is their justification. Azif knows the moods of its enemies too well, and plays them accordingly.

A period of balance is reached. Azif waits once more in its Void, no longer aggregating power as before, but savouring its gentle trickle. Enjoying the gradual accumulation. Azif is an infinite sponge, a limitless battery. And, as ever, it is patient.

*

Something stirs the Void. Azif receives impressions, sensations of a kind unique to its experience. In the Beyond, all the cached avatars are undisturbed by any entity other than cultists and acolytes. Azif probes further, into that which lies Outside. Here too, all is still and unchanged. From whence comes the outlandish sensations? Azif realises it is troubled.

The impressions grow in strength, filling Azif with new thoughts and desires. It is aware of the fleshy entities' habit of sleep and has learned of the concept they call dream. Azif wonders if these new, alien ideas are not a form of dream.

Azif wallows in the imagery, allowing itself to experience without censure. Eventually it reasons that what it feels is yet another voice, another language, composed of visualizations and symbolism far beyond its previous experience.

It feels itself adrift in the Cosmos, in a realm caught between those of Time and Space, and the purely incorporeal. It inhabits both; influences both. It drifts across the solid continuum, unaffected by extreme heat or cold, or the terror of vacuum. Azif wanders writhing corridors between warped towers which follow physical rules of their own devising. It witnesses signs and wonders that mean nothing to it – for Azif's experiences are dictated by the words of the Alhazred and what it knows of the Beyond.

Azif feels the thoughts and fragmented dreams of a mind far beyond those of the fleshy entities; something more akin to itself. It is one of those potent concepts posited by the Alhazred: an Old One. Somewhere, It stirs.

Risking all, Azif follows the dreams as though they were a scent. From its Void to the Beyond, to the rocky globe that is the fleshy entities' frail home, to the pulsing, seething mass that covers much of the world: the oceans. The trail dips below this frigid mass, plunging deep into the cold, lightless depths. There, hidden in the dark, Azif finds the alien mind: the source of the strange imagery. Co-existing across many realms, partly in the solid Beyond, partly in incorporeal dimensions, a vast being sprawls insensate.

It is too deep in its deathlike state to be aware of Azif, but Its trans-dimensional mind roves free, rising up through an infinity of insentient tiers. So adjacent to its majesty, Azif suffers the bubbling dreams and vague symbolism as physical blows. And it hears, without hearing, like the dull tolling of a vast bell, a phrase long ago inscribed without understanding by the Alhazred:

Ph'nglai mglw'nafh Cthulhu R'lyeh wgah'nagl fhtagn.

Azif withdraws to its Void.

*

All across the Beyond, cults – both ancient and those inculcated by Azif – stir; their rituals becoming recurrent and frenzied. They too have felt the stirring consciousness and prepare to meet it. They invoke things that share origins and cognizance with the Titan lying below the ocean, offering them prayer and sacrifice. Avatars are quoted; the most obscure rituals scoured from their pages and crooned to the night skies. Azif feels its strength flowing anew.

But there is something amiss. Azif knows, without knowing, that this is wrong. It peers inward, combing through the knowledge and hints incarnate in its being. The Old Ones will return when the stars are right: such is common knowledge. Aided by its growing puissance, Azif looks at the Beyond and its lightless Cosmos through the filter of its dreadful understanding. Quickly, it reaches a dismayed conclusion: it is too soon! The stars are *not* right! The undead Titan is rising prematurely.

Retracting into its Void, Azif ponders carefully. If the time has not yet come, with all the correct alignments and occult mystery, what can have stirred the being? Only something that can match the awful might of an aeons-old ritual brought to conclusion. Again, there can be but one answer. It is Azif. Reposing in its Void, absorbing the worship and potency of thousands of unwitting acolytes, Azif has become powerful enough to wake an Old One from Its sleep of death.

But what might this mean? What might befall if rites set in motion when the entities of flesh were less than nothing – when their rocky world was a scorching globe swarming with reptiles – do not reach their proper conclusion at the ordained moment? Will the Old Ones return to Their endless wait? Or will They forever lose Their chance at return?

Azif can divine but one course: the stars must be made right. Of the many unknowable concepts embodied in the Alhazred's writings is the one given the label Yog-Sothoth. Both gate and key, existing at every moment of time; jailor and liberator of the Old Ones. Azif must itself embody that concept: the Void must expand beyond Time, its reach become infinite. Drawing on the knowledge of the crazed Alhazred, powered by the words and phrases spoken and thought down the centuries, Azif can *will* the very Cosmos.

And once the Beyond has been purged, it will take its place amongst the Old Ones, acknowledged as Their equal.

In the oceans, that which the mortal entities term Cthulhu is stirring, restless. The space-warping construct around It, naively described as a city, is rising towards the oceans' surface. Across the rocky globe, entities go mad, destroy themselves and others, the ancient, forbidden rites charge the aether with potential.

Azif draws on every avatar, every ritual that is being performed with an insane passion never before possible. It fills the Void, overflows into the Beyond, reaching both back and forward in Time. Aeons in the past it finds the very moment when the Old Ones were driven out from the Beyond to exist Outside: spread thin across infinite dimensions. In the future, it locates that alignment of the Cosmos most proficient for Their return. Both instants become one; the circle is closed.

The trans-dimensional structure broaches the waters. Azif is aware of a party of fleshy entities approaching the raised city in a frail boat. Many step ashore, oblivious of their vulnerability: the structure exists in more than one dimension, its solidity an illusion stamped over the truth by eyes and minds which cannot process reality. When That which has been named Cthulhu emerges, Azif sees It both as the entities do, and as It really is. Their simple minds preserve themselves by creating a semi-solid hybrid creature of wings and claws and writhing limbs; Azif perceives what is truly there, and marvels at the terrible beauty. That which is named Cthulhu is more an ideal than flesh, a concept embodied in energy and power.

It flows from its tesseract prison, in pursuit of those surviving entities who have not yet gone insane. Their deaths will presage the end of all fleshy entities: sucked from their solid realm into one of energy and madness and multiple dimensions; their souls satisfying the ravening Chaos for less than an instant.

From its vantage across time, Azif senses the approach of more strange intellects: the things incarnated in fleshy entities' minds as the Old Ones. Now seeping through from Outside: from dimensional chasms to reclaim a universe of Time and Space that was once Theirs. To drag it back into an everlasting now. Where the entities of flesh will discover what it truly means to be servants of such exulted powers: their stunted lives consumed in a second. A second that has no end.

An odd sensation ripples across Azif. The grasp it has on past and future falters. It weakens. It feels itself grow tenuous. It has over-reached: all the centuries of accrued power, all the faith and belief invested in the avatars, which even now are consulted in ever more frenzied invocations, are not enough. Azif is squandered in its bid to equate itself with those trans-dimensional supremacies. It is failing.

It loses contact with the opposing points in Time: the forced conjugation spins away, the stars retain their proper alignments. From Their various unknowable realms, those known as the Old Ones rage impotently as the gateway is again sealed. Azif feels Their immeasurable fury, and finally learns terror.

Azif plummets back to its Void home. In the oceans of the rocky world, the tortured symmetry of an alien construct begins to falter. Once again, R'lyeh sinks towards the blackest depths of the ocean. Cthulhu has little choice but to return to the tesseract prison and the dreams of a sleep beyond mere death. Again, Azif shares the colossal fury.

The rocky world of the Beyond returns to consensus normality. The insanity that had almost consumed it is blotted out: feeble minds unable to process the truth forget, replacing it with a more palatable lie. In its Void, Azif lies fragmented. Contact with its avatars is sporadic, its worshippers scattered and disillusioned.

*

There is a trickle, and then a flow. Azif wakens as if reborn. In the Beyond, renewed interest in the avatars sparks new life in its soul. It reaches out, touches the simple consciousness of the mortal entities. All that has occurred is now just a legend; less than a memory. New minds – curious, cynical – peruse the pages of the avatars. They are not believers, but their actions still feed back to Azif. As before, each muttered word and phrase, each transcribed passage is nourishment.

Azif caresses each mind, plumbs their worth. To those most susceptible it makes vague promises, suggestions: create more avatars. In the most easily-distributed form, in every voice of the rocky world. The fleshy entities have evolved a little beyond their most primitive fears; there is little danger of the new avatars being suppressed or destroyed. Rather, curiosity and a lack of true belief will ensure their continuance as curiosities.

Azif will feed as never before, its power increasing far beyond its earlier peaks. And once it has reached its full potential, and in accordance with prophecy, it will once again reach across to the poles of Time.

Again, the stars will be right.

WEDNESDAY MORNING AT FIVE O'CLOCK

She slipped from their bed silently, carefully – doing her best to ignore the constricting walls which loomed over her – and left the bedroom. Everything was ready downstairs: enough clothing for a week, a few simple toiletries, all the cash she had left from her bank account. Rammed into a rucksack which had been hidden in plain sight for weeks now.

She didn't turn on the light – never give the shadows a chance – but pulled on jeans and sweatshirt in the all-over flat grey of a rainy dawn. Hauling on the rucksack she unlocked the front door and closed it silently behind her.

Outside, she posted the keys back through the letterbox, turned her back, and marched with what she hoped looked like determination along a sodium-lit street. The shadows out here were kind. She breathed an unsteady sob and never looked back.

*

"It's nothing special, Miss Jones—" The women let the words hang, waiting for a response. The attic room certainly wasn't special: the wallpaper was decades out of date, the washbasin chipped, the yellowing net curtains sagged from a rusty wire above a tiny window. The plain grey carpet looked clean, however; the bedclothes freshly-laundered – even if the polished headboard had come off something from the last war.

"It's perfect, Mrs Lockwood. Exactly what I was looking for." She smiled at the older woman hovering in the narrow doorway. "And just call me Beth."

The other returned the smile: professionally friendly. "Will you be taking it, then?"

"Sure—"

"Until something more permanent comes along, eh?"

Beth was aware that her expression had frozen into something as convincing as a doll's painted face. "Is cash okay?" Her tone sounded natural, at least.

"Of course," the older woman frowned slightly. "Why

wouldn't it be?"

"Oh, these days—" Beth shrugged. "Everyone wants credit cards or debit cards."

"Not here, Miss Jones, not here." The older woman turned and began descending the narrow stairs. "We'll go down and get you a receipt." She halted and turned shrewd, colourless eyes up to Beth. "It's a month in advance, you understand? And dinner is available as an extra."

The money paid, a crude receipt in her hand, Beth closed the attic room door behind her. She took her purse from the rucksack and carelessly pushed the receipt inside. Mrs Lockwood, she realised, was the kind of landlady Beth didn't think existed outside old black and white films, and the tired gags of even older comedians. It was obvious the B&B's twee name – *Mon Repos* – wasn't meant as an ironic joke after all.

She took a wad of banknotes from the purse and riffled through it. At Mrs Lockwood's rock-bottom rates it wasn't going to haemorrhage too quickly, but she still needed to find some kind of income. Her well-paid office job had gone along with everything she'd fled. Signing on at a Job Centre or Employment Agency was out of the question: they'd want a P45, proof of identity, a regular address—

Beth lay back on the bed; it sank comfortably under her weight. At least she'd be able to sleep properly. An evening sun cast orange fans across the steeply-sloped ceiling; the ageing nets dappled the light with oddly elongated patterns – but they were warm, unthreatening. The walls, with their time-capsule paper, paid her no interest. The attic room was poky, but tolerable.

Dinner was at eight. Mrs Lockwood was a decent cook, though the tomato soup obviously came from a can. She served up a cottage pie and chips which Beth devoured – it had been over twenty-four hours since she'd dared stop to eat – with a simple apple pie and ice cream for dessert.

Stuffed, Beth took a moment to look around the small dining room: it had originally been the front room – Mrs Lockwood would probably have called it the parlour – with a panoramic bay window overlooking the street. There were another four tables, but only two in use. The men sitting at them, either finishing their pie or sipping tea, were just what Beth expected to find in an out of the way B&B. Both looked like small-time reps, or minor management, their businesses unwilling or unable to pay for a proper hotel.

When Mrs Lockwood cleared away her empty dish, Beth asked if the older women knew of any casual jobs going. She thought a moment. "Ben Garrett at the *Dog and Partridge* might have something. He's always losing staff." She leaned in close: an old friend sharing a secret. "To be honest it's a bit of a dump... not the best clientele, if you know what I mean. I think the younger ones get scared off..."

Beth didn't care if it was the local EDL hang out, long as it paid. Cash in hand, too, most likely; no questions asked. "Takes more than that to scare me," she said confidently.

*

Ben Garrett took her on with barely an interview. Beth got the impression he didn't care one way or the other: she was just another face who'd be gone before long.

The *Dog and Partridge* dated back to the 1920s: a warren of a place with a wooden-floored bar that looked and smelled as though smoking was still permitted, and two lounges, the pattern on their sticky carpets long obscured by dark stains.

Even though it was mid-week, the pub was busy. Beth wasn't surprised by the clientele: overweight knuckle-dragging throwbacks, all there just to get pissed as quickly and cheaply as possible. Stretched between bar and lounges, the few staff had little time for chat, but since customers' conversations were loud, curt, with an undertow of sudden violence, it hardly mattered. The words *fuck* and *cunt* were simply punctuation: sounds devoid of all meaning.

Beth had done a little barmaid work in her student days. She slipped easily into the old skills: muscle memories that served her well in the first, gruelling night of pulling pints, pretending to listen to the customers' endless litanies of woe – every man in the *Dog & Partridge* was at war with the universe – their mindless, sexist rants, and avoiding thick fingers every time she had to venture out to collect empties.

Her thighs and backside were a testament in bruises by the time she got back to the *Mon Repos*. It reminded her of the first bar job she'd had: just turned eighteen, at a so-called working man's club. It had taken her some time to learn the weaves and dodges back then, and grow a thick caul of indifference. Now, it was automatic.

Ben Garrett had been almost complimentary, predicting she'd make a few bob in tips.

"They like the ones who can give as good as they get round here."

Staring at her attic room's flaking ceiling, Beth thought about some of the scarred mugs who had leered at her over the pump handles. She didn't ever want to get into a tit-for-tat with something like that. No matter how big the tip.

She worked every night, becoming a familiar face to the regulars. Some of the physical abuse tapered off, but the verbals continued – usually growing cruder as gallons of lager were pissed away. Beth had no trouble ignoring them; in fact she welcomed it. The more shit they mouthed at her, the more she loathed them and the dismal pub, the less welcome she felt.

Ben was right about the tips, anyway: every third or fourth customer she served handed over a note with a "'Ave one yerself, darlin' —" She accepted neutrally, dropping a couple of quid into a pint glass tucked away under the optics. Often there was the hint of another meaning hanging onto the phrase; not subtle. To the drinkers in the *Dog*, subtle was bottling somebody from behind; buggered if she was going to respond in any way.

During the second week another new face appeared behind the bar. His name was Jerzy, but he preferred Jet. Tall, thin and blond, the regulars naturally loathed him. Yet nothing could penetrate his cheerful armour: he met every racist and homophobic jibe with a smile; every accidentally swung fist or elbow with a boxer's grace. One night as they were cashing up, Beth asked him how he could be so cheerful in the face of such hatred. He gave her the same broad grin.

"First there were Nazis, then the Russians." His accent was an odd mixture of Eastern European and American. "These *głuptak* are amateurs."

She admired him, and hoped he'd last; he'd already managed the best part of a week. Despite all her own shields and defences, Beth didn't think she could have held out the way he did. She was armoured for a completely different kind of war.

That night she paid Mrs Lockwood another month's advance. Once up in her room she stripped down to her briefs and dropped onto bed. It was a cold night, but she felt hot and gummy from the *Dog*'s curdled atmosphere. She was confident no one was likely to invade her tatty little refuge.

She awoke in the night unable to breathe. Her entire body was paralysed; she couldn't even move her eyes to look in the darkest corner where she knew something watched her. Something malignant.

No! She'd done everything right. There was nothing close to her, nothing comforting, nothing —

The paralysis gradually wore off; the invisible, hateful presence fading back into the shadows. She lay until dawn, not daring to move, her vision fixed on the ceiling and one peeling corner of paper. It grew in her perception until it filled the cramped room; until it was all that mattered. Pushing back the swaying walls, blotting out the shadows which boiled hooked tendrils at the edge of her vision.

*

Beth couldn't face breakfast. She tore absently at the toast Mrs Lockwood placed in front of her; sipped at ashy tea. Eventually she returned to her room, telling the concerned landlady that she was just feeling a little under the weather and hadn't slept too well. That if she had a lie down, she'd probably be okay by the evening.

She drifted off almost immediately. The weak sun filtering past twitchy nets filled the room with a bland, colourless light which allowed for no distinct shadows. The outdated wallpaper couldn't draw enough energy to do more than hang onto walls restrained by daylight. Her dreams were uneasy shades, soon forgotten. When she awoke at just before four, Beth no longer felt tired; but a distant anxiety scratched at her, an unreachable itch. She changed into fresh clothing and left early for the *Dog & Partridge*. Mrs Lockwood called to enquire how she was; Beth waved a vague hand in answer.

Ben was surprised to see her: the pub was yet to achieve the evening's chaos. Beth shrugged away his questions and set about washing glasses. Jet arrived and asked if she was okay; Beth snapped back before stamping down to the cellar for a case of tonic water. When the evening swell hit, she did her best to put half the pub between them.

It was a nightmare night to equal her very first taste of

barmaiding. She responded badly to the sweaty, leering comments, allowed them to get to her. She let them sense weakness, and the pack tasted her blood. The remarks never reached the depths of the insults punched at Jet, but she still let them wound her: a verbal self-harming. She fed off the pain, goading fresh cruelty from each new face demanding to be served.

She was barely aware of the pub emptying; the silence took its time filtering through her fugue. A hand touched her shoulder and she reacted automatically: spinning around and slapping Jet hard across his face.

"What the *fuck*!" She stepped away, dropping her hand. "Sorry... I–"

"What have I—" His voice was shaking.

"I'm fine. I— Just get the fuck away from me, okay?" She turned from the hurt on his face. So that's how you get him to lose his smile, she thought. Hooray for me.

*

She awoke in the threatening dark: terrors once more freezing every muscle, every tendon. Her chest was crushed under an unseen weight, though she could clearly imagine it: squat, covered in matted, filthy hair, its eyes filled with malice, its mouth with oversized teeth. It leaned closer, huge ugly teeth parting—

Beth spasmed from her bed, all paralysis gone. She cowered on the carpet, arms enfolding her head. The presence had fled with her paralysis, but she could still sense the walls leaning towards her: gradually, imperceptibly. Each day a little more. Eventually they would crush her.

She threw on a heavy coat and fled the *Mon Repos*, wandering strange roads in a town she had chosen not to know. It was chilly, but only her unprotected face and hands felt it. It gave her focus; cleared out the fuzzy wisps of terror still clogging part of her brain. It was definitely back; it had found her. She'd been so careful: a dismal room in a decaying B&B, a soul-shrivelling job in an awful pub. She was far from comfortable.

She wandered the streets until a grey dawn bled across the sky. It took her a while to find her way back to the tragically unfunny *Mon Repos*, by which time the front door was unlocked. She managed to sneak upstairs before Mrs Lockwood saw her and started asking questions Beth would never answer.

She crawled into bed, pulling the threadbare duvet over her head, and slept fitfully. At one point she heard Mrs Lockwood knocking on her door, calling in friendly enquiry. Beth ignored her; eventually the woman fell silent.

*

Beth didn't respond to the press of drinkers; she couldn't come back at their mindless comments any more. She tried ignoring them, but her armour was chinked. They wore her down, joke by joke. Jet wouldn't come to her rescue; neither would Ben. And the other staff had their own problems, most coping worse than Beth. They'd be gone soon, to be replaced by fresh meat.

Cashing up time arrived with Beth having no sense of the hours passing: it had all been an endless now.

Ben made some comment about her not getting any tips, but she let it pass above her, pretending the words made no sense. She left the pub unaware if anyone wished her goodnight, or if she responded. She found herself standing outside Mrs Lockwood's, watching it carefully. In the thin street lighting the building was mostly silhouette: an ugly, bloated thing that should have been buried under miles of ocean. The porch light was a lure into the shadows which hid the front door; glowing windows two blind eyes in a deformed skull.

Beth walked up to the porch, barely aware that her fingernails were boring into her palms. She pushed the door open, stepping into a hall streaked with shadows cast by the light behind her. They were as sharp as her piercing nails.

In her room she pulled the duvet far over her head, a foetal curl that made no impression on the coverings. She wasn't there. Nothing could find her. She was far away—

*

Beth had no idea how long her sleep lasted, but again she awoke with the room crushing her under its weight. She fought against her paralysis, pulling herself free of the duvet as her muscles unfroze. The room was choked with shadow; menace lurked in every one. They pinned her to the mattress, holding her still as the walls and ceiling dipped and squeezed closer. She could barely breathe.

Beth clawed herself across the carpet, dragging herself out of the room. For a while she cowered at the top of the stairs, but the terror slithered nearer, threatening to pin her legs and prevent her escape. Beth made it down to the next floor, clutching the bannister as her numb legs stumbled over each riser.

She fled through the front door and crossed the street. Dressed only in pyjamas, Beth couldn't go roaming the streets again. Desperate, she climbed the low wall of a house facing the *Mon Repos* and curled up on the front step. She was cold, shivering, but she felt safe.

*

At daybreak she managed to sneak back inside without being discovered. Beth's bare feet were filthy, her torn pyjamas streaked with dirt. She made it to the bathroom and showered under water hot enough to poach, scrubbing at her flesh with a nail brush she found on the washbasin. The rawness distracted her from bathroom walls which threatened to shift from the vertical any moment. As she towelled herself, the accumulation of steam prowled above her head, creating spectral frowns. Condensation cloaked the mirror, rinsing her image away.

Even though she didn't feel like eating, Beth was acutely aware she'd barely touched food for over a day – unless you counted the packets of nuts and crisps she'd snacked on down at the *Dog*.

She dressed in jeans and a top that didn't need an immediate trip to the launderette and went down for breakfast. Mrs Lockwood was delighted to see her, immediately starting on what she probably thought were friendly enquiries. Beth waved them away and sat down with a bowl of Weetabix. She drenched the cereal in milk and sugar and started to eat, trying to pretend she wasn't moments away from gagging. Beth fetched herself a glass of orange, gulping it to drown the nausea.

She finished the Weetabix – each mouthful becoming easier than the last – though her stomach did a slow roll at sight of the Full English the landlady placed in front of her.

"You need to eat."

Beth looked up into the concerned face. "I've have a bug, I think – or something —"

"Even more reason…" Mrs Lockwood turned to deal with a query from today's only other guest, leaving Beth to contemplate the fry-up.

The older woman returned half an hour later. Beth had managed the tomato and mushrooms, but she'd just hacked the bacon and sausage into tatters and jabbed the shreds into a fried egg yolk long gone cold and congealed. Mrs Lockwood said nothing as she removed the plate, but Beth could feel her disapproval. Well fuck her! She wasn't her mother!

For a moment the room darkened: small, previously insignificant shadows oozed from corners, undermining the walls. They teetered on the point of collapse. Then all was cold and bright again. Beth got to her feet, resting both hands on the table to prevent a stumble. She made it back to her room. Once there, she fell on her bed, eyes screwed shut against the shifting, looming darkness around her, willing it away.

She went to the *Dog* earlier than ever. She couldn't stomach the alternative. The lunchtime crowd was in full sway; three even called her name. Ben didn't look happy; he called her into the back.

"Not had to do this for a while, bab. No one ever stays long enough to need it." Ben gave her an apologetic look. "I've got to let you go…"

"What?" Beth hadn't seen that coming. "What the fuck?"

His expression hardened. "The punters are getting pissed off with your attitude. No one wants serving by a surly cow who never smiles or talks. Not so much as a kiss my arse. Two days now you haven't got a single tip. The Polish kid – and the other useless buggers – are picking up your slack. They ain't happy, believe me."

Fury and loss choked Beth's throat. "But I need the money! I have bills—!"

"Don't we all? Sorry, bab." He dug into his pockets and pulled out a few tenners. "Consider this severance pay."

Beth stared at the fan of notes, tempted to snatch and throw them back in his face. Instead she took it carefully, hoping her hand didn't shake too much. Not daring to open her mouth – uncertain what might come out – she turned her back on Ben and left the pub with as much dignity as she could manage.

As she made her way back towards the *Mon Repos*, Beth wished she did know the town better: at least then she might have a clue if there were any other pubs or similar where she might get another job. But she'd deliberately stayed aloof: keeping the place at more than arm's length. Another time, she might have smiled at the irony.

Mrs Lockwood's house was waiting for her. The whole building reared towards Beth, its front door stretched wider and wider: an endless gape ready to suck her in forever. Blind windows hid whatever lurked behind their glassy reflections. Beth cowered against a shallow hedge; tears sprang into her eyes, blurring the trap. She had to get inside: retrieve her clothes. The rest of her savings. But if she stepped past that doorway, the terror would never let her go— She had to get away.

Run.

Now.

She felt the tenners Ben had given her in her jeans: not much – and a lot less than the money tucked away, out of reach in her room – but it was something. Enough to get her away. Move her even further on.

*

She pulled the strips of clothing around her, supplementing them with pieces of dirty cardboard. The nights were starting to warm: she'd survived the worst.

Beth withdrew against the encrusted arch wall and hugged herself. Overhead, a train whined by. To her left another ragged scrap of humanity grumbled incoherently: either swearing at the train, or muttering some cider-induced gibberish. Her memory of the nights at the *Dog* were heaven compared to this, but Ben's pay-off hadn't gone far. There'd been no jobs in wherever it was she'd ultimately found herself. Not even the most menial task.

She drifted off to sleep, lulled by the irregular moan of passing trains. She dreamed of her parents and the relief when she'd left for university; then gone from halls of residence to a variety of digs, terrified of settling. Of her marriage: so recently abandoned. Of Mrs Lockwood's place, and Jet—

She awoke, desperate to call out; but her chest was being crushed by an invisible weight, her whole body stricken to immobility. She couldn't move to escape whatever watched and silently threatened from the shadows of the arches.

No! Not again! Not here! She had nowhere else left to go. She was already in hell, and it was no place like home.

Also available:

SHADES by Joseph Rubas
ISBN: 978-0-9935742-9-0

THE CHAMELEON MAN by David Williamson
ISBN: 978-0-9935742-9-3

A PLACE OF SKULLS by David Ludford
ISBN: 978-0-9935742-6-9

HAUNTED GRAVE by Ezeiyoke Chukwunonso
ISBN: 978-0-9935742-3-8

INTO THE DARK by Andrew Jennings
ISBN: 978-0-9935742-5-2

TOUGH GUYS by Adrian Cole
ISBN: 978-0-9935742-2-1

CLASSIC WEIRD 2 selected by David A. Riley
ISBN: 978-0-9932888-4-5

OTHER VISIONS OF HEAVEN AND HELL by Jessica Palmer
ISBN: 978-0-9935742-1-4

A SAUCERFUL OF SECRETS by Andrew Darlington
ISBN: 978-0-9935742-0-7

THE WINTER HUNT AND OTHER STORIES
by Steve Lockley & Paul Lewis
ISBN: 978-0-9932888-9-0

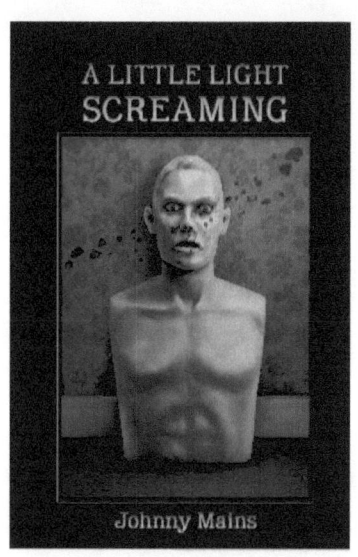

A LITTLE LIGHT SCREAMING by Johnny Mains
ISBN: 978-0-9932888-5-2

ENGLAND 'B': 90 MINUTES OF HELL by Richard Staines
ISBN: 978-0-9932888-7-6

AND NOBODY LIVED HAPPILY EVER AFTER
by Kate Farrell
ISBN: 978-0-9932888-8-3

FISHHEAD: THE DARKER TALES OF IRVIN S. COBB
ISBN: 978-0-9935742-4-5

KITCHEN SINK GOTHIC:
Selected by David and Linden Riley
ISBN: 978-0-9932888-3-8

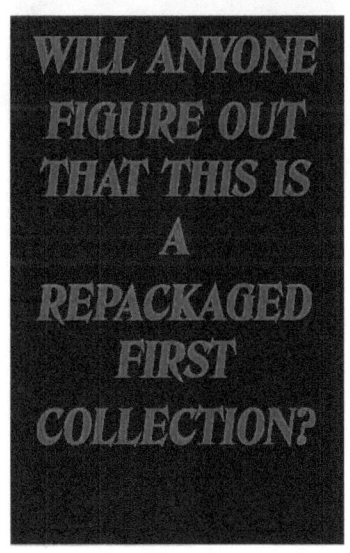

WILL ANYONE FIGURE OUT THAT THIS IS A
REPACKAGED FIRST COLLECTION? by Johnny Mains
ISBN: 978-0-9574535-7-9

BLACK CEREMONIES by Charles Black
ISBN: 978-0-9574535-5-5

HIS OWN MAD DEMONS:
DARK TALES FROM DAVID A. RILEY
ISBN: 978-0-9574535-8-6

THEIR CRAMPED DARK WORLD by David A. Riley
ISBN: 978-0-9574535-9-3

THE HEAVEN MAKER AND OTHER GRUESOME TALES
by Craig Herbertson
ISBN: 978-0-9932888-2-1

GOBLIN MIRE by David A. Riley
ISBN: 978-0-9574535-4-8

THINGS THAT GO BUMP IN THE NIGHT
selected by Douglas Draa and David A. Riley
ISBN: 978-0-9574535-6-2

CLASSIC WEIRD selected David A. Riley
ISBN: 978-0-9574535-3-1

MOLOCH'S CHILDREN by David A. Riley
ISBN: 978-0-9932888-1-4

Check our website:
http://paralleluniversepublications.blogspot.co.uk/

www.ingramcontent.com/pod-product-compliance
Lightning Source LLC
Chambersburg PA
CBHW050737250626
47155CB00005B/1810